'For ten years I'd shirked
the memories. I always felt them
scratching at the darker corners of
my mind, still feral; but sitting on
a tree stump in the gathering dark,
all of it – the space, the fear, the
sorrow – all seemed to find me
again. It was as if the past ten
years I'd only been standing still
and I was back in a mess with
a boy who only sees ghosts.'

Fiona Melrose was born in Johannesburg but has spent the majority of her adult life in the UK, first in London and then in East Anglia. She moved to Suffolk to concentrate on her writing and it is there that *Midwinter* was conceived. Previously Fiona has worked in academia, NGOs, public affairs and as an emerging markets analyst. She continues to keep a foot in both continents and is currently spending the majority of her time in South Africa.

Also by Fiona Melrose

Johannesburg

MIDWINTER

Fiona Melrose

corsair

CORSAIR

First published in the UK in 2016 by Corsair
This paperback edition published in 2017

1 3 5 7 9 10 8 6 4 2

Copyright © Fiona Melrose, 2016

The moral right of the author has been asserted.

A CIP catalogue record for this book
is available from the British Library.

ISBN: 978-1-4721-5180-3

Printed and bound in Great Britain by Clays Ltd, St Ives plc

Papers used by Corsair are from well-managed forests
and other responsible sources.

Corsair
An imprint of
Little, Brown Book Group
Carmelite House
50 Victoria Embankment
London EC4Y 0DZ

An Hachette UK Company
www.hachette.co.uk

www.littlebrown.co.uk

To the foxes of the Finn Valley for calling me and giving me courage to return that call. And for Maggie and Phoebe. In their company I walked hours each day across every field and forest path no matter the weather, excavating Suffolk's temper and tone. Without those walks this book could not have been written nor its sentences have found their breath.

Prologue

Think about a fox.

The vixen knows when to let her kits fight it out. It's with the push and the pull that they learn when to hide, when to growl and claw, and when to sit so still a bee might mistake small whiskers for a dandelion.

She'll not leave them entirely, mind. She'll keep watch.

I was gone, but I never really left you, heart. I never will.

Chapter 1

Vale

The shock of the water hit me like a hatchet. It felt like my ribs had cut clean through my skin and come out my throat. And almost as soon as I was in it, the tide ripping and heaving, I felt Tom's wrist slip from my grip as he got pulled away.

I swam as fast as I could. I yelled for Tom. I could only just see the boat in the dark and rain; hear Tom's voice bellow out, disappear and then come up again. I was hurtling along towards the river mouth – and beyond it the sea.

I tried to shout but almost as soon as my mouth opened it filled with water. I knew if I could keep going, the water might rush me back towards the boat.

Suddenly I seemed to be moving faster, skimming along the top of the river. I thought I saw Tom's arms reaching through the surface of the water. He was closer than I thought.

'The boat, Tom. Swim towards it!'

I was rushing at the stern and somehow, climbing up through the water, I threw myself towards it. It was my last chance. My left hand hit something hard. Then my right arm whipped up and found a rope, a rail, something, it didn't matter. I just had to hold on to it, tight, with every last bit of everything left in me.

'Tom where are you?' I couldn't hear him, nothing. Just sloshing and wind, then—

'Help me, man.'

He sounded nearby but I couldn't see him.

'Tom I'm here. Grab the boat.'

'Can't. Boat's moving too much.'

It was. Not just from the choppiness but left and right in the wind.

'Hang on, just don't lose me. I'll get you in.' I didn't know how.

I took the biggest breath I could and heaved myself up the side of the boat. I didn't make it all the way in but it was far enough, and with another push I went over like a fish on a line and all the water with me.

It took me a moment to find which way I was facing.

'Where are you?' I was trying to look over the sides to see where Tom was. 'Tom?'

'Fuckin' hurry up, I'm here.'

He was right up towards the bow, hanging off something. I couldn't see what.

'What are you holding? Can you climb up it? I'll drag you over.' Suddenly I felt the boat rotate sharp towards the peninsula. 'Are we moving?'

'Of course we're moving, everything is fuckin' moving. Jesus can you just help me?'

Scrabbling around for a life jacket or something, I found some nylon rope.

'Tom, I've got rope. I'll make a loop and you put it under your arms okay?'

4

'Shit I'm getting tired, man.'

'Keep talking to me while I do it.' The rope was all frayed but long and that was good enough. I made a noose best I could with one end and then tied the other end around the planks that made a bench across the width of the boat. I could hardly feel my hands.

'Are we out at sea, brother? It feels different, I don't feel the gully anymore.'

I looked around. I could make out land I hadn't before. The wind was getting worse. A few times gusts nearly knocked me clean over. 'I think we've moved towards the beach again. I'm going to throw the rope now. Tom, can you see?'

'Lower it.'

If I leaned right over I could see him, close but still too far to grab hold of. The rope got caught by the wind as Tom waved a free hand, trying to snatch at the blue line. Finally he got it.

'One arm at a time. Can you do it?'

I couldn't hear his reply.

He was struggling, hanging on the side with one hand and trying to get the rope over his head and free arm. It wasn't heavy enough for the job.

'I'm in!'

'Can you let go? I'm going to try and drag you round to the stern. Then I can get you in.'

'Brother, there's rocks here.'

'Can't be.'

'My feet keep hitting something'

'Then the boat would hit them. Tom, are you ready? You have to let go but swim hard and stay close. I'll pull you along.'

He did. And he didn't. I don't know what happened. But he got himself pulled away from the boat again, out along the rope, and the next thing he was screaming all hell about rocks behind him. And in the same moment there was this almighty bloody gust out of nowhere and the boat swung, hard and quick towards him with the rope still holding him to it. And he fucking disappeared between the boat and whatever was behind him. He was gone.

I'd fought with Pa. We fought about stuff all the time, but usually one of us had to stop because neither was going to be the first to use Ma to score points. Not this time; we both took the brakes off. I was shouting and hissing and I heard myself saying things I should never have said. I felt this fuckin' mad rage in me. There was no way of taking any of that back. And then I saw his hand coming at me. Came at my face like a hoof. The surprise meant I didn't know what to do. I don't think he did either so I left. I went out for a walk.

It wasn't slow like my walks usually are. It was angry. My shirt suddenly felt like it didn't fit. While I was walking, past the tractor sheds and out across the fields with my arms all stiff in their sockets, I must have dug my nails into my palms because when I uncurled them to open the gate, they burned like crazy.

It was early. The sun was low and a big dry moon was coming up the back. I got to the fallen chestnut and sat there looking down at the dogs sniffing and carrying on. Never understood how that tree kept living. It came over in a storm a few years back. We'd found it the next day, Pa and I, lying there with all its legs in the air and out the soil but it survived. Must have been because enough roots were still stuck in the earth and it had the water ditches feeding it. Anyway, it was still there and its branches made a big arch that was just right for resting on. I pulled my jacket close and stuck my hands in my pockets. Ma always said if you know where your roots are, you can survive anything. When I hated how things were my mind always turned to Ma and how she was before everything happened in Zambia and we came back here.

Ma was beautiful. Soft and sweet smelling and covered with flour. I knew this wasn't quite right because she couldn't have always been baking. I remembered her sitting at her piano, in her dress with zebras on it, and I knew she would have been making apple pie for me or nut bread for Pa. Her novels were always covered in flour too. She'd stand there kneading the dough with her library books to the side of the board reading away and sometimes she'd say 'Oh, that Mr Darcy, now there's a man for you.' Pa would tease her and say she only ever liked a man in breeches and he didn't stand a chance with her what with his overalls. I always pretended to look away when they kissed.

My chest ached from the cold and my head. I get headaches from being too angry. Felt like the inside of my skull was all red and raw. The dogs were fed up as well so I started back to the house. We'd been out so long that by the time we were making our way past the horses I could see Pa had put the lights on. I could make out the shape of the house against the sky. When the sun went down and the warm went with it you could hear the last hope of heat crack as it hit the horizon. It made me wish I hadn't cut my hair so short.

I put the dogs in through their door, all wet from the grass, and stood outside. The house looked warm with all the lights on. Ma always said it was pretty and I suppose it was. She liked brick houses. Looking at it I thought, maybe this time I'll leave.

So, I stood there feeling the kind of sorrow that stuck in my throat. I didn't cry and I kept standing still. Then, for no reason, or maybe because I just didn't know what else to do, I made a deal with myself or God or some bullshit like that, that if Pa came to the window and looked out before I counted to one hundred then I would go back in. If he looked for me in the night outside, I would go back inside and tell him it was okay, that I didn't blame him. I wanted to tell him I missed Ma too. But he didn't look out and I knew I could never say it anyway. When I ran out of numbers, even though I counted longer than I planned, I turned away. I walked up our track until I reached the road and started for town.

By the time I found him in town, Tom was already talking stupid and acting worse. He was wheeling around slopping his pint, acting like a loon. After our farm and the Admiral, the Old Anchor was his other home. He and the guy pulling pints were telling each other dirty limericks and Suffolk rhymes. Tom would start to laugh even before he got to the last line. He was always pleased with his efforts. He took a swig of his pint.

'So, Beccles for a puritan, Bungay for the poor.' The barman joined in. 'Halesworth for a drunkard and Bilborough for a whore.' Tom never tired of that one.

I was used to him being like that and mostly he made me laugh. Only a couple of times did he take it too far. Like the time he was trying to grab this girl. She told him to fuck off and he suddenly got right angry. I had to pull him off her and slap some sense into him. I wanted to tell the girl we were sorry but she had run off, and now she hates us. It didn't look like this night was shaping up much better either. Tom was all swagger and spit and none of the girls were having any of it. The Anchor was heaving with the usual Friday mess, someone was having a birthday too, so I needed to use my elbows like crowbars just to get to him.

'As I live and breathe, it's brother Vale! Glory be, what happened to your face?'

He was funny that way, always talking strange, especially when he got oiled up. Some of the guys called him Shakespeare because of it. He got his way from his Ma who fancied herself an actress though really she was just an usher at the town cinema. These days no one even knew where she was. She just floated in and out of town and then was gone again. She'd had some sort of breakdown a few years before. Tom still loved her like no one else. He'd do anything for her.

'Hey,' I said.

'You look like a man in need of a beverage.' He squinted at my face which I knew was swollen even though I'd tried to hold snow around my eye. 'Ugly stuff,' said Tom, 'we'll need to discuss that.'

I nodded over the noise.

'Get this gentleman a brew!' He just kind of bellowed it into the air but I guess somebody heard because soon enough, a jar slopped over the counter and then Tom was clunking glasses with me and making the kind of hoo-hahr types of noises the army blokes make. When we were a bit younger Tom had a cousin who did that all the time. I didn't like it and I didn't like him – but I still felt bad when he got his legs blown off in some raid in Afghanistan.

The whole town was like a barracks some nights. Especially after a tour got back. Tom could get into trouble quite quickly when that happened. He was always saying he was more of a man than they were. One time he really went at this one guy

9

who everyone was saying had medals and was a proper hero and Tom said you don't need a war to be a hero and he could fight the Taliban in his underpants and still win. It ended badly of course. I didn't know what I was, but it wasn't a hero.

The base was the other side of town towards the Forest. Some days, you'd have armoured vehicles and travellers with horses and a few tractors one after the other, all fighting for space on the same narrow road.

Tom and I had a few more ales. He was better practiced than I was, so I got pretty bad pretty quick. I know I was ratted because when Tom suggested we find some girls, I thought this was a good idea. Tom had shagged lots of girls, me, only one, and in the end, I don't think it really counted. Also, it was Tom's sister so I could never tell him about it.

In the end we never found any who would talk to us let alone go with us so we bought some bottles with what was left of Tom's wages and walked out along the harbour past the secondhand boat place. We carried on past the huts for the rowing teams to the river quay. Tom thought we would have better luck at another place we knew down there. Tom's logic was, go to a real dive and the girls would always be keen. When we got there we found the doors all shut up. We were cold and still had our bottles with us.

'Let's get in a boat,' said Tom. 'Be warmer.'

We looked around a bit. They were mostly too fancy to be any use, all closed cabins and the like. Most of the pleasure boats were already out the water what with winter coming. Tom said this was on account of them being owned by 'townie frauds who would piss themselves at the first sign of a decent swell.'

'Or maybe they just don't like the cold.' I said

'Fuck off,' said Tom. 'Which one we having?'

I liked the look of a small wooden dinghy, it was blue and had a big thick tarp we could crawl under. Tom said it was a girl's boat. In the end we settled for a bigger one with an engine out the back and enough shelter and canvas to keep the wind off us while we drank. We swung down along the planks and ropes and after some wrestling with the cover found we could make ourselves a nest.

'You can't be cut up about your Pa you know,' said Tom. I'd told him about the fight as we walked.

'What do you know about it anyway?' My head was swimming all around and around as bad as the water under the boat.

'I feel you Brother, but in the end your Pa's your family. Like me and my lot. My mother doesn't even live with us and some days I hate them both so much I could beat in both their fuckin' heads with a shovel.'

'You're too drunk to do anything with a shovel.'

We thought that was funny.

'When we get back I'll have a word with Pa Midwinter about it.'

'What you going to say?'

'That you're already ugly and if he keeps this up you'll never get laid. Ever.'

'But luckily I have you right?'

'Exactly.' Tom tested the wheel. He swung it left, then right. 'Shall we take this fine vessel a-sailin'?'

'Sure.' I said and stood up to show my willing. I didn't feel too good.

'Whoa there sailor.' Tom leaned over the side of the boat. 'Yup, tide is up so we are good to go!'

'What you know about tides anyway?'

'Absolutely sweet fuck-all. But I do know sometimes, the sea comes up the river to this here town, and sometimes, it goes the other way.'

'But which way do we need it to be going?'

'Well,' he was getting all ponderous, 'Everything is back to front with boats. So I figure, whatever direction you think it doesn't need to be going is the right one. Got it?'

'Er. Yeah.'

'Good.' He was one triumphant sailor.

We were all kinds of merry, unhooking the tarp from around the boat, Tom finding a tin of tea and some matches in a box, me pointing out that we had lots of rope. For a moment I wondered what we were doing.

'Let's head for the peninsula.'

'Aye captain,' said Tom. 'I say we have a jolly old picnic when we get there, like we do in the summer.'

Half way along the river, off to the left, was a long old peninsula, with some old Second World War bunkers. It was now some secret bird-nesting place but everyone ignored all that and just used it as a beach. If you walked right over it to the other side, which took less than ten minutes, you could swim in the sea. You'd have to really want to, though, shrivel cold even in the summer.

As we looked out into the black we couldn't even think which way the ocean was.

'See where them gulls are heading?' said Tom, pointing up.

I couldn't see a thing.

'We're sailing that'er way.'

He was a clever salty that Tom.

Somehow we got the boat out into clear water, mostly by pushing away the other boats and dragging ourselves along the pier ropes until we were clear. It wasn't pretty but it was effective and then we could hoist the sail. I was thinking less and less about Pa and the troubles we were having and starting to fancy a life beyond the farm. A life with boats and booze and company.

We were making good progress and because the tide was high we knew we weren't about to get stuck on sandbanks and crap like that. Tom was pretending he knew all sorts of sailing songs and was singing like there was no tomorrow. I knew he was just making them up as he went but I liked hearing them and he liked singing them and I guess that's what friends do for each other. We shared another bottle of beer as we went, and passing it between us made me feel like my cousin probably felt when he talked about his army friends, brothers in arms and all that. It made me wish I'd had my own brother. I had Tom though. That was good.

By the time we got to the peninsula we were frozen. We had crouched down in the boat as far as was safe with a hand on the wheel. A few times we forgot which way we were meant to turn, with boat steering working kind of backwards, but we did a good enough job in the end. Tom was going on about navigating by the stars and us going off to find new worlds. In the end we just found the peninsula and that was fine by me.

We stood to throw the anchor over. We didn't get the rope out all the way.

'Think it matters?'

'No, brother, it's in the drink isn't it? Hold the boat steady.'

'Okay. Quite windy though.' It was whipping off the ocean like a row of ice picks.

'Boat's going nowhere. But we are going a-picnicking. Come on.'

There was a pause when we realised we'd be needing to jump over and wade in onto the stone beach. We didn't have a dingy.

'What you think?' I said. 'How will we get back? Tom?'

Tom was leaning over the stern. Next thing, he disappeared over.

I had to follow. I was only in half way up to my knees but as the water hit me I felt the air being sucked clean out of my chest. Ahead of me, Tom was holding his tea and matches over his head. By the time we reached the shore, and it wasn't more than twenty yards, we had both sobered up by at least two bottles.

'Fuckin' burly out here man,' said Tom.

I had taken off my socks and boots before leaping over so. Once I put them back on, Tom sent me to find kindling and a can to fill with rainwater while he tried to get his feet warm.

'You keep singing so I can find my way back, okay?' Tom nodded and piped back up. His singing voice was a little thin now.

'Yeah, like that. Keep at it and find some driftwood here and don't go wandering.'

'Jesus you're a bossy old bitch,' Tom said.

I leaned away from the river, towards the sea and set off across the flat.

'Tom! Sing!'

Tom started up. Even with my head all gummy, I knew where I was going. We came here nearly every weekend in the summer. The rocks on the north side made shallow cups for rain water and we'd scoop it out with whatever tins other people had left there. It wasn't far to go but the wet and the dark weren't helping. I imagined the telling-off Ma would give me if she were alive. 'Not your sharpest choice was it, my heart?' The last time she'd said that was out in Kabwe on the day she died. She found out I'd hidden a scorpion in my bedroom and the lid had come off the bottle.

I found the water and some tins and wood easily enough, I was used to scratching around for stuff. Getting back to Tom was harder. I guess it was the wind but I couldn't hold his voice. Sometimes he would sound out ahead of me but then turn up behind me. I felt panic rising and wished like hell we hadn't come. What the fuck were we thinking? I spilled some of the water tripping over. I had to go slower. There wasn't much of a moon but it was all I had.

'Tom! I can't hear you, sing!'

Tom struck up again and this time I knew I was closer. I shuffled over a little ridge like a hobbled donkey, to see Tom hopping from foot to foot trying to get warm. He had set some reeds on fire.

'What took you so long?'

'You're fucking crazy, you know?'

I couldn't feel my hands as I let the pile of wood fall. It was starting to feel like the longest night of my life.

We drank the tea when it was just about hot enough. The water was all full of the leaf bits but we didn't care. We never said it but I reckon we both felt like those American cowboys, all booze and cold black nights and smoky fire.

The wind was stacking clouds like a mob of crows. No sign of stars now and the air was starting to clot.

'Feels like snow,' said Tom

'Hail probably.'

'What's the bloody difference? If it comes we're in trouble. Nowhere to hide here and with the tide we'll be stuck for hours.'

'We'll survive.'

'I will, you, not so sure. Don't forget Old Riley.'

Three years previous, one of the old duffers from town had got caught out on the peninsula in a storm and by the time they found him he was stone cold. Dead.

'Maybe we should face the river again? Get the boat home?'

'That's very sensible of you, brother. And I don't much care for it. Still, something coming.'

We stood to put out the fire. My legs felt like they had seized up for ever. Tom decided to keep his boots on but I took mine off and the shingle dug deep into my feet as we walked down to the water's edge.

'I admit I do not see our sailing vessel,' said Tom.

'Me neither.'

'Where'd it go?'

'Don't know.'

'We in the right place?'

'Reckon so.'

'You're a whole lot a help, brother.'

'Well, I'm seeing what you're seeing and I'm not seeing the boat.'

'Fuck this.'

'I'll say.'

'We can't be in the right place.'

We squinted into the black water. There was nothing that told us where we were or how far away the boat might be. I started to feel tired and then just beaten and angry.

'We shouldn't have come.'

'Yeah, first-class, fur-lined, five-star, ocean-going stupid idea,' said Tom.

'Your five-star stupid idea, you mean.'

'My? My stupid idea?'

'That's what I said.'

'I don't fuckin' think so, brother.'

'Yeah, you were all, hey, let's go a-sailin' and all that crap.'

'So what? You do everything I say? Anyway I never said we had to come here. We could have gone up stream, not out here in the middle of fucking nowhere in a fucking storm to have a goddam picnic did we? No. We didn't. That, brother Vale, was your genius. So, for once, just stop fucking whinging and man up.'

'You sound like your Pa.'

'Thank you, brother Vale.'

'I wasn't being nice.'

'I know.'

'Okay.'

'Okay.'

'And, it's fuckin' pitch dark and I can still tell you look like shit.'

'Thanks.'

'Your face hurt?'

'Can't feel my face.'

Tom thought that was funny.

Then we were quiet a little. We were both suddenly feeling the night.

'Looks like witches' piss out there,' said Tom.

'I'll say.'

We agreed to wander up the shore a little to look for our boat. It was a stupid idea given we were both still hammered, and I was walking like a crab with three feet. We'd sometimes catch sight of ripples as a cloud shifted a little. No boat.

'Must be the other way.'

'Yup.'

Back we went the way we had just come and well past where our fire had been when, there she was. We could just make out her shape, way down the river toward the sea and much further out than we remembered.

'Oh man.' I said.

'Oh jeez.' said Tom.

'What you think?'

'I say we do it.'

'Really?'

'Really.'

'I don't know.'

'A call to valour, Vale Midwinter. Our finest hour. It can't be that far. It's got the anchor and all.'

'True.'

'You okay?'

'Sure.'

'Say it like you mean it then.'

'I can't. I'm not. Shit, Tom.'

'I'll wade out and let you know how deep it is.'

'That's crazy, we go together, that way if it's deeper than we think, we got each other.'

Tom threw his weight at me and nearly crushed the life out of me. He smelled like a brewery.

'I love you, brother, I do.'

'Okay, but we still got to get to our boat.'

Tom nodded. We were neither of us in a good way to be swimming in the dark, but then again we could hardly stay there. Tom took his boots off in case we had to swim. He left them on the water's edge.

I hardly felt the water rise this time. I was numb already. Tom roared 'Fuck!' as the water hit him. By the time we were in up to our waists we realised what we were in for. Turns out, when the river goes back out to sea, it takes everything with it.

'Tom, come closer. We'll do better together.'

Tom had to lean his weight into the river to get to me. My pulse was up in my throat. It was difficult going even for those few steps. We linked arms.

'Jeez, where's all this water going in such a hurry?' He was shouting.

'Back out to sea, and we'll be going with it if you don't look sharp.'

'Boat's not far. Water's not too deep.'

And he was right, we could see the boat and we were only in it just at our waist. Tom was a little deeper because of his height. As if to make up for it he started with his sailor songs again. We waded deeper and deeper in. All the while the river dragged its great heap under us.

Then it felt like we had been going all night. I had to think about every step. Tom was getting tired too. We were linked through our arms. We stopped singing early on. We were headed into the middle of the river where we knew there was a fucking huge gully. There were rocks there too. The back-rush of the water in there would be a beast. As we edged closer we could feel the drag getting worse.

'I don't think I can do this, brother', said Tom.

'You have to mate, we're linked. You drop, I go with you.'

'I think we should go back.'

'Are you crazy? It's taken us how long just to get out here and now you want to get back? And then what, we sit there waiting in the storm like old Riley and the boat just heads out to sea without us?'

'That's what I'm thinking. I worry we're on that boat when it heads out to sea.'

'No, we need the boat. It's got a motor and when the tide changes again then we get pushed back up the river. We can't do that swimming.'

I was trying to sound confident but who knew how I sounded. I was just trying to shout through booming wind, with my teeth half frozen in my face.

I would just as easily have gone back and sat on that bit of rock until someone came to get us. Maybe even Pa. But I didn't fancy our chances waiting for someone to find us with a couple of matches in a thunder storm. Tom was starting to get that weepy look old drunks get. I was having none of it.

'Come on Tom, hoo-hahr!'

I let it out from inside my belly somewhere and fuck me, Tom straightened and gripped me closer with his arm, though I'm sure it was aching like a bitch. We took another step before finding our balance again. The river bed was solid enough but we knew it would suddenly drop away into the gully where the boat was resting and when we felt that rush we knew we would be done for if we stepped in. The wind was thickening and it was raining harder too. It might have been hail. We were wet through and too tired to keep on. I knew what we had to do and I knew Tom wouldn't like it. I didn't like it either.

'Tom we're going to have to swim. Together.'

'Are you crazy?' Even in the dark, I could see Tom was panicking.

'We can't beat the gully. We'll be sucked out to kingdom come. We have to go in further upstream and hope we get washed toward the boat. If we go in here, right next to the boat, we'll be washed past it in 5 seconds.'

He didn't say anything, we just stood there shaking and leaning into the tide to hold our ground.

'I don't know.' said Tom.

'Water'll wash us at the boat. When we see it coming, we got to push up out the water and grab hold. Got it?'

'Jesus fucking Christ. We just walk in?'

'Tom, no, Jesus, listen to me. We have to swim, stay on the surface, keep our legs out of the drag underneath.'

'Jesus.'

'Come on. Just don't let go of me.'

'I won't let go. Aren't there rocks down there too?'

'That's why you have to kick. Stay on the surface.'

'Okay, okay.'

'And prepare for the cold.'

'Okay. Shit. Okay.'

Nothing prepared us and we lost each other just as soon as we hit the water. The gully beat us and beat us again. I was just struggling to breathe. Then I heard Tom choke and rasp, and suddenly felt a huge weight. I thought I was dying then, but I kept fighting. And I still don't know why.

I got us home. Me and Tom. I got us both back on that boat and the motor going. I don't know how. The wind was screaming and Tom even louder. I wanted to tell him to shut the fuck up; but I knew he couldn't. Then we hit something in the water, got shaken quite hard, and he yelled out and then went totally quiet. I thought he was dead. Jesus Christ, I panicked. I had to take my jacket off and loop it through the wheel to hold it in line so I could get to him at the back of the boat. It made no difference to me whether I got back home, I would have just let myself drift out, but I had to help Tom. I was so cold I was on fire, burning right through, and it felt like I had a shard of glass stuck through my shoulder. The deck was wet and there were bottles and things rolling around on it. I nearly landed on Tom, slipping and getting my feet caught in the ropes.

'Tom?' He just lay there. 'Wake up man.'

I shook him hard and he shouted out as his eyes opened suddenly. He was fucking terrified. He looked like a pig when you get one trying to bolt from the runs at the abattoir. His skin was so white I thought I could see right through it.

'I'm getting us home. Can you hear me?'

He was clenching his jaw for all he was worth but he nodded.

When I'd finally pulled him out the water he was a dead weight, his body did nothing to help. His arms were pulling at the side to lift himself but the rest of him just hung there. The sides of the boat were so deep and he finally came over like a huge sack of lead, screaming all hell. It was ugly but he didn't go out in the tide, I'd not let him go. That was good.

Hearing his grunting and shouting and passing out and coming to made me panic some. I just wanted to get somewhere where someone would know what to do with him.

'You got to hang on.' I tried to cover him with the tarpaulin. It didn't reach all the way over him, but maybe it helped. I guess I should have done it before, to keep the wind off him.

'I have to go just up there to steer now.' I pointed towards the wheel as I shouted. 'You hang on, okay?'

My jacket sleeve had done okay holding our path but we'd drifted a bit. I felt beaten. I could see the harbour lights but I couldn't judge how far we had to go. Sometimes they seemed to disappear, and then I panicked some more and thought maybe I had gone half a circle and was pointed back out towards the sea again. I hurt everywhere, too. Mostly in my shoulder. I had to take my hand off the wheel because the engine was shuddering along through it into my bones. It hurt like hell. I knew there were better ways to get in to the harbor, all to do with floats and sand banks, but I didn't know what they were.

I wondered if Pa knew where I was. But, instead of wishing he was there and feeling bad for everything I'd said earlier that night, I thought that if me and Tom died, then that would teach him a lesson. I thought if I died then maybe once he had lost his whole family, Pa would know how I felt when Ma was killed. I should have hated myself for thinking it. I didn't.

Tom's shouting had stopped. Instead he was grunting like a dying horse. All I could hear other than him was the water sloshing and banging on the side of the boat and the empty bottles rolling from one side to the other. Tom was crying too. I didn't know how to help him. The rain kept on.

The water was syrup. Pa always said about boats, to send them out you have to work hard, charting the course and stuff, but for the most part, if you just give it some push, a boat always finds its way home. Same with horses. I didn't give a shit about horses and I was well past ever wanting to see a boat again. You always hear about the speed of light travelling at this and that, but that night I knew for sure that darkness just stands still.

'Tom you have to do it.' I said that mostly to myself.

I think he said, 'I can't.'

I shouted out with all the lung I had left. There was no one else to hear me but you always hope someone will. My voice didn't even go very far. It froze right up under my chin somewhere. There was no space for it in all the rain and ice. I shouted again. Nothing.

I stopped. And in that same breath the wind and rain fell away.

It felt just for a few seconds like when Ma used to say 'angels are passing'. That hush. Just the slopping and washing of the water.

Then I saw the lights. They were right up ahead, closer than I had thought they were. I stood up so quickly I nearly threw myself overboard.

'Tom! Tom, we're close, we'll make it. Did you hear that?'

I was shouting at him over my shoulder. I didn't want to leave the wheel now I was trying to get us straight to the lights. I could see them clearly and I knew where the buoys were in the water. It was okay.

The lights got bigger and clearer even through the rain. I heard a man shouting, someone other than Tom. Tom was groaning and then he'd suddenly bellow like a bull being branded. Even with all that I was pretty sure I could hear someone else.

'Hello? Hello?'

A big light swung round. It was so bright it was like staring right at the sun. It swung again; left, then right and back again. All the water ahead of us lit up. It was a search light from the harbour master's cabin.

I shouted for all I was worth. As we got closer I could just see him on the edge of the quay. I shouted and cried even more and shouted at Tom and at the guy. I've never been so pleased to see someone before. And that light, guiding us home.

As we got nearer I could hear he was giving instructions to get the boat in close.

'Are you alone boy? Are you all right?'

'No. I'm all right, but Tom is hurt.'

'What you say?'

'Tom. He's badly hurt.' I was yelling at him. 'He needs to go to hospital.'

'I've called them.'

'What?'

'I've called the services.'

I didn't know what he was saying about the services. I was so busy watching him and the big wall of steel and concrete starting to shade one side as the boat got nearer the moorings. I didn't want to screw up getting us in and miss the tie-up or we'd have to go round again and circle back. I knew I couldn't do that.

'Tom? There's people to help you.' I grabbed at the ropes but I couldn't feel them in my hands.

The master called down to me.

'Wrap it round. You have to grab hold and wrap it round.'

'I can't, I can't hold it.'

I was stabbing at it but couldn't close my hands around. I felt the boat starting to drift.

'Grab it boy.'

'I can't. My hands are gone.'

'Jesus lad, grab it.'

Chapter 2

Landyn

Kabwe, Zambia. The three of us sat there like we did every night, dining table laid out, me at the head, Cecelia to my right, running her thumb over her wedding band as she always did, and Vale, ten years old at the time, sitting to my left. Somehow I always remember the table, big and trustworthy, mahogany. At night the house was always heavy with the smell of citronella, to keep the biters and the bugs away. I could smell it even as I came across the garden towards the low light of the place, all spread out like a long train carriage in the trees, one big umbrella tree out the front, always full of monkeys and birds.

Vale was quiet as usual. We two had finished with our plates, and Cessie was waiting for him to finish before she rang the bell for the girl to clear. The girl had been with us for nearly the full two years we were out there by then. We called her Sara though she had another name too.

That night is was another battle with me saying Vale, why aren't your grades improving when I spend all this money on lessons and Vale saying he didn't know.

'That's not really an answer.' I said.

The boy just got quieter and quieter swinging his legs under the table and stabbing at the green beans one by one until I told Cessie to ring the bell.

'Vale's not done yet, Land.'

'He has no plans to be done. Do you?' The boy ignored me. 'Ring the bell.'

The lights from the ambulances were flashing through the rain on my windshield even before I was half way down the old road to the quay. My stomach rolled in on itself like a big oily eel in a jar. The old body remembering dread. There I saw my boy huddled up on the side of the quay, all soaked and blue with cold and covered in blankets. You'd have thought from looking at the lad that he came out the water dragging them all behind him on the back of one of those mossy tides.

Of course, of course, there were those who would say it was bound to happen. I could almost hear them, dropping their voices as they tried to disguise talk as caring. Shame about that boy, they would say, and his poor old father after what happened with his wife, bless. Terrible, so terrible, and now this, they'd say. Gossip. From where I sat, I could see all the ways I might have prevented it. The words I might have chosen with more care. Not let myself get so riled up. Perhaps I might have gone to find the boy when he went off with the dogs that night. He might have done different too, of course. He might not have said what he said and could have come indoors and not gone to town, might not have drunk so much with our Thomas. All the things you could have done differently, that can keep you awake every night.

Don't I still think how things might have been different for his mother? Some nights I dream things turned out well for us. Then I wake full round and as I fall back into my sad old skin, I remember myself again and know it not to be true. This is a cruel trick the mind plays. Like a sly old ferret those hopeful thoughts burrow in there. And then, when you're getting all cosy, they turn on you and rip you right open with their sweaty little teeth until you feel your guts are spilling out all over again.

When I rolled up at the quay, I couldn't see what was what, though I knew in the instant the little huddle was Vale. I'd know him if he was a speck on the moon. The rain was coming in like the waves had begun to escape the sea. Ice in it too. I hoped my old wagon would keep itself going in such a drowning. There hadn't been the pennies to give it the attention it needed the past months. I admit I sat a second with the engine on to settle my dread before I faced it all.

I'd felt this before, and known it before too, the sickly feeling before opening the door and seeing what had to be seen. Back then, in Kabwe, it was in early morning, just past sunrise and already the sky was bleaching into nothing like a bit of old parchment, cicada beetles already up and out, all screaming so as you could hardly hear yourself think. I stood there for God knows how long and in the end it was only because of the policeman that I went in and saw what had been done to our Cessie.

Now, even in the motor, the noise of the rain on the roof was deafening. My hearing isn't too good either, that's how bad it was. I knew those boys must have been well oiled-up to even think to go out in that squall. I got myself together.

Vale was sitting on a wall where all the rowing boats are moored. They'd covered him up. There were folk looking on and some we knew, too, though none had gone to him, to offer some comfort. He sat there in the rain all bundled up like a boy with no home, and in that instant I saw him like he was 10 years old all over again, sitting there after the business with his Ma all white and drawn for what he'd seen; and, of course, God help us, it was all of that darkness that had brought us back to this. You can set the dark aside for just so long before it comes after you and rolls you back under its weeds and rocks. Can't outrun this stuff and looking at my boy at the water's edge, I knew I was a fool to ever think we had.

He saw me, I think, but not a word came out. His mouth just moved open and shut again the way the terns do when they're bibbling in the shallows. I thought maybe he did not know me so I said my name over and over and gripped him to me. I said;

'Vale it's me son, it's your Pa. It's your old Dad here.'

All he did was shiver and shake with such an ungodly violence I could hear his teeth knocking against each other. Perhaps because I felt desperate the way you do when you know you might have lost everything, or perhaps just because his mute shock called for something honest, I said, for what might have been the first time;

'I love you Vale, I love you son.' He didn't say anything, so I just kept holding the boy close as I could and I thought to myself, that we had been here like this before. Him all fallen apart, just a mite back then, and me hanging on and hoping it would all be all right in the end.

Behind him I could see through the rain to the quay where there were some lads getting the boat back in and tied up and Kevin, being the quay master, a good fellow, was walking along it looking at the bow and running his hand along the gunwale. He rapped the boat with his knuckles like boat people do, some sort of habit they have. I'd not even thought about the boat. By rights they had stolen it.

'He'll need to come along now, Sir.' It was the medical lads.

'With you? Can't I bring him?'

'No Sir. He has to come with us so we can keep an eye on the way.'

'Keep an eye? Is there something wrong.?'

'No Sir, I'm sure not but we need to monitor him and get his temperature up. Pulse is a bit dickey, he's been out there a while. It's below freezing tonight isn't it?'

'Right, right. Can I come with him?'

'You can follow on behind and meet us there.'

'If you say, if you say.' I turned back to Vale.

'Will that be right with you, son? You go with these fellows and I'll be right behind.' No response. 'Son, do you to hear me. Can you go along with me behind? Will that be something you can do?'

The boy turned his head to me, lips like slates and eyes as dark and empty as they were deep. His face was bluer for all the flashing lights and I held it firm in my hands to make sure he would look at me and hear me. I could feel his jaw bones resting cold in my palms and the ghosts gathering up behind us.

'Can you do it?'

Dear God, and those tears came. He let the one out and the rest just followed on like sheep flowing out of a pen and across a cold, cold field at daybreak.

He had never cried back then, never cried for his Ma. God knows I did, for weeks and weeks so I sometimes thought I couldn't breathe, but the boy never did, not that I knew anyway.

He nodded.

'Good lad, good lad.'

Then, through the wind and all the lines pinging off the metal masts and all the chaos, I heard a bloody great animal roar behind me, angry and deep. I turned to see someone, being lifted up on a stretcher. It was young Tom. The rain was coming down so hard around him and it looked like he was fighting every last drop. God almighty he was crying out. I didn't see his father. He was probably face down on the floor of a pub somewhere.

'Shall I go to Tom? I'll see how he is.' Vale nodded. 'Good then, I'll be back, I'll just see to our friend.'

When I got to young Tom, I knew there was trouble there. He was straining in his face, his veins coming out his forehead, blue and ripe to bursting.

'Tom, lad, it's Pa Landyn. You're okay lad. These fellows will help you.' But I knew even then they might not help him. Tom grabbed me round my collars, with big hard fists and he just hung on and looked at me with his red eyes, staring and burning. He held on for all he was worth that boy and only when the fellows took him away did he let go.

'I'll be along to see you lad. I'll come along to the hospital.'

He just kept staring at me but spoke no word of a prayer. I dare say he was shocked right down to his marrow with fear or pain or both. Even as they loaded him in he just kept grunting through his teeth and straining even though he had stopped fighting them.

'Will he be okay?' I asked the fellows. I had to raise my voice with the wind as it was. They only shrugged. I didn't like that. Not for their resignation and not for what it said for young Tom.

'Where you going with him? Which one?'

'Suffolk Coastal.'

'I'll be right behind.'

The lads were taken through big swing doors. I sat a while on those hospital seats, all clung up with damp and a great tiredness came over. Like a big heavy dog blanket had been thrown over me all of a sudden. I wished for all my life I wasn't there with everything dyed that strange green that was also blue. I've never cared for it. I tried to get a response off the people there, but there was just no hurrying them along. There I was waiting to hear something about my boy and no one doing anything to help except say, 'You may as well take a seat, it will be some time.'

'It is my boy they have through there, and his friend, young lads,' I said.

'I understand,' said the heavy nurse, hiding behind her counter.

I could tell she bloody well didn't understand. Not one bit. Any woman worth her salt would know that my boy was suffering something through there, some tremendous fate that had nothing to do with his temperature or his shoulder or his pulse they kept checking every time I caught a glimpse through a door.

It seemed the tides, or some darkness, had conspired to bring us all to this place; me, Vale, Tom, even Tom's useless, drunken father none of us could find. I could shake that fat woman right out of her shoes to make her listen. It was no use, I knew she had already decided I was an old duzzy whoop and young boys up to no good and had what they had coming to them.

I went out the front of the hospital to escape the waiting. It was bitter, but there was shelter enough to smoke and breathe some air in. Everything smelled of the coast. It's like that in winter, the sea finally takes over the land. In the summertime, that's when the earth can claim its place, and push its shaggy boundaries right out, all fat and full of green.

On that night, out there, watching all those rag-edged

characters coming and going under the hospital lights, all hunched against the wind and rubbing their hands, I longed for warmer days and easier times. Those late summer evenings when the air thrubs with the sound of harvesters and tractors and bailers, their engines going right through the night that follows and their big lights blaring down the fields to gather their fruits. A man too old and tired for the work can sit a while, with his dog sitting as close as he can, both feeling the warmth of the late sun on their bodies and be carried off by the smell of crushed onions that cuts through the air for miles. So full and rich is the earth round here that they harvest more than the lorry backs can carry and they spill over, and get smashed, and let out their sweet vinegar.

You would not want to wait too long though. A man of my years cannot sit and face a setting sun the way a young man can. When you're young it means the work is done and with that comes the night. There are adventures to be had when you're all roar and stupid. But seeing the sun falling like that, so you can near count it down as it drops, leaves a man such as myself with all manner of regret and longing. Perhaps for another pop at it, where you might be braver and quicker, more bold in the round.

I could have done better, it's true, but I lost my folks young, so I had no time for all that. Had to work to keep the land going, teach myself most of the business end of things and I guess didn't teach myself so well as it turns out. My Ma and Pa were the best a boy could have and losing them as I did meant I had to teach myself to live too. But I did make it all work, to a degree, and I wasn't going to throw it all away. All the working and the trying meant I forgot to get married of course, as you do. When I met

34

Cessie, quite a bit later on, she asked why a fellow such as I was still on the market and in truth I had to admit I had forgotten to take a wife and make a family and next thing I was forty-odd. The farm had settled and I'd made a good concern of it and what with a few hours here and there that I then had to myself, I'd begun to notice the lack of company.

I recall it was old Dobb who told me I'd be old before my time without nippers about. And he was right.

Now though, Vale was up there in the wards. We shouldn't have quarrelled as we did. Even for our fractious ways, we went too far the night before. Too far.

He cut me right where he knew there was fresh meat, the type that doesn't knit. He sat with his dirty boots on his mother's tapestry footstool and I had asked him twice already to take the boots down or just take the things off, which he normally does anyway. But he just carried on rolling those cigarettes, as if I weren't even there. I pointed out that he was disrespecting the memory of his mother.

'Your mother put each of those stitches in herself. Took her a few months too. You respect your mother's memory, Vale.'

'If it wasn't for you, I'd still have a mother to respect and not just a memory, wouldn't I?'

Just like that. Out of the blue. Like he'd been saving it up all these years and finally he couldn't keep it in any longer and it didn't matter that it was only dirty boots and furniture, something snapped and he just had to say it. Just like that.

'What did you say?' I said.

'You heard me.'

'What is it you're saying then?'

'We didn't need to go there but you made us. Ma got killed

because of what you did, not for anything she did.' He didn't look at me when he said it. Pup-dog jumped off my lap as I stood.

I should have known this was his pain speaking, because with him it always is, but it got to me and I said, 'How dare you speak to me like that?'

'What you going to do?' He stood up. I saw his boot scrape wet dirt on his mother's stool as he did.

'You think you know it all? You were a child. I know how hard it was for you. I do. It was for us all.'

'Yeah, right.' He was spitting.

'You know why we went.'

He said nothing, but his cheeks were red and he was biting on the inside of his mouth like a raging horse trying to throw off its bridle.

'It was a good opportunity, a fine one,' I said.

He shot round. 'How? What was good about it? That Ma was killed? You pissed all those men off and then where were you that night?' He was puce, weeping, outside of himself. 'You were nowhere. You left us alone and that's why they killed her.'

I struck him.

I struck my boy and got him hard. Across the face with the back of my hand and I did it for his mother as much as for me.

He grabbed his face with his hand, his eyes blazing. He laughed too, just to himself, to make sense of it I guess, but he wasn't done and he came like a viper for the final blow. He pointed at me, his nose and eyes streaming where I had hit him, I could see his left cheek swelling.

'You know what you did. They killed her because of you.'

He left, out the door, leaving me there raging and aching. And I stood dazed until I noticed that Pup was cowering next to the wall, shaking all through. When I went to her to make it right she ran away to hide under the kitchen table. The others gave me a wary eye too. I tried to coax her out and had to get down on all fours to see her.

'I'm sorry, little one, I'm so sorry. I didn't mean it. Come on out.'

But she wouldn't. And only hours later, when I'd gone to bed with a shroud of shame and misery all about, did I feel her weight flop onto the bed next to me.

It was well after two when Kevin called to say the boys had been found, with Vale trying to get the boat alongside and tied up in a gale and screaming out that Tom was hurt, and badly so.

I was finished with my cigarette, and went back in through the big hospital doors to check on Vale, but he was asleep and there was nothing more I could do for him that night. The nurse said he'd be fine after some rest. He would probably be out by the Sunday. There was nothing too terrible, though his shoulder was ripped. Thomas was bad. He'd hurt his spine and his legs, and word from Kevin was that his father had been found but he wasn't fit to visit.

I drove home; the longest drive. Snow was coming and the heating in the motor did nothing to help. The lights only picked out what was falling right in front of them and it was hard to see too far ahead up the lanes. I came through the grove, just before the straight, open stretch to home. As I flicked the lights onto a full beam, through the rain, I saw a great white tipped copper plume shoot into the hedges.

My fox. Ah, there she was.

My boy would be okay.

Chapter 3
Vale

'Wake up, you're okay boy, help is here. What's your name? Can you remember? Take another deep breath.'

A man was holding something over my face. I tried to move but I felt nothing. I saw the man, and I knew he wasn't the harbour master so I thought maybe it was Pa but then I looked properly and saw it wasn't him either.

I said, 'Where's Tom?'

And he said, 'Off to hospital.'

'Is he going to be okay?'

'Can't say,' said the man.

'I got us home.'

'Right about that. The Master says your father's coming.'

'Okay.'

'Can you tell me how old you are?'

'Where's Tom?'

'How old are you? Do you remember? Keep breathing lad.'

'20. Will he be okay?'

'Good. So you're 20 years old, and what's your name?'

'Vale.'

'That's good too Vale. Now, your other name, family name?

'Midwinter.'

'Can you follow this light with your eyes.'

I couldn't.

'Midwinter,' I said.

'You stay there. We're going to get you in the ambulance. First PC Brown is going to ask you about what happened.'

The light behind me appeared and then got blocked out again.

'All right there son? So you're Vale Midwinter?'

I nodded.

'You boys got yourselves in quite a mess tonight. Your friend should be okay though. You feeling better?'

'Yeah.' I was burning right down into my muscles.

'So, big night, been drinking?'

'Yeah.'

'How much? Do you know?'

'Few jars.'

'A few?'

'Yeah, well, maybe four, or six. More for Tom.'

'Get in any scraps last night, you know, have a go? Other lads there?'

'No.'

'You've got a bit of a shiner on your face. That from before?'

I remembered Pa. I nodded.

'Had anything else? Smoked something?'

'What? No.'

'That's not your boat down there is it son?'

'No. We. No.'

'Do you know whose it is?'

It was the first time I'd thought the boat belonged to someone. I looked up at him. His nose and moustache underneath had made a way to part the rain coming down his face. It made me think of Moses from the Bible story. Which was stupid.

It was difficult to think. I was thinking about Moses. 'Oh.'

'Oh's about right.'

'Tom's hurt.' I don't know why I said that. 'He still here?'

'He's going to hospital, they need to get a move on with that one. Incomplete spinal. Possibly.'

'What?' I didn't know what that meant.

'Your dad's been called. Okay? He's on his way. The medics will come and get you in a minute. Need to get you warmed up. Anything else I need to know?'

I didn't know what more he wanted and I couldn't speak anyway. Couldn't move either, I was all wrapped up in God knows what. Heavy stuff. It was like I had sunk into the peat out at the marshes.

We had a milking cow that did that one year, got stuck so far in she near killed herself trying to get out. Struggling and fighting until she was so knackered she just lay there and waited for the end. Then the sun started to come up and the mud and peat started to dry around her and she nearly died. Mostly because she just didn't have any more fight in her legs to get her weight up. We got her out with six guys and ropes and a tractor but she didn't even try and help herself. That's how I felt.

I don't know when Pa arrived. In between it all and feeling how I did, I forgot I hated him because maybe I didn't. In the wet I could smell the tobacco on his coat. It was good. I wanted to say I was sorry. I tried to move my mouth but nothing came out. It never did when I wanted to say something important.

We sat together for a while like that even though it was pelting down and I had those stupid thoughts you do, that nothing bad had happened between us.

I woke up later the next day. It was afternoon a nurse told me. I was alone in a ward. There were two other beds between mine and the window that were empty. I didn't know where Tom was. I was attached to one of those drip bags and I could feel the needle going into my hand. My shoulder hurt the most though. I remembered pulling it when I was dragging Tom out of the water. I was thirsty but I couldn't see anyone around.

'Hello?'

My voice was gone, broken and rough like it had been cut through with a hand saw. I tried a few times. When my voice did come out I didn't recognise it. Finally someone came in to help. A nurse brought me tea. She loaded it with sugar and helped me drink. It was so good. Burned my throat the whole way down. She couldn't give me news on Tom which pissed me off. I told her everything was hurting. I must have fallen asleep again because I kept thinking I was back on the boat rocking this way and that with the bottles rolling around just not getting anywhere. When I woke the windows were dark and a light was on. Pa was there in a chair in the corner. He was snoozing sitting upright like he did at home with his Pup on his lap. It was strange to see him without her.

I knew he'd be thinking he should be home to see her. He had worked out she was nearly eighty in human years. He always said it would soon be time to call the vet. But he never could. She had gnarly feet, like oak roots, Pa said. He got her when we got back from Zambia. I guess he needed a friend.

Pa's face looked grey and hollow. I shut my eyes again. I didn't want to talk to him if he woke up. I had nothing I knew how to say.

Chapter 4

Landyn

I was in a bind before we had even sat down to eat. It was still hot and the day had been long and difficult. Out there it worked differently. Thousands of acres and teams of labourers who all lived in villages nearby and a few on the land itself. They arrived as the sun came up, all sitting in a huddle at the gates. We'd open up and they would file past, all rag and muscle. We were there over two years and still, I couldn't wrap my head around it all. Back home if I wanted something done I'd do it myself. Out there, though, you do nothing for yourself but all the time you were trying to get everyone else to do it how you want it done. None of them were farmers. They were just selling their hours of work. And though he lived on the land, the same applied to the man Chisongo.

The house was a sanctuary. I felt more like myself there. Some nights Cessie and I would sit out once Vale was asleep, and we could hear the singing coming up from the villages below. A little encampment of rounded huts with thatch on top, chickens in and out the doors, always the smell of a wood fire no matter the time of day or season. At night great rolling melodies that came right out of the belly of a man. They all sounded like love songs or songs about longing and they could all but break a man's heart. We two had sat out, our chairs pulled up together facing out into the dark and listened.

Cecelia stretched her hand out to me as we sat. I took it and we sat like we hadn't for the longest of times.

But, that night, sitting around the table, was a darker night.

I thought we'd outrun that history. Wasn't I just an old fool to think it? I thought it wiser to move ahead, leave it all behind and time and season would plant over the top of all the peaty stuff and better things would grow.

But then with what Vale said, all mauling and dark and the quarrel we'd had, I was starting to feel like a rabbit on the run. A great beast for a plough had gone over the back of that field and turned over all the darkness again. A man of my years might start to wonder if there's some dark magic in it all when there's one trouble and another and then another right there on its heels. Suddenly the night is full of owls.

We went out there, to Zambia, to make our lives fresh, start again after some terrible troubles with money and the other stuff. You think you aren't the man who will let that sort of thing break him, you think it won't stretch your centre until it is too thin to hold, but in the end you are, and it did. It made me into a man I would not choose to befriend.

Difficult years. Snow and drought and snow again, one after the other making fodder and the like twice the normal price. We managed I suppose but with every passing season we were a little closer to empty. And then, the last blow came when some new fellows came into town, contractors, bit of money backing them up. People needed a break and here it was. Big companies, food chains, renting land off the farmers who owned it. They just had to plant what was asked for. I didn't want to. It wasn't right. You can't go on planting and planting in the same old field one season after the next and never let it rest. Not a fallow field in our valley after that lot moved in. None of those great hot poppy fields you used to get. No flowers at all to speak of.

So, the other fellows took advantage of the good money and planted to order and I carried with my old ways. Old fool. Soon enough, I had one harvest season left and I'd be finished. That was the start of it all with me and Cecelia too, I suppose. Everyone has a fine and deep-bedded family when the cash is rolling in but take that away, and you'll find out soon enough how well the centre holds. And it shames me to say, we found out who our worst selves were too.

Before we eventually decided to go to Africa, we messed about with all kinds of schemes to try and save ourselves. Our farm wasn't worth much, only the subsidies it came with and those barely covered the cost of maintaining it. Still there'd be enough to keep us alive awhile if I sold it and could hire myself out as labour. I'm not smart with money, never have been. I had enough and lived okay, only I never had any long term savings for pensions and the like. Never put a mind to it and you don't, not until something goes wrong. I had an idea we could sell the house and a portion of it all and set up in the cottage on the far side. It needed better electrics sorted and the pipes were shot, but we could stay in there and make a go of the orchard and the fields that fell to the south side of the Hill. There was good earth in there.

Cecelia cried, oh she cried, wailed even. It was the Irish in her I don't doubt. And the farm was the only home she had known since leaving her own after she'd quarrelled with her family back in Larne.

'We can't leave the house Landyn. What of our roses? I won't leave those. If we have to leave here, I'll take every last one of them with me.'

'Cessie don't.'

'Don't what? Don't you dare. *You* get all stuck in your ways, *you* don't take a good thing when it's offered you – and it's your *wife* who has to leave her roses behind? I don't think so. I do not think so.'

'I've worked my fingers to the bone haven't I though? I've been honest, done all I could. Worked day and night. You do know that?'

'Don't I just? I see you so rarely I'd not recognise you to see you in the street.'

'I'm doing it for us, love.'

'Well. Now we're to leave our home apparently. So you've done that for us too, haven't you?'

I had nothing to reply with. She was all venom.

'Cecelia, don't be like that. I'm asking you to come to a new house in the same valley. That is all. If you'd rather go somewhere else then that's good and fine, but I won't let you take my lad.'

'What have you said to me?' She was on her feet.

'We have no choice. Do you understand that at least. We cannot stay as we are. So we have to move. If you say you will not come with me then that is the end of us.'

'Don't you dare say that to me Landyn Midwinter. I am your wife. And you threaten to cast me out and take my child?'

'No, you've not heard me. No. I want you to come along, try over...'

She turned away from me, back to the feed ledger where she was trying to make the numbers look better, hoping there was more than there was.

She never spoke a work to me for over three days. Left the room when I walked in, pretended to be asleep when I got to bed. I dare say our Vale learned some of his games from her.

A full week later, she wandered out to the barns where I was offloading feed for the piggers. Never forget it. She stood in the door, a cup of coffee in her hand. My cup.

'I'll be needing roses Landyn.'

'I'll make sure of roses.'

'What are we to do about Vale? This is all we have to give him.'

'I don't know.'

'Landyn, I know why you resisted the contracts, I do. I even love you for it. But you can't stop the world. Your fallow fields are fattening all the butterflies and bees, but they aren't keeping us in honey, are they now?'

I rested a while that evening, thinking about what Cessie had said, what I was asking her to do. I sat on the wall that overlooks the horses and then across the fields out to the woods. We'd laid potatoes there that year. Plain old potatoes allowed to grow to any old size they chose, not a regulated size for cutting into factory foods. It had been a wet spring, unusually so, so we'd taken a chance on them, and it had paid off handsomely. The plants were high and full and the purple tops made a lovely cover. They were planted from the paddock wall all the way back until they reached the trees. It was something special to see, and to think a thing so pleasing on the eye was working all the while, forcing out those fat little tubers under the earth, rounding out all plump and thick and multiplying. We'd sell those of course, but it would never be enough.

I sat so long on that wall, feeling the damp and cool from the flint coming through my seat. I couldn't face Cessie, working away at the numbers in the kitchen. I couldn't tell her that in spite of it all, I blamed myself, that perhaps I had been foolish. I had fields at rest but in full meadow-bloom and no money in the bank. This land, given to me by my father after he had bought it field by field off the man he worked for, had come to nothing. And the house too. I was born there back when it still belonged to the large estate and my Pa was managing the landowner's fields for him. He worked hard and laboured away until he had the house and enough land of his own to make a go of it. And here I was, not that many years later, throwing it all away.

I turned to look back at the house. It was all soft, sitting there, like it grew right out of the earth even though it had a bit added on here and there. I could see Cessie at the kitchen sink and young Vale behind her doing his homework, probably getting all his sums wrong. Poor bugger, clever with his hands, knew the land like I know my own heart and loved a good story to read but numbers got him in a right pickle. He cut a scrawny shape, leaning over his books with his tongue pointed at the pencil tip. I wanted him to have the farm. It was his birthright, it was, and he would be good at it, I knew it. Even at that age, no more than seven or eight he'd say:

'Let me try with the tractor.'

He'd climb on my lap and off we'd go down the fields. I'd want him to have a good time so I'd say, 'Shall we go faster then?'

'No, we'll miss out some.'

'Some what?'

'Some barley.'

'Oh, we're harvesting are we?'

'Yes, we're harvesting.'

'Are we getting a good load this year?'

'No, too cold.'

And he'd shake his head like an old otter who'd seen one too many winters. That was him all over. No fripperies, all business he was. Back then his hair was still reddish, like his mother's. He had a few of her freckles too.

But for all the soft evenings and plump potatoes, the money was still gone.

Bleak old morning by the time I was sent away from the hospital, on account of there being no real news on Tom, and Vale being on the mend but needing some solid rest. Cessie, Vale, Tom all ghosting around my head, I went home a weary man, feeling the weight of that bleak trinity.

I'd rushed out the house in such a hurry when I got the call, I'd left a whole row of lights on and no heating. Even as I tapped the wet from my boots at the door I could hear the dogs' noses under the door. A fine welcome and one I needed. My Pup was there too. Lovely old lady she was. I opened up and they all ran out into the wet and dark.

Pup stood there, her efforts at wagging nearly knocking her off her own feet. I could see she'd messed. I cleaned it up and her too. I put the kettle on while I made up a fire. There weren't too many logs. That would have been Vale, he stormed off before the wood was done. And who could blame him? The shame, the horrible shame of striking him came back to clobber me, as if I had struck myself as hard.

I'd just sat down once he left, his face raw and cut. Even Pup didn't dare come close. All I could think was that I had struck my boy and then I remembered what he'd said. I knew it to be true. He did too. Once you speak what you only dare suggest to yourself, it becomes truth: I had angered Chisongo and he had come looking for vengeance.

I ached from it all. Sat with my Pup awhile. I don't feel myself when I'm apart from her too long, it's like losing your own shadow or walking with one shoe on. She was messing herself a bit these days, I knew it was time to get the vet round. But when is it the right time? She seemed happy in herself, trotting around, always looking for a bit of fuss. Still, been with me since Cessie passed. I dare say she helped me raise young Vale.

'Not sure we got it quite right there, Pup. All a bit of a muddle aren't we?'

That dog saved me from myself some nights. You need another body breathing close by when you're driving yourself mad with thinking. You can be up all night trying to make things right but then that hour before dawn there's a special dark that comes. Occult black it is, and dense, and your mind can play a trick so you think it's all down to your own dark self that crows are mobbing. Pup always lay close, offered a little lick. Just the twitch of her bony legs was a comfort. Funny little paws like shelled walnuts, oak roots even, and a brave terrier heart.

Early afternoon I went back to see Vale. He was sleeping like a baby and I didn't want to wake him. Hadn't been off the boat 24 hours yet and he looked it. I put down a chocolate bar and I'd brought him a paper, though he generally didn't read them and this one had got a bit wet and wrinkled on the way. As I laid them on the steel cabinet he opened his eyes for just a wink and I thought he said something.

'What's that son? Do you need something? Some water?'

'Sorry.'

'Don't be sorry, don't say that. You're a good lad. It's me who's sorry.'

But he was gone again and I had to wonder if that was what he had said in the end. He could have said anything and I'd have loved him for it.

I decided that when he next woke up, I'd be sure to have news of Tom, even though no one would tell me anything, not being next of kin and all. I even explained that the next of kin was probably unconscious from drink but no one cared to listen. I'd need to see him for myself. I left Vale and made across all the hallways and passages to find Tom and could feel the aching all through my feet as I went. I had thought he would be in the areas for broken bones, orthopaedics, what with his legs being the problem, but it was through big double doors saying 'neurology' that I was sent.

There was young Tom. He was strapped in and tied up and plugged in to God knows what. He was sleeping though, which was a good thing, nice and quiet, eyes closed, mouth open. He made a great lump in the bed. Built like an ox that boy. Always had been and with an appetite to go with it. He wasn't a fattie though, solid as they come, and strong too. Could eat a loaf of bread and a jar of jam with it and it'd not even touch sides. One night he'd had another almighty row with his father and turned up in the kitchen around supper time, ate a whole chicken, two potatoes, a leftover sausage pie, two jars of beer and then, after ranting and raving and sharing his wisdom on the benefits of early planting, went back home to finish off the fight. We'd have needed another bank loan if our Vale had eaten like that, and a set of locks for the refrigerator door too I dare say. But he was a good boy Tom. Got in trouble mind, but mostly it was because he just didn't know where to put his anger and his feeling that he didn't quite fit. He was just too large for the town. I dare say in a city he'd have gone unnoticed. Out here he was an oddity. Got it from his mother. Funny woman, always dressing in costumes and quoting poetry. For a big lad who didn't know any social niceties, Tom knew a lot of fancy verse.

'You'll be okay young Tom.'

'Pa Landyn?' He'd almost opened his eyes.

'Didn't mean to wake you lad.' He was mighty groggy, thick eyes.

'S'okay.'

'Just checking in on you. You need anything?'

'My Pa come?'

'I don't know lad, I'm sure he's been though, you've been sleeping a good deal. He'd have come earlier.' It seemed better to just lie to the boy. No one wants the truth when they look like that. Well, I wouldn't.

'Okay.'

'Hurt?'

'Nope.'

'That's good.'

'Doc says not.'

'Oh. Sorry, son. You need anything you tell them to call me up on the old telephone. How about that? Your father's so busy.'

'Yeah, he's busy.'

'He is, so you tell them to call me. I'll leave the number at the desk.'

He almost managed to nod in that contraption they had him in. God it was awful.

'Vale okay?'

'He's sleeping still. You'll be all right.'

'Okay.'

'Good lad. Tell them to call.'

'My Pa's busy.'

'That he is.'

'Okay.'

'Yes. Good lad, Thomas.' He'd fallen back to sleep already.

When I left him it was all I could do not to well up. I had no idea who he was. Not a hint of the swagger and joust I knew from him. One stupid night of high jinx had changed everything for him and he knew it. The devil had got in him, I could see – he had some darkness settling in his gut. Takes some nerve to outrun that kind of misery.

I left him. I didn't go back to Vale, just checked on him with a nurse. She seemed like a nice woman. By the time I got back home to Pup and the others again, I was spent from all the to and fro, and I laid out on the sofa to sleep the sleep of the dead.

I woke to the dogs going at it and only after I blinked a few times and saw it was dark did I hear the knocking. It was almost four in the afternoon.

'I'm coming, I'm coming. Shush yourselves you dogs.'

Opening the door let a blast of ice air in. It was a Domino brother, Neil. He was a man who always looked as if he was peeling

55

away from his own bones, saggy-skinned but thin. We all called them Dominos because if one drank a glass the others had to have the same and they all went down as hard as each other. Their family name was Webb but I don't think anyone remembered that anymore.

'Come in Neil.'

'Ta for that Land.'

'Come in. Cup of tea?'

'Bit dozy there Land?'

'Had a snooze, bit of a long night.'

'I heard that Land, heard it down the pub now. Fuck me. Fuckin' horrible. Thought I'd drop by.'

'Right. Thanks Neil.'

None of the Dominos could speak without cursing. I always considered it a great failing of their mother, God rest her. I put the kettle on.

'How's your boy?'

'He's at the hospital still. He's resting up. Take a pew Neil. Mind out for old Pup with your feet, she'll be under the chairs.'

I pointed to the table for him. He had to wade through the other dogs, Jessie trying to lick his hands as they passed, but I reckon if folk don't fancy my pack, they shouldn't stop by.

'And young Shakespeare? The Walker boy?'

'Not so great for him. He's in a bad way. You haven't seen his old Pa on your travels round the pub have you? You take sugar?'

'Fuck me. Two, ta.'

'It's a bloody disgrace if you ask me. He needs to look to his boy.'

The Domino looked awkward.

'Well, Landyn I've come with news on old Walker. Roy found him and gave him the bad news about young Shakespeare.'

'Right?'

I handed him the mug and sat down with mine.

'And he was too far gone to know what it was all about.'

'Right.'

'He managed to say the lad had it coming and you could sort it out. Something about Thomas preferring you anyway.'

'Oh for God's sake. And why wouldn't he? With a useless old fool like Walker for a dad, who would stand a chance?'

'Well I won't lie to you, he was right fuckin' out of it. Worse than usual if it's possible. I heard it off Roy, he said to me he said, Neil, best make sure Land knows about this sooner than later. The lad Thomas will be needing some pals.'

'Roy's a good man.'

'Those boys were unlucky. Sorry Land. Fuckin' horrible.'

'Oh I know, you don't have to tell me.'

'I've done worse on a fuckin' Sunday morning before church.'

'But you're still a good fellow. And Roy.'

'Shit. Sorry Land. Thought you should know about Walker though. Let your boy know we all asked after him too.'

'Thanks Neil.'

'Yeah. Good cup, thanks.'

The Domino left. I gave him a bottle of our cider.

'Ta Land, that's my Saturday night off to a good start.'

'Just stay away from boats will you?'

He was good to come and warn me about Tom's father being in no fit state to help him. No true surprise.

There was still some hint of day on the far side of the sky. Just a hint mind. It was starting to snow. A few flurries and not landing, but enough to warrant a trip to the sheds and throw some extra straw at the chickens. I thought too that the horses could do with some hay. I was glad for having them up nearer the house that night I can tell you. Pup decided it was a walk worth taking though I told her not to bother. Perhaps she sensed I was low. It was bitter. The wheelbarrow was hard in my hands. I was thinking about Neil Domino. Good fellow.

The horses were crushed in close together under the oak. You could smell what was left of the heat come off them as you got near. Their coats would be steaming. I tipped a bale off the barrow and spread it around for them. They'd be pleased for that. None of them were young ones anymore. Flurries were coming down more steady now. Big fat ones. I wondered if the beet would freeze in the ground that night. The year before we'd lost the lot from the earth being frozen and then thawing too quick, rotting them all.

I sat on one of the big old branches that had come down the year before. Pup came along and I lifted her into my coat.

'There you go little one. Nice and warm in there. Seems we're all in a muddle again.'

She turned her head up, wet nosed, licked my chin and then burrowed right down so she was hidden away from the cold. I got a cigarette out my pocket. Smoke hit the back of my throat like a prayer. It was good to sit out there, cold and quiet as can be. Good to get my feathers together when the rest of the world seemed to be moving too quickly around me, present and past all rolling in on one another like foxes play, so as you can't tell when the game ends and the fight begins. Tooth and tail all the same.

For ten years I'd shirked the memories. I always felt them scratching at the darker corners of my mind, still feral; but sitting on a tree stump in the gathering dark, all of it – the space, the fear, the sorrow – all seemed to find me again. It was as if the past ten years I'd only been standing still and I was back in a mess with a boy who only sees ghosts.

Ah, but then, across the paddocks, through the snow she came. My fox. Quietly out the edge of the woods, straight line from her snout to her tail like an archer's bow, tight and sharp in the front and ending with the spray of quill. The last lick of light caught her side. I'd known her a few years. She'd had some pups in her time, three that last summer. She stayed along the fencing, where the trees still offered some cover. Pup didn't stir and only one of the horses gave the fox a passing look. She would have been a hungry fox. Rabbits were mostly gone at this time of year.

Short steps she took through the grass that was just about getting a covering now. Oh, she was fine, sharp as a whip, keen-eyed and sleek. She stopped a while and with a quick turn looked right at me.

She looked right at me.

Later that night I made the journey to see Vale. Thank God and everything else I found him sitting up a bit. Had some colour but wasn't eating too well. None the less, he could come home the next day. I wasn't sure how that would go. We'd not spoken really. He wasn't saying much – too tired was my guess – and I didn't know what to say to the boy, after everything that had passed between us, and the long night and Tom.

'I saw my fox this evening, Son. You remember the year I had to leave food out for her, poor thing? I know she knows me. Came out of the night and looked right at me. Come to check we were all doing okay. Beautiful.'

I knew I was babbling. The lad said nothing, only fiddled with the bed sheet. His colour wasn't right yet and we'd be needing to see the doctors again even after he was released. And he carried the mark of my anger, his eye still swollen. He carried on rolling the hem of the sheet into a little peak between his thumb and forefinger.

He made to clear his throat a little. Didn't look up through. 'It's not her you know?'

'What's that?' I had to lean forward to hear him.

'It's not her. It's just a fox.'

Chapter 5

Vale

They let me go home after a couple of days. When I got there I just slept mostly, for a few days more. I wasn't even tired. Maybe it was the medication but I didn't mind. Time I was asleep was time I didn't have to deal with anything. Even when I was awake I was only really half there – somewhere in-between conscious and not. I had dreams about Ma and Zambia, dreams about Tom and me fishing and stranger ones to do with white birds that were trying to tell me something. But all of that, even dreaming maybe Ma was still there, was easier than being awake in the world and in the house with Pa.

Then one morning about a week after the accident I woke up and knew I was done sleeping. I decided to organise things to go to work a late beet harvest with Mole and some of the guys from Blyth. As long as the snow held, we'd get the job. Though it was bitter, the ground hadn't frozen yet. My shoulder still hurt some but it could hardly be worse than staying home with Pa. He didn't say anything but I knew if I gave him half an inch he would try to start up about going to see Tom. News was bad. What was I meant to say anyway. 'Sorry your legs got smashed, I pulled my shoulder?' It was bullshit. I knew I'd have to see him and I did want to, I did, just not then.

When I got up to work the beets the next day, Pa was trying to find his pen, searching all over the place like a stupid old hen. I was feeling punchy. He had a pen in his jacket pocket but I couldn't be bothered to tell him.

I knew he hadn't eaten yet because his coffee cup wasn't out. He only ever used the same one.

'You can only use one at a time.' He got that from his dad according to Ma.

I suppose it was true. It wasn't the logic that pissed me off, it was the fact that he did the same thing every day, same cup, same plate, same everything.

I took some bread and went to spoon on the jam we always got from old Dobbler's daughter, damson, apricot, all kinds. We were down to that last jar. When I opened it I could see there was just about enough for both of us if I was careful how much I took. Not a lot, but enough. I paused for less than a second, then I scooped the whole lot out and loaded it high onto my wedge of bread.

We had a solid day ahead with a few acres to be done. Everything was lined up to go. I was to drive the tractor pulling the harvester – I could do it with one arm and just rest the sore one on the wheel a little if needed. The tractor was a big beast, one of the new ones. We'd scoop up the beet behind me. It would climb up a shoot that, at the top, would bend to hang over the side of the machine. Then the beet could fall into a trailer trolling along besides, pulled by another tractor. Only issue was Mole Boy would be driving the truck with the trailer besides me and he tended to doze off a bit and not keep alongside the way he should.

'Hey Mole.'

'Hey there. G-g-glad to see you out and ab-bout.' Mole Boy was dressed up for a blizzard.

'You ready?'

'Always, always ready.'

'You better keep up, right?' I knew some other guys were listening.

Mole nodded. He was trying to grow something on his face. Looked stupid. Mole Boy always looked like a baby compared to all the other guys even though he was older than some of them. Ma always said he stopped growing out of fright when his brother died. He stopped talking for nearly a year and when he started again he had a stutter.

'If you get too far behind all that's gonna happen is I'll be dumping a few tons of rock hard sugar-beet on the roof of your truck.'

He opened his mouth to laugh or something. Fucking idiot.

'It won't be fuckin' funny when it happens, will it?'

I just walked off. Don't know why I was such a shit to him. He got me the job after all. He was always looking for work and got it too because he grafted hard and was honest and also people felt sorry for him and his Pa a bit. Sometimes I just hated him being so stupid and slow. Hanging around him made me feel, I don't know, less. Less everything.

While I was walking away feeling all riled with Mole but still feeling like a shit for how I treated him, the guy we were working for, Randall, came up to me.

'Midwinter.'

'Yeah?'

'A word.'

'Okay.'

He had a face like a leather hide, like he baked himself in sun and ice and nothing in between. Had the nose of an old boozer too.

'You driving?'

'Yeah.'

'I know about what you and Walker did to that boat.'

'Right.' I could feel him edging in on something, like a dog stalking a rat.

'And while I'm sorry for what happened to Walker, I'm watching you, right?'

'What do you mean?'

'Stealing, boozing, all that crap, I'm not having it here.'

'What?' I could feel my spine rile up on itself.

'I'm not having any shit from you, Midwinter. You do the job, you do it right and that's that.'

I was screaming inside, like I could beat the crap out of him then and there, just smash him. I couldn't say anything. I needed the money.

'I'll do it right.'

Mole Boy kept up though and was on the mark when I emptied the bin up through the shoot. The sound of all those beets bombing down into the empty metal trailers was deafening. You could feel it in your skull and in the hollow of your chest. When Tom's cousin who had his legs blown off came back from the Iraq war, he said that's what it sounded like to be under fire only it didn't ever stop. The bin never emptied, it just kept on. When I first heard that, I thought it must make you crazy. It's not like it's a day's work with a crew, it's always thinking you're going to die and just because the day ends, doesn't mean the noise will. I couldn't imagine that really.

He was in one of those raids with mortars and shit. One of the guys he was with had his arm blown off. Tom's cousin couldn't see anything and he was trying to help the guy get under cover or something. They got trapped up some valley with insurgents just hammering them from the ridges. That's how he told it. He said he couldn't think which way to go because of all the noise and he thought they'd said to go but they'd said to hold and then he got fuckin' hit and lost his legs. No one knew how he survived. Probably be better if he hadn't, not after all that. Best I could think was that maybe he didn't remember it. Sometimes you don't. Tom used to ask what I knew about Ma and what I had seen. He knew I was there. It was all of it bad, like you need to teach yourself to un-see it. Mostly that's what I did. I told Tom I saw nothing.

When I heard the noise in the Kabwe house, I knew what it was, and also what it meant, even before I saw it. I had locked myself in my room like Ma had told me. She told me to hide in the big wardrobe but I wanted to see where she was. I looked through the cracks in the door panels, even though I knew she'd said not to. I couldn't see anything so I climbed out the wardrobe. I opened the bedroom door and looked down the corridor towards all the shouting. Then I remembered that the house was fitted with panic buttons. I knew there was one in Ma and Pa's room and I ran to find it, to push it, knowing if I did that Mr Kraus from just along the road would come and help us.

I remember what happened to Ma but I can't remember if I saw it or if I heard it and added the pictures to the sounds. I heard Ma shouting out. I knew Chisongo was there because I would know his voice anywhere. There was so much noise and so many voices. I didn't like it. So I went back down the corridor to my room, and crept inside the wardrobe and lay down. I know I was still holding the panic button and I went to sleep. There in my nest, in that most terrible moment, I slept like I never should have. I slept peacefully.

I only woke up when Pa found me. I knew exactly what had happened. He put me in my bed, and lay there with me. The whole house was alive. Cars and men coming and going and neighbours – Mr Kraus was there like I'd known he would be – and I could smell coffee, which made things feel oddly normal. Eventually I slept some more.

I woke again, washed and got ready for school in the little green bathroom that was kind of mine. All the bedrooms and bathrooms were down the one end of the house. It was a long house and all on one level with a 'verandah' all the way along it. Ma loved the word 'verandah' and she said it 'verrrandaah'. Pa liked that.

I could still hear voices all around the house and there were men in the garden with pens and paper pads writing things down and looking at the earth and picking things up and handing things to each other and talking some more. Nobody was paying any attention to me. I had a sort of a nanny out there, Maria. I went along the corridor to find her but then I heard some noise from Ma and Pa's bedroom so I went there instead.

I tapped on the door with the end of my finger then pushed it open a crack. Ma lay on the bed on her back as she usually was when she was asleep, but covered right up to her eyes with sheets. Some of them looked like plastic. I knew that wasn't right. Her eyes were closed. I saw her there and remembered the sounds that

I had heard, terrible sounds, and I knew that she was dead. Pa was lying next to her with his head alongside her shoulder and his big brown hand resting on her. He just lay there, as still as if he had gone with her, his eyes all glazed and strange so it took him a while to notice I was there. And Dog was there too, curled on the bed like he always was, his eyes all big and wet like he was crying.

When Pa eventually noticed I was standing there he looked embarrassed or something and pulled himself up and got on his feet and said,

'Vale son, you're awake. You shouldn't be here. Your Mother is…'

'I know.'

'You do. I'm sorry son. I'm sorry about your Ma.'

'It's okay.'

'Would you like to say goodbye?'

I just stood there and looked at her. I didn't know what to do, so I said, 'Goodbye, Ma.'

I know that was stupid because she was already dead and couldn't hear me or anything. Then I felt Pa put his arm around me and pull me into his waist. And he said,

'We're going to be all right, son.'

I guess I nodded or something.

'Do you think you're finished?'

I nodded again.

'I don't think Dog is. We'll leave them awhile.'

When I thought about all this after, I was worried Pa thought I didn't love Ma and that even Dog loved her more than I did. It was too late then to say:

'I'm not finished.'

When it comes to your Ma you never can be. I guess the few

minutes just standing there at the door with the rug she wove on the floor between us was enough. I kept looking at the rug so I didn't have to look at her. I wanted to touch her to see how she'd feel and also just to connect myself to her again, but I knew better than that and let Pa turn me away. He held my hand like I needed to learn to walk again. I suppose I did.

The house was a mess. Everything was wrecked and broken. Lamps over and pictures down. I always try and remember it, which isn't right I know. I know how the shades were bent and the pillows from the sofas were all over the place and the cabinet was smashed and there was glass everywhere. There was a lot of glass. Because the house was long like that, we had to go through all the mess in the living room and hall and along the corridor to get to the kitchen, passing all these big fat guys with moustaches and glasses and guns at their waist. When they saw us, they stopped their conversations midway, leaving half-finished sentences hanging in the air. Stuff like 'fucking horrible' and 'poor woman' and some things in their own language that I understood even though I didn't recognize the words.

Mrs Kraus, our neighbour, was in the kitchen. Maria was there too. Mrs Kraus came forward to hug me.

'Come child, come let's pray to the Lord for the passing of your Mother's soul.'

I hated her. She was always telling Ma off for not sending me to Church and Pa for letting me play with the farm kids too much. I ducked under the fat pink curtain of her bare arm and ran to Maria and stood behind her at the stove.

'Come,' said Maria, 'have some hot chocolate milk. I have porridge.' She pulled out my chair at the kitchen table like every morning and I sat down and waited for my breakfast.

'Vale, I've already telephoned for the Doctor to come.' Pa said from the door.

I must have looked confused, or hopeful or something, like I'd misunderstood Ma's condition because he said,

'He can't do anything for her now but he still has to come and do some things and write things down. He will be here within the hour and then he will take her away with him. So, just thought you'd need to know that, Vale. So as not to be surprised when he calls in.'

'Okay.' I nodded, so he knew I understood.

'You might want to be in your room when he comes. I don't know though. I don't know how it all works.'

I noticed Pa was rubbing his eyes a lot with the heel of his hand and stretching out the bottom of his nose by slowly wiggling his lips.

'The doctor will know how it works, Pa.'

'He will. The doctor will know. That's why I called him.'

Maria put my porridge in front of me. When she leant down to make a circle of honey carefully on the top, I saw she was crying but trying not to, and one of her tears landed in the porridge. I wondered if I was meant to be crying. Everyone else seemed to be, or trying not to but I couldn't, so I just ate and Pa kept walking up and down and once he stroked my head which was something he never did.

'Hello?' said a man's voice from the hall. I could hear his shoes crunching on glass as he walked.

Pa said I should go back to my room and I could take the rest of my milk with me. I thought I might spill it, so I left it on the table. I remember all this stuff, small stuff and sometimes I wish I wouldn't.

I could hear Pa going out to meet the doctor. They were talking so I ran back along the corridors towards my room. I wanted so bad to go in to see Ma again, but when I got there all I could do was stand in the doorway, looking at her with the big rug between us. I didn't know what to do, so I said, 'Goodbye.' And then I turned and went across the hall, back inside my room, behind my door and leaned up against it to keep it closed. To keep me hidden.

It felt like I was in there forever. I was still at the door, listening. I could hear a man say, 'Terrible, terrible.'

Ma's door was right opposite mine so if I put my eye wide at the keyhole I could kind of see what was happening. I could see the doctor on the edge of the bed, careful not to disturb Ma and how neat she was. Pa stood there, his back to my spy-hole, cupping his elbow in his other palm and chewing on his finger nails. They were talking all soft and low but I could hear the doctor saying they would find the savages and kill them and Pa was saying nothing, just rocking back and forth. The doctor said some other things I couldn't hear and then he leaned over Ma and pulled the cover all the way over her face and Pa let out a noise like a dog baying and then his face was in both his hands and he shook and cried and sounded like he couldn't get breath in. It was horrible.

I ran all the way to school. No one had seen me leave the house and I hadn't stopped to fetch my bag from the kitchen. I just climbed out into the garden and ran as fast as a kid can run when he knows has seen things he shouldn't.

By the time I got there I knew I was three hours late. I could see my friend Gekko sitting at his place in the window along with all the others. Gekko might have been in the classroom, but his mind was always on girls or motor bikes. He was a bit like Tom I guess, always in trouble. The alphabet meant he was often sitting right behind a girl called Kikanda-May. She was always laughing and teasing and none of this did anything to help Gekko in class. He was either fighting with her or trying to get her to join us on the wall at break-time but it was Chipo she fancied. Chipo's dad had a big farm and ran the co-op in Kabwe.

Gekko was already looking out the window when I came careening through the gate, running flat out and on my own with no schoolbag.

I stood outside the class door a whole long time trying to catch my breath and thinking maybe I should have stayed home. Then I decided that getting in trouble at school would be easier than facing what was going on back there. I made myself straight as I could, knocked, and as I opened the door the room moved towards me like one big animal. Miss looked right at me from her place in front of the chalk board. We called her Hippo behind her back.

'Well, there you are Midwinter.'

I don't know if she just meant to state it as a fact, but it felt like a finger being pointed and a detention order. I stood there like a fucking idiot. She told me to take my seat.

'You talk to me after class about this.'

I slid into the desk and sat there like a dope holding my elbows still trying to breathe properly. Miss called out, 'Turn to page ninety-seven and Vale, you can read from the first paragraph that starts with Oliver.'

I remembered I had no books with me.

'You can start to read, Vale.'

'I have no books Miss.'

'Excuse me? Where are your books?'

'I didn't bring them. I didn't bring my bag.'

'You come three hours late and you have no books?'

'No Miss.'

By now the whole class had turned around and was looking at me. All either smirking or frowning, depending on whether they liked me or not. Most of them didn't because I was English and foreign and some sort of enemy or something. I wanted to tell them to leave me alone. I stared at the varnish cracking off the yellow wood on my desk.

Miss asked if I cared to explain. I just sat there so she ordered me to leave the class and I had to wait outside the door. I suddenly felt so tired standing there. I wished I had finished my breakfast but then I remembered why I hadn't, and for some reason that made the standing feel okay. It seemed like I was on the wrong side of all sorts of doors that day, trying to get in, trying to get out, told to stay in, told to get out. I was a fucking mess and I was starting to feel like maybe Pa should be there to sort it all out and wondering why he wasn't.

The school bell made a terrible sound. I stood looking at my feet and thinking Ma would have something to say about my shoes being so scuffed after running like that. Everyone filed passed me and no one dared talk to me. Gekko said nothing either but he made sure he passed close by me and tapped my foot with his so I knew he was there and that was good. When they were gone Miss called me in. I stood next to her desk where she was making ticks on a long list, which seemed a waste of effort. Her big pink arms wobbled as she marked. She didn't even look up from her stupid ticking and said, 'Well?'

I couldn't always hear what she was saying. She had a funny accent. Gekko said she was from South Africa. She made me never want to go there.

'I'm sorry I was late Miss and about not reading out loud.'

'I am more interested about where you were. Three hours late, hey? You can't turn up three hours late and just say you've lost your bag. Those books will need to be replaced, you hear? And you have no excuse have you, hey?'

'No Miss.'

'Do you not like to read and learn? Are you so disrespectful of my class and your schooling that you think it's okay to be so rude and lazy?'

'I like to read Miss.'

'Then what have you got to say for yourself?'

Turns out I had nothing to say for myself and instead, out of nowhere I felt my guts reach up into my throat and try to choke me. I heaved just the one time before all Maria's porridge and chocolate milk came up and out of me and all over the place. It just kept coming up and kept trying to come some more even when there was no more left in me.

I was all shaking and cold as I sat in the nurse's room. I could see vomit on my shoe. I liked the nurse, she always looked clean and busy and Pa always said to trust a busy woman. She wore a white uniform and a bright cloth wrap around her head. Always different colours. She said she would call my mother to come and fetch me so I said that my Pa might come if he wasn't too busy with the doctor at the house.

'Is your father ill too? You got sick from him.'

'No miss. The doctor came about my Ma.'

'Oh shame, shame, shame boy, so your mother is the one who gave you the sickness. I see.'

'No. She didn't.' I said

'I will go and call your father.'

'He doesn't know I'm here. I was meant to stay in my room 'til the doctor was done with Ma. But I didn't mind because Mrs Kraus wanted to hug me and pray to the Lord for the passing of my mother's soul.' I said the last part quickly so she might not notice if I got any of it wrong.

'You say what child? Your mother has passed?' The nice nurse leaned into me.

'I suppose so. Pa called the doctor. He doesn't know I am here. I was meant to stay in my room.'

'Sweet mother of Jesus,' said the nurse, crossed herself, and hurried out of the little white room.

After a while she came back to the room and sat with me. She just sat next to me and held my hand on both of hers, squeezing my fingers and rubbing her big thumb over the top of my hand and talking to herself a bit. I think she was praying. Then, after a time, Pa came and fetched me and took me home and he kept saying, 'I'm sorry. I'm sorry I left you, Son. I'm sorry I left you.'

I thought it was strange that he was feeling sorry, because after all, it was me who climbed out and left him there alone with the doctor and those men who stood around the black van smoking.

In the end I guess I was some sort of sick because when Pa had helped me bath he tucked me in my bed like a kid half my age, he held me close and I cried and cried and cried, like a boy who has just lost his Ma, and Pa cried with me so my pyjama shirt was wet through with both our tears.

* * *

I stayed in my bed for three days. Dog stayed with me all the time and Maria would come to my room with soup and then when I felt a bit better some toast and then some chicken pie. I would eat and Pa might talk a little and sometimes we would just sit silent together and watch Dog dreaming and twitching. Sometimes, when I was meant to be asleep, I thought I heard Pa crying in the room across the hall. I didn't know if I should go to him or not. I wouldn't know what to say to him if I did but I did know that he missed Ma something terrible, and maybe that made it okay for me to miss her too.

About a week later the local policeman came to the house and said, 'Found them.'

And Pa cried again. We came back to Suffolk three months later.

Mole Boy was keeping up with me and we did a whole field before we took a break.

'You did well Mole.'

'Thanks. You too. I was worried you c-c-couldn't keep up.' He looked surprised that he'd said it. The other guys thought that was funny and I guess I did too. I pretended to hit him.

After a smoke, Mole and I walked back to the trucks.

'You b-b-been okay?' he asked.

'Yeah. You know.'

'I can help you with stuff if you like? On the land and stuff. Just until Tom gets b-b-better. He'll be better soon.'

'Don't think he will.' It near stuck on my throat to say it. Mole felt it too.

'You can finish that before we start again,' he said, before I stubbed out my smoke.

'Thanks.'

'Sorry 'bout Tom. I know he's your b-b-brother.'

'Yeah, guess he is. You miss yours?'

He nodded.

'Sorry mate. Bad times. But, thing is with Tom, he's going to get better. It's not like he won't be able to walk again. They'll fix him up.'

Mole said nothing. I stubbed out my cigarette.

'Come on. Let's work.'

We lined up the trucks for the next field, we needed to get a shift on for the light. I tried to remember if I'd asked Mole about his brother before. Probably not. Couldn't really ask a guy that kind of stuff unless he raised it and with Tom there it probably wouldn't come up. I'd known Mole Boy as long as Tom but somehow Tom was family.

After we got back from Kabwe, Pa was off trying to earn a few pounds working on other people's land, hauling for the Dominos. He even fed some hobby farmer's pig's each morning. The guy couldn't be bothered to drag a bucket of pellets a few hundred yards to his own pigs. Either way, Pa was busy, so I just did my own thing and hooked up with Tom again. I was ten.

Mole Boy was always nice to me. I guess I felt like I should be friends with him because of it. He still annoyed me with his slowness though.

Tom never mentioned my Ma but I knew he missed her too. One day about six years after we got back he asked me what happened and I told him, mostly anyway, what I remembered. I told him about Chisongo and the guys coming to the house, Pa not being there. I guess Tom was the one that started it. Not like he meant to, only suddenly I asked questions, or remembered differently.

'They just came to your house?'

'Yeah.'

'For no reason? No brother. No one picks a fight for nothing.'

'You do.'

'No. Dave Robins on Tuesday, insulted my mother. Neville what's-his-name yesterday, called me soft. Reasons.'

'Well I guess Pa used to get after Chisongo quite a lot.'

'See? What about?'

'I don't know. He wouldn't turn up some days, stuff about money. And then he got upset that night also. To do with his girlfriend. But it was stupid stuff. In the kitchen.'

'Well, I know how I can get.'

'What are you saying?'

'Just a theory right? Maybe, maybe, your Pa upset the workers and then there was whatever happened in the kitchen, and then that one guy got drunk and brought a gang to your house to teach Pa Landyn a lesson. But he wasn't there. And they found your Ma instead of him. Jesus brother Vale, that's heavy.'

'No, Tom, you're not telling it right.'

'Yeah, but it was your Pa they were after, wasn't it? It's just he wasn't there. He was the one they had beef with.'

'What you saying?'

'Just a theory. Your Pa set them off.'

'Bullshit. You saying it's his fault Ma's dead?'

'No, Jesus, brother, I would never say that. Just saying no one picks a fight without a reason. Forget it. Forget I said it. I'm just talking shit.'

But I couldn't forget it. I was spitting angry with him. We nearly had a proper fight over it again a few days later when I asked him why he'd even said it if he didn't think it was true.

It was like he had let this beast out of a cage and there was no way of getting back in. I'd never seen it all like that before but once I did suddenly I couldn't see any other explanation. Pa had upset them all so they'd come back to settle the score. He was so fucking arrogant and full of it that he'd turned us, Ma, into some sort of target. If he had been there that night, he would have had his gun ready, he always did out there. You had to. Bad stuff did happen, but mostly up North nearer the border. Where we were everyone was relaxed, that's why Pa said it was safe for us to go there and the government knew the farming would be good.

The evening Pa hit me, I had just come back from taking the dogs for a burn across the fields. Across the sky, a late arrow of geese. Ma always said it was good to be a goose. You always knew where you'd come from and where you were going.

The older ones had been lagging a little as usual and so was Pup but she just sat down by the bridge and let us go on and ahead. When we got back to where we left her, she'd had herself a little snooze in the leaves and was ready to join us for the couple of miles home.

Pa called to me when he heard me tapping my boots on the wall outside the kitchen door. He wanted a fire so I went to fetch some wood in. It was a chore, I was too cold and too tired, but without the wood the house would be an ice chest. The pile was all covered in cobwebs and dust that had settled over the summer so I did what Pa hated and took logs from the bottom. Beetles had got in so that some of the logs felt more like cork. I only got a small load, enough for that evening and another small fire in the morning. I was delaying going in. Sometimes when I got back in the house after being out and free, I felt the air was just too heavy and the rooms too small for breathing. Out in the fields, you could walk until your legs stopped caring where they took you. Inside there is always something to bump into. Pa doesn't seem to mind, but then he's much more quiet in himself.

I went in and started to stack the logs next to the fire, lumping them down in threes and fours just to get it done.

'Go easy there son. Keep it neat. Smaller and shorter on the left, long burners on the right. Oh, not too close to the stove, don't want it smouldering.'

'I know what I'm doing.'

'Only trying to help.'

'Only trying to make sure it's done your way you mean.' Pa didn't respond and I knew I'd been too sharp .

'True,' he said, 'only wood.'

He always did that. Agreed with me when I was already annoyed with him. Somehow it made me feel guilty and pissed me off even more. So then I'd fix the logs and feel fuckin' crazy about it because I knew he would be watching me and I knew he would be feeling some kind of smug from it.

Pa wanted Pup on his lap. Pup couldn't jump anymore so he had to lean forward to lift her. Pup padded round and round, curling herself tighter and tighter until she lowered herself. Because we had been out she had all those burs in her fur. She had whole clumps behind her ears and in her tail. She sat all patient as Pa teased apart the hairs. Sometimes you have to do it just a couple at a time, to get the stuff out. His big old hands all careful and telling Pup he'd soon be done and making easy conversation with the dog to calm her saying,

'Got a couple more in there, right in behind your ears, old gal. I'll go gentle.'

Pup, who sometimes had the fucking devil in her, would just take it, and even lift her legs up to the side so Pa could reach under the belly to do the job better.

The longer I watched him the more I raged. He was wearing his gloves without the fingers and half the burrs he took off just got stuck on those.

I was done in from the day's cold. Once it got going though, the fire was warm. It was good to sit. I'd forgotten to take my boots off and I couldn't be arsed to get up and take them off. I was sure my feet were frozen into them anyway.

Pa told me to take them off and I thought, Christ, leave it, just give me a fucking minute. When I didn't budge, he kept on at me. Somehow, the more he asked, the less I wanted to do what he wanted. I felt like he was pushing me and pushing me, and I could feel this almighty rage building in my chest out of nothing. I could hardly hold it.

Then I said 'You killed Ma.'

I tried to stop the words from coming out but I couldn't. My head was screaming and the words just kept coming and coming and then I felt his hand across my eye. Bam, quick and hot. Like a fucking poker across my face.

I was blinking at him and trying to understand what had happened. I knew it and didn't know it at the same time. For just a second maybe even less, he looked exactly like he did when Ma died. It was fear, or something like that. I didn't understand how he could be more afraid than angry. I was angry all the time but mostly he just looked like a fucking stupid animal in the road hoping someone would run it down and put it out of its own misery.

Chapter 6

Landyn

The whole blessed day had been upside down: labourers fighting over women the previous night meant two of them were still too drunk to turn up. Others were missing for no reason at all, and one of those was Chisongo, the boyfriend of Sarah who worked in the house. When he did eventually turn up I told him to go home. He didn't like that. It meant no wages and he had no doubt already drunk the money from the week before. By the time I got home I was done in.

After dinner, Cessie went to the kitchen about dessert. Vale and I sat in thick silence. His grades were getting worse, despite the extra lessons we were paying for. I remember running the back of my knife over the bumps the lace table cloth made. Up and down. Funny thing, the way something like that can be so satisfying when you are stuck with a situation you can't see a way to fix. Like cleaning a gun or punching holes in a leather strap.

Cessie came back, sensing the tension, trying to make everything right in the room.

'Boys, there's a lovely apricot tart Sara made. Just coming out of the oven, and custard. Your favourite, Vale.' She rubbed Vale's shoulder with the flat of her hand as she passed him. He smiled at her and as he did I felt a monstrous rage brewing, the type that bubbles up, rolling and spitting, and will not settle down again. Then I heard a great crash from the kitchen.

Our three fat Suffolk hens gave up on laying. Just like that. Seems they can bear to lay just so many and then one day, enough is enough, they just can't take the damn futile disappointment of it all and give it up.

The lad had been home now well over a week. He didn't have much to say for himself, lurking around in a constant mubble-fubble. My spirits were low too, I admit. All I ever saw when I looked at him was the bruising around his eye.

Being down a few chooks we'd need to head for the Ashe Auctions, held on Wednesdays for donkey's years off the big double road past the marshes. We'd usually go together, Vale and I, and although the lad was smarting, I did trust a little that he would do his old Pa right and give me a hand.

The trust I had, have always had, in the boy came down to trees. Say you want to plant a pair of saplings, as I did the other year. You dig perfect and identical holes, fill them up with manure and bone and set the roots in each one, good and deep. You wet them down well so they can really soak their feet all the way into the meal of the soil and take their fill. You give them each a neat stake to hold on to, tethering them at the base so you know they'll grow straight and true. A few months will pass, then a year – and you'll see how nature works.

One of my saplings already has the look of a tree for the centuries. It grew smart, using its wits, looking for the sun but not rushing, putting out some good branches, long and low out the sides and just enough on top to cover them. And in the earth, where it's all full of the stuff of it, the roots are digging well, burrowing and mining for life. That tree will give names to towns, act as a landmark to travellers. A strong tree can suffer a bad frost or loose a full branch in a storm, but the roots are what keep it true. That's how it was with Vale.

The other tree though – now that's a different story. Even though it's tethered just as firm, watered just as long, its roots are fickle. They could never decide which way to reach, changing track with the tides. That was like Tom: all over the place, looking to fix on some horizon but never quite finding it. He was always running and hiding from his father's miserable rages, and when his ma ran off with the out-of-towner, any hope for him left with her. He came to rely on us more and more, and when we eventually went to Zambia we knew that we were leaving him to fend for himself.

In the beginning, Kabwe was all a huge adventure. This despite the sickness I had felt as we landed and the door flung up to show nothing but a bleached hot sky that went on forever. It was a place to shift your being. Your sense of where you fitted in the world. Even in the first two weeks out there, we all had a purpose to our days, where before perhaps we had just drifted a little, rolled along.

Cessie set about making the house our own. Took her three days to work out where we could get paint to clean it up a bit. It had a tin roof and was roughly plastered on the outside and painted sky blue. We hadn't been there half an hour, deciding which rooms were for what, when she found a spider the size and touch of a field mouse. The house seemed to come with its own dog too. Big fellow, coat like a ginger biscuit. No one knew who he belonged to, so we kept him for our own. The housekeeper Maria called him Dog and from the day we arrived he was Cecelia's constant friend.

I never fully understood it but the house came with people who cooked and cleaned and kept it going, and the land came with labourers too. The property had changed hands, (you had to wonder how many had come and gone before us), but the locals all remained. Still, the people there were good and worked in a way folk never worked back home because when the day was done, there was the business of living and carrying and walking for miles and miles.

The housekeeper Maria, her helper Sara, Sara's man Chisongo and a few others lived in a long row of cottages out the back, up the hill a little. Maria and Sara were related it seemed but I never worked out how. Sara and Chisongo had a child, about three years old when we arrived. Never knew what a sweet girl like Sara saw in that man. He was a funny one right from the off. He never seemed to belong. What I later took for insolence and eventually viciousness I initially saw as sadness or its milder cousin, disappointment. I asked after his family once. We were out in that God awful sun, trying to get the water tanks next to the house fixed. We needed them to catch any drop of rain off the roof.

'Got family near these parts Chisongo?'

'No.'

'But you're from Kabwe?'

'Now I am from Kabwe.'

'No family?'

He turned away from me and scratched the back of his neck which he always seemed to do when he had nothing to say.

He didn't like me, or at least that was how it seemed. Everything about our interactions felt like a joust, right from the start.

Vale and I sat next the fire. He was reading his book and running his hand over his head. I don't think he was used to his new short hair. Wasn't sure I was too fond of how it made him look, all old and tired. But maybe he was and I'd just not noticed before. Strange too, I felt I wanted to reach over and touch his head myself; run my hand over the prickles and feel how they were, to feel how he was under it.

'Want to come along to the Ashe in the morning son?'

He shrugged. 'Could do.'

'Could choose us some new chooks.'

The boy just nodded.

God. We were in a messy place all right. All moss and tangle weed and every log I turned threw up more dank rotting bark but I did hope a little trip up along the coast road might be just the tonic. I left it that I would be up and in the kitchen early enough to get to the Ashe and I'd either find him there or I wouldn't.

The night was deathly. Even under all the old quilts and blankets my skin felt pinched. I could hear the big brown owl that sits out the back. Long black calls through the sky he makes, black as old blood. I was grateful for my old Pup under all that and I dare say she for me.

I felt as though my eyelids had only just connected in the middle when light woke me. It came through the bedroom door from the landing and I knew Vale was up already. I could hear him letting the dogs out below. I rolled over with some pain to find my clock on the side table – four thirty – and there it was. My cup. White with blue roses and a small chip on the far side on the rim. He must have brought it in to me. I breathed in the coffee steam, deep and encouraging, and thought I might dare to consider it an offering.

God almighty the effort it took to get my frame from the bed and downstairs all correct and present in God knows how many layers so as not to make the boy wait. There was toast on the table and at a rook's breath past five, he was back and we were in the truck. Not a word had been spoken.

Vale took the keys to drive and I didn't stop him. The fog was still low and the headlamps made little difference so we went slow and steady through the sop of it all. The livestock in the fields were huddled in deep together, using their outside flanks as some sort of shield against the damp. At least the winds had died down.

He did well on the curves.

'Good going son.'

He didn't respond but I kept on anyway.

'It's like a big old grey rabbit just sat down on our corner of the earth this morning. Have to dig our way out from under her.'

He just kept a grip of the wheel and stared ahead into the dark and wet air. With no conversation on offer, I concentrated on what was passing out the window. The fog started to burn off a touch once the light got itself going and by the time we got towards the marshes, the day was already rolling over to stretch its old legs.

Marshes are not for me. Nothing honest in them. You can't trust the earth under your feet. Years back, when they were building town here, there were hundreds that died just dredging it and shoring up walls to ease back the sea. A folly if ever there was one, as if the sea would approach a little row of stones we'd left and take a decision to go back the way it came. None the less, the madness continued for a full few decades and so many were drowned or died of misery that a church was erected just to pray for the souls that perished and to appease the ones that remained. Our Lady of the Marshes. Still say the Sandlings prayer every Sunday, for all those who died, so I hear. The place looks like a great old hoary battlement over the flat reeded basin. You get wide and noisy clacks of birds out there come autumn time. Dark black clouds of them gather on the wing like the very souls of the perished marsh men. They move this way and that with the tides – the water is always shifting its form around like a sly old hag, taking the ground with it.

Cessie thought it the most beautiful place for miles, so when we got her back from Kabwe it was there we took her to be buried. I felt Vale's eyes shift over, towards his mother.

'Shall we visit on the way home?' I said.

'No.'

It was still bitter when we arrived at the Ashe auctions. First sniff of air felt like a witch's slap. I took my gloves off to light a smoke and my hands came out like a dead man's claw, wrinkled and blue in the nail. A few minutes more out of the wool and they'd be blood-fallen.

The Ashe was mess and order at the same time. Piles of stuff you never knew you needed, all lined up with tags on and lot numbers, and someone with authority wandering amongst it all, telling you the bleeding obvious.

'Nice piece of plough that is, good come time for potatoes.'

'Nice boar here, easy to handle and no nipping. You don't want a boar with ready tusks.'

Groups of old Suffolk boys like me stood around with caps and woollens on chatting and smoking and shifting this way and that to keep from freezing solid. Roy the Domino was present, if not necessarily correct. Always a bit frowsy of a morning – they are not a family well suited to early starts. He was muttering about beer. I swear, the worms will have had me and somewhere a Domino will still be muttering about beer. Good lads those. One of them had thought to bring a flask of coffee. Probably a kindly wife had packed it up with some sweet bread for the ride to counter the wet in the air. I spotted Dobbler.

'Morning Dob.'

'Morning Landyn, Mister Midwinter, Sir.' He offered a bow. Made me chuckle did Dobbler.

'You old fool.'

'Old fool, but wise.' He smiled to reveal he had lost another tooth since I had last seen him only a few days before.

'What's going on in your tater-trap Dob? Lost another tusk?'

'Wasn't using it.'

'Fair enough.'

'You remember I'm over at yours for the piggers soon?'

'Haven't forgotten.'

'How's the lad?'

'Just maundering about really. Tricky one.'

'Shame. Time and space I dare say.'

'Here's hoping old pal.'

We both turned as Vale went off in the rows looking at the boxes on the tables that held the smaller stuff.

Dobb shook his head. 'Oh deary me, got yourself a big old bear with a sore head. And wants you to know it. Well, later then Land. Got my eyes on a nice old harrower over there.'

'Later.'

Vale was picking through the bits: tools, knives, novelties, toys. Long pale ghost of a boy, bent over a little on top, skinny but strong. He was pausing at the knives, unfolding a few and testing the blade with his thumb. He took time over a small one. I could tell he liked it.

I guess he knew I was watching because for no reason he turned towards me. We just stood there in the wet air looking at each other with all that hurt between us. The whole morning held its breath.

In those early days in Kabwe, we were confident we had done the right thing – not without misgivings but there was hope and abundance in the fields and in our bellies. That doesn't mean it wasn't strange, alien really. It wasn't our natural habitat and there were things we couldn't quite understand. After our first trip in to town there I was so overwhelmed I had to go back to bed. At one stall you could buy snacks, phones, ladies' make-up and cigarettes which were only sold one at a time. The same man could send money out of the country in dollars or sterling and arrange transport for anything to anywhere else on the continent. His brother ran the barber shop next door, which amounted to an upturned beer crate under a jolly umbrella, a mirror hung on the fence and some clippers plugged into a car battery. The barber shop was a great social hub and card games and beer bottles were in constant employ there. Both places did roaring trade.

People shouted when they were only two feet apart, children would simply leave school to work for their parents or because it was this or that family occasion, funerals went on for days, and everyone knew everyone else, although perhaps that wasn't too different from home. All of this conspired to set me on the back foot from the time I woke until the time I slept.

Our piece of patch, over one and a half thousands acres of it, had near three hundred fellows working on it, local men. One would come and then his brothers and cousins and uncles would join the troupe too. Everyone seemed to know everyone from somewhere and all seemed to be related through blood or marriage. I never worked out who was who in the whole tangle of it. When another lot came looking for work the ones that were there already sent them off. If a fellow didn't turn up for work he might just send someone else in his place, often much younger and of unclear relation. I found it all so loose, so fluid; there were no clean lines in the way I was used to.

My troubles with Chisongo began early. He had a swagger to him – not unlike Tom and our Vale walking into a pub late on a Saturday night to be honest – but he was a smart fellow too. He knew me for an impostor and I knew him to be a rotten apple. When there was misery with the other chaps, I could always trace it back to him. He would disappear for a few days then roll in on pay day demanding full wages. The other fellows would have to pick up the slack when he didn't turn up and he'd pick fights with them over nothing, accusing them of stealing cigarettes and small change. I don't know why I didn't turf him out. Perhaps to keep Sara and Maria happy because they were a support to Cessie, and she liked them.

Only once was there an incident between Chisongo and Cessie. Cessie was on her own in the garden. I'd taken Dog that day. I was with Kraus tracking and then shooting baboons who were attacking villagers and raiding their food stores. Not uncommon in the dry season. Dog was a handy warning shot for the baboons, so deep was his hatred of the buggers. Cessie was trying to revive a rose she had forgotten to water – it had suffered in the heat. She'd cut the wilted flowers and leaves off and was giving it a good drink. Chisongo approached her, but came from the side of the house so she never saw him coming.

'You don't give me enough' was his greeting, according to Cecelia. Gave her the fright of her life.

'Chisongo? What do you want here?'

'You don't give me enough money.'

'It's three days to pay day. It's not long.'

'I need it now.'

'No. And anyway I don't have money at the house. We still need to go to town for wages.' She said she could feel the adrenaline beginning to bristle.

'I need it.'

'Chisongo, I heard you. But now you need to hear me. I do not have money to give you. There is no money kept in the house.'

Then he hissed something at her. Not in English. But she felt its harshness and its heat and knew it was directed at her. Then he spat on the grass right next to her feet and walked away.

I should have taken a hard line and sacked him right then. And don't I think about it again and again. In the end, in my impotence, all I did was go to him and explain that there was no money in the house and that Mrs Midwinter had nothing to give him. I was weak when I should have shown strength. It was a polite discussion from my side and sulking silence from his. I was never a man to risk a fight. Added to that, out there I felt I didn't know the rules. Still, I'd felt the old eels in my belly from the get-go. And when the eels tell you something's amiss, you trust them. I know that now.

* * *

The chickens were some of the early lots. I went to find Vale.

'Be needing to choose our hens then.'

'Sure.'

'Shall I leave it to you'?'

'You choose.'

'You sure son?'

'I'll bid.'

'Either. That'll be grand. Let's go see the birds then.'

Dear God, there I was, talking about chickens and walking on egg shells. We went over to the cages. Poor wretches, all packed in behind the wire. One ginger hen had been all pecked behind her head and was bleeding. She was in a bad way poor love. Hens always seem to bleed thick for some reason. The blood sat proud on the feather grease. She was small too, a good target, and the others knew that getting rid of her would free up some space for them.

'The girls in there look angry, eh Vale?'

Vale didn't reply, just wandered ahead a little to peer in the other cages.

He pointed to a clutch. Good fat birds, nice healthy beaks. He'd chosen well.

'Yes, those. Good spot, son. They look fine. Good spot.'

The auction was a good one, fast and quick. We huddled close, all pinched buttocks and steaming breath. The angry hens came up before ours. There were five of them and the bleeding ginger one was taken out of the offering though she remained in the cage with her tormentors. She crouched there, either too shocked or too scared to move. Her one eye was coming out a bit. I couldn't bear to look. Some small-holder from past the Sandlings took the lot.

'You get our birds for us son.'

'Pa?'

'See you at the truck.'

The Sandlings man was swaying off towards the car park. He walked like a fisherman at the end of a long, cold crab season. I ran to catch him.

'Excuse me Sir?'

'Yeah?'

'Did you have any plans for that there ginger bird'?'

'Yeah, mate, for the dogs. Too scrawny for the pot and too dumb for laying.'

'Oh for sure, no good for any of that.'

He made to move off.

'I was wondering if you might consider giving her to me. 'I'd pay you of course. You'd make a little profit, her being thrown in the lot for nothing.'

'Why?'

'Uh, ferrets.'

'Right, right'

He opened the box with one hand scooped in to get her with the other and handed her over. She didn't even bother to move. I wasn't sure she was still alive.

'Give you two?'

'Sure.'

I handed him some cash. The hen felt warm. I was sure she was still breathing. I put her inside my coat and went back to the truck. No fool like an old fool.

'Pa?'

It was Vale with our clutch. We'd gone for three and come back with six fat ones and one near dead one.

'I got the ginger one.'

'What?'

'Another little lost one for your mad old Pa,' I said.

There. I'd caught him. He forgot it all and let slip a small upward curl of his mouth.

We drove the long road home like that, Vale looking straight ahead and me with the little runty hen warm in my coat.

'Son, you need to go to Tom. I know I have no place telling you what to do. I know you won't ever trust me to know right from wrong and this way from that ever again. If that's how it is then that's how it is. But listen to me when I say, that boy needs you now. For everything that's going on in you there's as much going on in him. He's your brother, son. He is that. If you think I'm a rotten old arse of a father then you need to look at the one he's got and know that however lonely you are he's as much and more. He's got no legs for God's sake. Will you go to him son? Or at least think about it?'

Vale reached inside his pocket with one hand still on the wheel. He took out a small bone-handled knife. He put it on the dash.

'I got him this. For whittling.'

The knife sat on the dash between us, glinting a little in the light and rocking back and forth on the blade. It was a fine-looking knife.

'You're good people Vale. Good people.'

I shut my eyes against the sun just about coming through the glass and felt a solid drowsiness coming. Just the kind you only feel in a warm car after an early start. It took all manner of aching away.

Chapter 7

Vale

I'd been out with the dogs. I couldn't sleep all day anymore, and walking was the only thing I knew to do when I didn't know where to be. I was dreading the day ahead. I had to go and see some counsellor lady about what had happened. The hospital had referred me. I didn't want to go, and should have said so when the doctor told me, but Pa was there and he agreed on my behalf.

'Sounds good son. Just half an hour and if you don't like it, we can put it down to experience. Best we do what we're told.'

When I got back to the kitchen, Pa was there drinking his coffee with Pup on his lap. I was dripping all over the place. My bones hurt, like they were bruised or something. My shoulder was still quite bad and my eye was still patchy.

Pa was being extra nice to me since I came home from the hospital, when really he should have been angry. I still hadn't gone to see Tom and Pa knew it. I had hidden the knife I bought at the market in the drawer next to my bed so I didn't have to see it.

'There you are Lad. Young Mole Boy called.'

'What'd he want?'

'Was just asking after you, really. He hadn't heard from you for a few days. Not since the beet haul. He'd called in on Thomas up at the hospital but the lad was asleep.'

I didn't feel like dealing with Mole.

Pa went on, 'Said he'd got himself a new contract at that big old manor up Playford way. Some London folk have it now. Nice piece of land they have and all the gardens too. Mole will have some steady pennies for a few months when the summer comes.'

'Right.'

'I told him he deserves a big contract. Works hard.'

I hated how Pa always went on about Mole Boy. He felt sorry for him so he always made him sound better than he was, more impressive. I don't know why he thought I wanted to hear it.

'Ready when you are, son.'

'I still need to dry off a bit.'

'I could use a bit of prinking myself. Best pass a comb through. Come on Pup, off now.'

I went to dry myself as best I could and tidy my head. It looked stupid. I turned my face to the side. With my hair all tidy suppose I looked a bit like Pa. Still, when I was younger he always used to say, 'You've got your mother's ears.' Usually I hated that. I reached up and traced my finger along the rim down to the lobe. So soft. I didn't remember ever touching Ma's ears but I must have.

We didn't talk much on the way to town. Pa let me drive. I don't know why, he probably had his mind on the jobs he needed to do at the bank. He was wearing a jacket over his blue jumper and though he was looking out the window I could see he was pursing and easing his lips as we went. Made me think he was anxious. The roads had ice up the sides. I was careful to drive properly so he wouldn't get riled, and I left the radio on his choice, but in the end I don't think he really noticed.

We parked up and I left Pa outside the bank. I didn't want him coming with me.

'Okay on your own?'

I nodded.

'All right then. Sure it will all be fine.' He was fidgeting and I suddenly realised he was worried. He thought the counsellor might ask me about my eye, that I would tell her about our fight.'

I could have said something to make him feel better. Instead, I turned and walked away.

Town was just one street, straight down the middle, and it ended at the quay. Whenever people come there and ask directions, they get the same answer; one road in, same one out, and boats and water down the end so you'll need to use your brakes. People said it so often that you'd hear old boys like the Dominos shouting, 'You'll need to use your brakes!' as they tumbled out the pub door at closing.

The counsellor was up next to the doctor's surgery, near the war memorial where all the smarter places were. I had to breathe in and out a few times before opening the door. I hated it immediately. It was too small and the carpets were the colour of dried blood. There was an older woman behind the counter.

'Hello, are you here for Caroline?'

I handed her the note I was given at the hospital.

'Vale Midwinter. That's right. Glad we could fit you in.'

I wanted to hide.

'You'll need to fill this in. Leave the last section open for me to do, all right?'

'Okay.'

I went to sit and fill in the form. Whole load of questions about who sent me and why. When I had finished with it I just sat all hunched in on myself chewing on my nails and knowing I was in the wrong place.

The room felt hot and close. I didn't take my jacket off though. It was all I had to hide behind. I could feel sweat gathering at my neck and on my lip.

'You done?'

'Yeah.' I handed it back over the counter.

'Good. I'll just tell her you're here.' She walked along a short corridor and tapped twice on a door.

'Vale Midwinter is here. Yes.'

Suddenly, instinct took hold. I got up, flung open the front door, and was gone. I was out and down the street so quick I didn't even hear the door hit the frame as it swung shut.

I walked fast and felt tears coming though I didn't know why. I just knew I didn't want to talk about any of it. I didn't want to explain why we went in the boat, why I ran away to find Tom, why Pa hit me, what I'd said. Most of all I didn't want to talk about Ma. In the end everything always went back to her. I didn't want to talk about her like she was the cause of every problem, and certainly not to some woman called Caroline who had never even met her.

I walked towards the water to cool down, smoking as I went. I knew there wouldn't be many people that way, just a few dog walkers. My hands were shaking. I managed to open my bottle of pain killers and swallowed a couple. By the time I got to the boat yard I had worked up a whole head of steam.

Sometimes I just got angry when I should have been worried or upset. It was like I only knew one way to feel stuff. Ma would have asked, 'What is it you're really feeling love.' And then I would realise I was sad or mostly, afraid. Afraid of all kinds of things, like looking stupid or failing at something. I tried to ask myself questions that Ma would ask but it wasn't the same. She would have taught me to find a way though.

I knew I'd have to fetch Pa outside the bank but I needed some quiet first. I sat low along the wall to get out of the wind, looking at the boats and thinking seagulls were noisy fucking bastards and wishing we'd never come in today. I also wished Pa would stop trying to talk to me about Tom. I didn't want to visit him. Like an idiot or a baby or something I just wanted him well again. And I wanted to say, 'It's not fair.' I knew that was stupid because what's fair anyway?

I leaned right back against the wall. I felt tired. Up over me the sky was grey and seagulls were all going this way and that, some were just floating on the wind. Just water and seagulls and lines pinging off the metal masts and the wind sort of brushing my forehead. I wanted the feeling to last. It made me feel like I used to when I was about to fall asleep and Ma would run her thumb across my brows until my eyes closed. It felt like that, like sleep coming.

By the time I got to the bank, Pa was resting outside. He looked sort of old. I suddenly felt sick seeing him there. I knew I'd done wrong. I wanted to make it right, but I couldn't.

'Sorry Pa.'

'All right son. Saw our Dobbler. Good man.'

'Okay.'

'He reminded me about the piggers next Monday.'

'Okay. Monday.'

'He sends his regards.'

'Thanks'

'I could tell he wanted to ask how it went with the counsellor. Instead he said 'You hungry?'

'Yeah.'

'Caravan?'

'Okay.'

Pa patted his pockets, like he always did, a weird, old-man gesture. I hated it. He and Ma only met when he was forty-something. She was younger. They were going to have another baby before me but they lost it. Ma wasn't too healthy after that. They probably weren't thinking to have another – but here I was. When I was still in school some people thought Pa was my grandfather. I didn't bother to correct them.

There had been a cafe in that caravan since I could remember. They may have swapped the trailer for a new one but nothing smart enough that you'd notice. Not much room, but good food. I'd only ever been there a few times. Always with Pa and always on days I remembered later.

First time was when we went to Grandpa's funeral. Pa cried that day. Another time was after the big storms which brought the whole barn down and I came with Pa to get a loan at the bank to fix it. We had come for breakfast with Tom a year earlier, after Pa had to bail him out of prison. Tom got badly oiled up and then put his truck through a wall. Pa knew it wouldn't do to phone Tom's Pa. He'd just go off on one and leave him there anyway. Pa and I agreed we had never seen anyone eat as much as Tom ate that morning. Pa liked to joke that every pig and hen in the county would start running for cover when they heard Tom had been on the tank the night before.

As usual there was a line of cars and trucks outside the caravan. Just before we went in, Pa turned to me.

'Son, I hope it went well. I realise I can't always help you how I should.' He was blinking a lot and couldn't look at me. 'So if the lady is a help to you and can do what I can't, then it's a good thing. And you should speak freely to her.' I could tell how hard it was for him to say it.

'I didn't go.'

'What's that?'

'I didn't go. I couldn't.'

'You needed to. The doctor said. They worked hard to get you a place.'

'I couldn't.' I was feeling some heat rising.

'But the doctor...'

'Screw the doctor Pa, I couldn't do it.'

The truth never helped me. Pa was being all anxious and kind so I thought I should be honest. I should have realised it would upset him again.

Two girls came out of the cafe. One of them worked at the pub. I'd always liked her.

'Hey,' she said as she passed.

I tried to reply but didn't manage. I turned my head to see her go. She was linking arms with the other girl but she looked back at me and saw me looking at her and we both quickly looked away. I wanted to think she was interested; but then I realised she was probably just staring at what a goddamned mess I looked with a whopping great shiner and cuts on my face.

Pa sighed.

'Come on. We may as well eat.'

He went up the steps hanging onto the rope railing. I had to follow him. The place was full and noisy. Not a place to go when you feel like hiding.

All four Dominos were there, packed into a booth, and they swung round to say hello. Roy waved at us with his fork. There was a whole sausage stuck on top. They were all ribbing Pa about wearing his jacket.

'Gettin' married Land?' Roger said.

'Who's the unlucky gal?'

We ordered our food at the counter.

'Go take a seat son, I'll square up.'

'I could wait.'

'Just do as I ask',' he said, more forcefully than I'd expected. Louder too.

He came over with a big tray of food, unpiled it and sat down. He didn't say a word and didn't look at me. Pa faffed around with salt and sauce. Then he sighed deeply. I glanced up and met his eye. He looked softer. His lips were pursed and he half nodded.

It was warm and clean in the caravan. It always smelled like coffee and bacon in the morning and vinegar for the rest of the day. We'd ordered steak and kidney pie. Pa leaned across and broke mine open a bit because I was still only using one hand and struggling.

'Tuck in, son.'

'Thanks.'

It was good to eat. I didn't even let it annoy me that he would say 'Mmm' as he ate. He always did it, because he liked his food, but it always pissed me off because he was doing it for no one in particular and he didn't know he was doing it himself. It was just a noise. Like an animal when it's sleeping. I hated it. We ate a lot and then Pa told me to get us apple pie too. When we were done I thought we should head home.

'No, come on.' Even as he was saying it he was brushing crumbs off himself and sliding out of the booth. He gestured for me to follow. He went to the back of the caravan.

'Kev.' He said. I hadn't seen the harbour master there.

'Ah, Land.'

Pa put out his hand. 'Thanks for what you did for us. For the lads. Here's Vale.'

'Ah you're looking a little better lad. Good to see you up and about.'

I put my hand out to shake his 'Thanks for helping us.'

'Not at all. It's my job. And my pleasure.'

'Yeah. Sorry to cause it all though.'

He tried to be light.

'Ah lad. We've all done stupid things. Still, I do worry for your friend. Popped by to see him day before yesterday when I took my old dad in for his checks.'

'Your dad fit enough?'

'Oh yes, just keeping an eye on his old ticker.'

'Glad to hear it. And how'd you find our Thomas?' said Pa.

'Oh not good, as you'd expect, right? Didn't chat long, just a look in, lots of doctors coming and going and he wasn't too wakeful.'

'I'll go again today then,' said Pa.

'Do that Land. He'll be needing his friends.' Kevin smiled at me when he said it.

I felt Pa's eyes on me.

'Thanks again Kev,' said Pa. 'We'll get you and the family round one evening for a meal. Not sure what you'll get, but it'll be hot and we'll have some grog.'

'Aw, sounds good. We'd like that. Give my regards to Thomas when you see him, will you Vale?'

Pa and Kevin shook hands.

Then, without looking at me Pa walked straight for the door and out down the little stairs. I took after him. He was moving faster than usual. I had to call after him.

'Pa wait.'

'I'm done.'

Pa kept walking for the truck.

'What?'

I could tell he was fuming. 'Even the harbour master has gone to visit our Tom. Every last Domino, Dobbler, Mole Boy, your dumb old Pa, but you, his only true friend in the world, will not go. I don't know what is wrong with you but you best sort it out.'

'I'll go when I'm fuckin' ready, okay?'

'You watch your mouth. I can just about stand you maundering about me and cursing behind my back all day and night but I will not let you drop our Thomas.'

'I said …'

'I don't care what you say Vale Midwinter. I care what you do. For your friend. The lad cannot walk. He cannot walk and he will likely never walk again. He cannot work and other than the two of us, he has no family to speak of. You think about that and then you do what's right or I'll have no more for you.'

'Pa.'

'No. No.' He was spitting. 'I'm tired. I've had enough and I want to get home now.'

Pa didn't say anything as we walked back to the truck. I knew I should feel bad and I did. But, I was also fucking hissing.

He opened up and got in on the passenger side.

'Did you want to get the fencing?' I said.

'No.' He slammed the door. 'Straight home. I need to see to my Pup.'

I didn't want to talk to him anymore either, my chest was pumping and tight as I started the engine. It felt good to leave Town, past the petrol station and out past the abattoir until it was just fields again. My shoulder suddenly hurt more. Pa was tapping his fingers on the window side and looking out at nothing through the window.

The rain was long gone. Some sun was hitting off the wet slick on the road and I had to squint to see right. All of a sudden I saw a big old rabbit flop into my path and I slammed the brakes. Stupid thing was all deaf and blind with disease. Didn't know where it was. Probably hadn't eaten in forever either. Even the foxes didn't want it, with its ears and eyes all swollen and full of pus. In a couple of days its brains would probably start coming out its nose. The disease meant they rotted from the inside out. Slowly I went round it.

'Run her down, son.'

'What?'

'Run her down.'

'But we've passed already.'

'It's not right to leave her like that.'

'You serious?'

'It's not right.'

'Pa—'

'Goddammit Vale, you run her down or you can get out and walk home and I'll do it.'

Pa was shaking and red and his eyes were watering. Everything felt thick. I could hear his breath all sharp and uneven through his nose. I felt afraid but not for me. Suddenly all kinds of stuff was sitting there in the car with us. All of everything from before was there, with us, engine running, two wheels in the dirt. I would have done anything to just keep on. I looked in the rear mirror. The rabbit was still there, dumb in the road. I shunted the gear and reversed. I think I got it on the way back. I made sure of it the second time. It hit the wheel then the undercarriage. I stopped just after on the side.

'Shall I check?'

He shook his head

'No.'

'I'll check.'

I got out. The rabbit was pulp. I'd hit it right. Blood and fur all messed up together, its innards ruptured on the ground.

I got back to Pa. He had his face in his hands. He was weeping. I started up the engine and drove on home. I had nothing I knew how to say.

Chapter 8

Landyn

Dear God I had the devil in me, and stood over the mess on the kitchen floor in Kabwe and demanded to know who had done it. My voice was dark, the anger bloody and full. Who had dropped the plate and broken it and ruined everything?

'Land it doesn't matter, it's just a plate.'

'I can make more pie.' Said Maria.

'It does matter. It matters that no one can be bothered to do anything properly, and everything is always taken for granted no matter the hours a man works. I am sick to death of having to look after everyone in this house.'

God forgive me, the words just came, big, heavy words, with history behind them. And even while I was saying them, I was watching, watching myself, the way you do sometimes when something bigger than you is about to unfold. I didn't know it then, not with logic or reason, but I felt it as I watched myself. I could hear those words coming out of me as if I was just a split second behind it all. And around me everything was silent.

Then, through this silence and my own voice I heard a noise.

Like the sort of small, short yelp a puppy makes. Once, then twice and three times and then it came again, and again and on and on. And then I see the child, Sara's daughter, that she had with that drunken lout. She was hiding like an animal that has been wounded and it knows it has to hide away or it will die. I knew it was her had dropped the plate.

And it made me even angrier, this small child's noise, these stupid hiccups. I shouted at the girl to stop, but it was I who could not stop. And some other part, older part, maybe the father in me knew something was amiss, this time, everything was wrong.

That blessed rabbit sat in the road like it had nothing left to live for. We had to help her. There's no man alive that I would call a friend who would leave her in that state.

If she felt some pain for a second as we hit her then that was all right too. Pain is not always the same every time you feel it. It has different moods to it depending where it began and where it has come to sit.

Only an hour or so before, I'd been in fairly good spirit all things considered. Though of course I had been worrying about Vale, feeling uneasy about him seeing a counsellor but all in all nothing I felt we couldn't manage.

Been in the bank and seen old Dobbler there. There's a friend for you.

'Ho there Landyn, old pal.'

'Oh. Oh morning Dob.'

'I've been meaning to call you up on the old telephone.'

'Oh? Tell you what, I'm needing to get a move on this morning,

keeping an eye out for my lad, so if you'd walk outside with me?'
Dob nodded.

It was so good to be out on the steps. Cold air hit my lungs and it felt like the first breath I'd taken all morning.

'Sorry about that Dob, needed some air. Busy old day.'

'I dare say, Land, I dare say. Did see your boy heading down the high street like a bear with a sore head. Looked like more of the same trouble. Sorry 'bout that Land.'

'That's appreciated.'

Dobbler meant it. He wasn't a man to go looking for gossip. Straight as a die that one. Probably the closest I have to a best friend. Seems right strange to think of him like that, but there it is. When Vale and I got back from Africa, there was none as solid as Dobb.

'So, to get your own head right, let's be sure we sort those piggers we've been talking about?'

'There's an idea.'

'Get them loaded and sorted. Be too late by end next week won't it? Too old by half then.'

'Too true. Good thing I saw you, near forgot the pigs again over the last few days.'

'I did remind you at the auction old fella but, you've been a busy man, bear taming and all.'

Dobbler winked through his wiry eyebrows. Even when we were all younger he had them. Great wild and hairy things. He could make them wiggle all round like those caterpillars. When Vale and Tom were youngsters they'd laugh so hard they'd cry and so he'd wiggle them some more.

'Ha! I dare say you're right. Bear taming. Got to find it and catch it first so best be on my way.'

'He'll be all right. He's a good lad. You've raised him good, Land.' Dobbler looked right at me when he said that.

'He is Dob. That he is.'

'All right then. I'll come round week today? Monday shall we say? Unless you hear different. Give you both time to get your feathers together.'

'Sounds Good. Monday.' We shook hands.

I knew he was right. Vale was a good lad.

When the lad came up the road towards the bank to join me, I looked at him real close, like you do a child when he's been unwell and is finally sleeping. The bruising round his eye was still thick and deep. Had some scabs and scratches too, along his temple and his forehead from whatever went on in that boat. It had only been three days since the accident. He was blinking away the smoke as he lit a cigarette facing sideways into the sea breeze. He had long horizontal frown-lines across his forehead. Pale as a lamb. There was some tiredness to him all hunched up in his coat. It used to be mine that one. The collar was fraying though and had come away from the sheep skin underneath it. I decided I'd try get some pennies together to get him a new one for Christmas. He'd like that.

'Caravan?' I said.

'Sure.'

We didn't speak as we made our way down there. Just the winter between us and the chestnut leaves on the pavement as we went. I could have walked like that with him forever. It was the closest I'd felt to my boy for years.

And now, straight back in the miserable brine that we had become. Sitting in the motor with Vale hissing and biting next to me, I could feel all the dust and grit rolling up over the deserts from Kabwe. It was as if from the moment I read about the place for the first time, the two places could never be separated again. I'd struck my boy and now we were all in this great sucking bog. Tom was in it with us. There was nowhere to go with all that. Nowhere at all. All the years of work to make things right, to save the farm, to get us back to where we were, before it all, come to nought.

For so long I'd kept Kabwe apart from Vale and me. No need to have any of that coming back here with us and start to unsettle things and yet here it was sitting in the car with us, squatting in the road half dead and needing to be run down.

Everything about that rabbit raised the ghosts in me. Its blood and death and hopelessness. When we'd left for Kabwe the farm was overrun with the buggers. And like the one in the road, they were all feeling death just over their shoulder. Creatures don't lie. They'll tell you where you are in life. When the half-dead ones start falling over at your feet, you need to look to how close you are to it in your own life too. If you try to pretend there's nothing wrong when it all falls about you, those animals will bring their message to your door. She was a spectre of her proper self. I knew her eyes were all full of fluid, a seeping brain, but she'd still be breathing and her heart pumping all the harder just to keep herself moving. I sat there feeling the engine thrubbing and Vale saying something I couldn't be bothered to hear.

We hit the rabbit.

I felt her little body thud into the undercarriage as it came off the wheel. I knew she would be split right open.

Another morning and Cessie and I had quarrelled. More and more we were at each other, the worst versions of ourselves. Having the excuse of the bank appointment was the only thing that had stopped the yelling that day. I don't remember where Vale was. I was in constant defence about the money, the lack of it, and even the slightest look from her could send me into a rage. And she, to show her disappointment or her wounding from my anger, would retreat into silences, chirping to Vale and the dogs with all the false jollity she could muster, but never a kind word to me.

Off to town and the bank, where I seemed to spend my every Monday and nothing in front but another attempt to beg the bank man for money. I took up the *Farmers' Chronicle* to calm myself. I flipped to the section on tractors, thinking I could sell one of ours and maybe rent instead, bit of cash in the pocket. And there it was. A little rectangle of words. Never forget it either.

Farmers Wanted for a New Life in Africa's Fertile Bread Basket

The government of Zambia is developing its commercial farming sector. Land, interest free loans, equipment, five years tax free subsidised program. Apply now. All who respect the values of our democratic nation are welcome.

There was a bit more text about who they were looking for and a tiny map of Africa with a little basket of wheat to show where farmers would be heading. The other side of the world. I didn't even like going down London way. Hadn't done for over ten years at the time and saw no reason to start, and there I was sitting in the bank feeling my chest start to thunder and my brow dampen looking at a little map of Africa, a place I'd never even given a second thought. Quickly, thief-like, I tore out the advertisement and tucked it into my wallet like a crisp new tenner.

The bank rejected my every suggestion and again, I went back home with nothing to offer any hope. Only, the little wheat basket on a neat map kept popping into view, just out the corner of my eye.

Of course I didn't dare mention it to Cecelia. She didn't much like me those days. And I can't say I blamed her. Every month we seemed to be closer to ruin. She sat adding things up and adding again and no matter how she did it, the pot was closer and closer to empty. She had taken a morning job cleaning at the Manor. Imagine it. I heard her telling Vale where she'd be going and why he'd need to be getting his own breakfast.

'But why Ma?'

'Because we need to pay for the jam and bread, heart, so I'll be up the road getting us some pennies. It's not far, so you'll know where I am.'

'But Ma you don't like cleaning.'

'That's a true tale. God knows. But I'm going to tell you something you'll need to learn for the rest of your life. Work is work Vale, there's never any shame in doing an honest labour.'

'Can I come with you?'

'No, you'll be busy with school, won't you? But when you get home, I'll be there to tell you how it all went.'

But she was shamed. She hated it so and at night she would sit, her back to me in front of the fire and rub her hands with ointments and creams to try and keep them pretty. Once soft and showing no mark but the farn-tickle of the sun, they cracked and puckered around the tips.

We bought nothing, we went nowhere and still there was never enough.

'Farmers Wanted for a New Life in Africa's Fertile Bread Basket.'

* * *

113

Could we go? No reason why not, although I didn't exactly know where Zambia was as compared to any other country in the area. It was never in the news, which was a good thing I supposed. I put the idea down, pushed it right aside. It was ridiculous to the point of madness. But, I'd be waiting for the truck to come back in a dark old field, or lifting bales into the trolley and all along my mind would wander back to the advert. Then, I'd allow myself another peak at the *Chronicle*.

Will be of particular interest to growers of grains and livestock.

I took to sneaking into the library once or twice. Just maps and pictures of the place. They made it look lovely, big and wide, but dry. Red sand and scrubby-looking grass with trees and houses in between. Hard to imagine anything growing there, but evidently it did.

But this was the truth, I was one failed harvest or late payment away from ruin and had a family that wasn't the same because of it.

For the difficulties of the land and the troubles of life, my own dad passing so early and me being not yet 25 when he did and my dear mother so soon after, for all that, it was the first time I'd felt so broken and without option. I was a little older than when my folks had passed on, but I had Vale and Cessie too, and they needed me to make it all right. I had even begun to feel as if I must be shifty in my ways to be in such a mess. Started to feel owls in the night's air, something dark moving in.

Still, I did some reading up over the next couple of months. Never told Cessie of course. I had tried to tell her, suggest it by showing her all the papers and information I'd gathered. She flat refused it. Another almighty row. Tears, more accusations.

But I kept looking into it. Good growing land, lots of tobacco and the like but a lack of food based crops, which was why the government was encouraging all kind to come and bring their expertise. Whole load of white fellows from over Zimbabwe way were relocating there or had done already. Zambia was welcoming them with what they had left to start anew after they lost their land to political troubles. You could grow a commercial crop like tobacco but a good portion of your land had to grow food in return. Seemed fair, and smart too. They had a hungry nation, youthful, growing and spent all their pennies importing their food. What did frighten me a bit was the size of their farms, hundreds of labourers needed and great distances to travel.

'Land, interest free loans, equipment...'

I tried to put it out of my mind for a while. I had to. It was too wild a plan, too mad an adventure for a family that hardly had the energy for a day trip to Norfolk let alone half across the globe. But our situation didn't get better. It only got worse. Cecelia and I were scrapping all the time or not talking at all which was worse sometimes. Often I'd take myself off to sleep downstairs in front of the fire and find myself waking the next day with only a collie dog for a friend. Vale had to forgo a school trip for lack of pennies, not once but twice and by the time the rains were late in coming we were flat broke.

I got in to the kitchen one June day. It was hot and dusty. Not a hint of those cool east-coast breezes. Everything was wilting. The mail was on the kitchen table. Vale would have brought it in when he came home from school. There on top was a letter for

Cecelia. I didn't know the writing. I lifted it up to get a squint on the post mark. Her home, County Antrim and on the back the address of her mother in Larne. They'd not spoken for over two decades.

And right then something she had said to me during one of our quarrels came back to me and I knew beyond doubt she was thinking to leave me and take my Vale with her.

'Landyn we can't go on. I can't.' She'd said.

'I'm doing what I can.'

'Are you?'

'What on God's earth is that meant to mean?'

'You do the same. You keep on doing the same, but the same doesn't work does it?'

'I don't know what else to do. I can't exactly throw in the towel can I?'

'Well maybe I will.' She had her chin out.

'What's that meant to mean? Do you threaten me Cecelia?'

'If you choose to see it that way, then yes I do. I can't do it anymore. I need, I don't know, something. I need a rest.'

'And exactly where do you plan to go for this rest?'

She paused, bristling but unsure.

'I'll go home to Ballymena. I'll take my Vale with me.'

I felt like I've been hoofed by a goddamned horse. Right in the softest spot.

'What? Are you out of your mind? You've not been back since you left as a girl and never a word passed between you and your good for nothing family since.'

'They're still my blood Landyn. And Vale's blood too. And the fact that I would even think to call on them should let you know how broken I am to be here.' She was in tears. She turned

116

and went upstairs, the bedroom door closed behind her. She had stayed there until the next morning. She told Vale she wasn't well and he had taken her some toast. I spent another night downstairs, maundering and hot.

And then, this letter from Ireland, a death warrant with a postage stamp. I felt great wheels were beginning to move without me and with it a monstrous, freighting panic began to rise like a horse trying to escape a burning stable.

Cecelia had left Ballymena under a low cloud. Just 18 years old and she'd fallen in love with an archaeologist fellow from out of Dublin. He was in Larne working on some diggings there. Her family were having none of it, wanting her to marry a nice local lad and not get all above herself and carrying on with some older fellow who was up to no good. When they once and for all forbid her from seeing him anymore and sent her to the priest for confession, she packed her bags in the middle of the night and chased the man all the way down to Dublin where he was back at the University.

Never worked out of course, broke her heart. And for shame and stubbornness, she'd nowhere to go. So she came to Suffolk to stay with her cousin Margaret who had a fair job with a smart family in Easton. One of the big old mill houses there. And Cessie came to look after the children there. Horrible pair as I recall.

I met her at Aldeburgh. She was taking the children out for a day on the beach. And I was there with Dobbler helping the Dominos' dad. He needed help fetching some nets for his boat. Or at least that's how I remember it.

Dobb saw Cessie first.

'Oh there's a fine one for you Land. One in the nanny uniform.'

'Cut it out Dobb.'

'She's too good for you, that's true, but probably worth a try?'

I turned back to the nets which were all a tangle and while I was trying to get the webbing straight, Dobb was off, crunching across the shingle towards Cessie. Next thing, he's giving her a bit of Dobb-chat and making her laugh and both of them looking at me and next thing he came back with her telephone number and said she was expecting to join us for a walk on the beach over the weekend and her cousin Margaret would be joining us too.

Women always loved Dobbler. Cessie said it was because he was easy and a bit of a shambles and the kind of fellow you could pass an evening with without feeling he was out for anything else but company.

That Cessie would rather go home to a family who she had not spoken to for near twenty years than stay with me forced my hand. And in the end the decision to go to Zambia came down to a strange game of chance. With every application and form to be filled and bureaucracy this and waiting for authorisation on that, I'd say;

'Well, if it doesn't work it doesn't work' or 'If it's meant to be it'll be.'

But it was so easy. After so much struggle, it was as if the stars had finally lined up in our favour – whole constellations conspired. After all the years of going nowhere suddenly everything was moving. It was all 'thank you for your application, we would be very pleased to offer you a loan with the South Zambian Rural Development Agency.' Visas to travel and appointments for medical checks all lined up as if they had been sitting in a row behind a closed door, just waiting for me to open it up.

Eventually though it came down to me having to be firm. As firm as one could be with Cessie. But I could not lose her and Vale to Ballymena. I was certain I would never survive it. A piece of paper came saying we needed to make our final application to the Zambian agency by the end of the next month if we wished to be considered for that year. If we missed the deadline, we would have to start the process again a full year later. Summer was coming to an end in Suffolk and our haul from the fields didn't look good.

Cessie was in her sewing nook, mending the bottoms of my trousers. She looked so calm in her work, focused and quiet. I took her a cup of coffee and a closed the door behind me. I sat.

She glanced up quickly to the cup.

'I'm nearly done here. Not perfect. But they'll have to do.'

She was whirring away along the seams, trying to hold all the frayed bits together.

'Cecelia. Stop for a moment.'

'Nearly done.'

'No. Stop. Look at me love.' I hadn't called her that in so long. She swung around to face me so our knees were touching. I could hardly find my voice. 'Cessie, let's go to Zambia. Together. Let's give it a try love. Give me six months. Give us six months. And if you don't like it, you go to Ballymena. Or back here. Wherever your heart will be easy.' She was watching me so closely I could feel my eyes smarting and wet. 'I know you don't like what I've become. God knows I don't like it either. I do know I've let you down love, I know it, but you have to let me try this one last thing for us. Six months.'

She swallowed and I could see her breath was short. She dropped her head away, frowning and rubbing her finger tips along her forehead like she was trying to resuscitate a memory or feel the shape of something she could no longer name. She looked up, as broken as I.

'Six months.'

Chapter 9
Vale

I felt like shit when we got home from town. All the running away from the counsellor and the rabbit and everything. I couldn't be in the house with Pa. I walked to the Admiral for a pint. It wasn't much past lunch time. I had a quarter-thought to visit Tom, but then I just chickened out like a fucking baby. I guess I just never knew how to fix things. I didn't know what steps to follow to get things back to how they were. And no one was telling me. I guessed he'd be asleep maybe. I wanted to see him. I needed his help with all the fucking mess and everything but I knew he wasn't able to do that. I didn't know what to do with myself without him.

'Hey,' I said.

'Hiya.'

It was the same girl I'd seen earlier. Seeing her where I usually did, behind the counter, I remembered her name was Beth. She was kind of plump and pretty and had long curly red hair. Even redder than Ma's ever was. Couple of times I'd seen her pass the farm on her horse. She rode like a fuckin' nutter. Open road, stubble fields, anything, she didn't care, they were all the same to her. Tom always told me to ask her out or something. Of course I never did and then after a while I hated going there with him because he always made me feel like an idiot.

I'd got to the pub pretty quick. There was ice in the ditches and a little cover of snow, but the roads were clear so long as I walked in the tyre tracks. It was okay. I liked going to the Admiral because it was good for little nooks and places to hide and be quiet.

The warm hit me as I opened the door. Nice big fire and the smell of beer made it worth the walk.

'Pint,' I said.

'Usual?' said Beth.

'Yeah.'

'You look frozen.'

'I am. It's nasty.'

'I love the snow. It's so beautiful. How you been then? Busy in town?'

'Been okay.'

'Really?' She looked up from finding a glass.

'No, not really, but, you know.'

'Sure.'

I didn't know what I was meant to say next.

'How's your friend? Don't usually see you in the day.'

'He's not here, he's not well.'

'Yeah, I know. Sorry about that. You can keep me company then. Got some leery old ones in.'

She gestured with her eyebrows behind me. I kind of turned.

There was a grubby lot all sitting round a table near the fire. Made me feel even more dodgy for drinking on a Monday afternoon if this was the company. They had enough pint glasses on the table to oil the entire army and the enemy too.

'Jesus.' I mostly said this to myself

'I'll say. They're drinking like it's Saturday night. Here's your pint. You know any of them?' She looked up.

'Not much, but enough. Know what I mean?'

'Yeah. I know them more than enough just this afternoon.' She rolled her eyes.

I didn't know what that meant but I let it go and it just kind of went quiet again. She was busy with glasses, drying them and lining them up on the shelves. She worked quickly.

'Your Dad comes in here sometimes. Where's he today then?'

'He's home. He's not feeling too good and his dog is old so, you know, he doesn't like to leave her much. It's stupid.'

'No. I understand that. When my horse had colic, I slept over in her stable with her. It was February.'

'You're crazy.'

We both smiled. It felt nice. I tried to get a proper look at her when she wasn't looking at me but then I just felt like one of the leery old perverts she hated.

'Which dog is it? The little Jack Russell?'

'Yeah.'

'Oh, she's a lovely little thing, he brings her in here sometimes. I see him sneaking her snacks.'

'Oh, sorry.'

'Don't be, makes me like him. Makes me think he's a nice guy.'

'Right.'

It felt so warm in the in the pub and it was kind of nice talking to the girl with no one else there trying to interfere. I could feel the whole horrible morning disappearing just from being around her. I liked her face. Her skin looked soft.

'So your friend, is he going to get better you think?'

'Well, they don't really know. His legs are pretty bad. He can't really walk.'

'Oh God, it's so, so horrible. I heard he couldn't walk but I guess I thought it was just temporary.'

'Yeah, well, no one knows yet.'

'Must be a comfort though, to have you visiting. He'd be glad for his friends. God, that's so sad.' She was refilling a jar full of straws.

'Yeah.' I knew I was being dishonest, but I wanted her to like me and I didn't think it was a bad thing, just wanting someone, a girl like her, to like me a little. If I told her I hadn't been to see him yet, then she'd want to know why, and I couldn't have answered that, because I didn't know either. But it wasn't like he was doomed. There was stuff the doctors could do. I read a thing about a guy who everyone thought would never get up again and next thing he was walking and playing football and everything.

I guess I just thought that when I saw Tom I would know he blamed me, and if he did, then no matter what the truth was or how it was wouldn't matter because I'd still be guilty. I didn't know if I was to blame. I said for us to go in, to get in the gully to get to the boat, but then when we got in the water and it was so cold, then I don't know who did what and how it all happened because it felt like there was something else out there controlling everything. I couldn't tell Tom that because that's a cop-out. It was all so fucked up. As long as I didn't see him, and know he blamed me, then I could just keep replaying the whole thing over and over looking for something I could remember that would prove to me that it wasn't my fault. That it was an accident. It was.

Beth was dealing with an old guy who was counting out every

last penny for his ale. I wanted to ask her out. But I didn't really have money for that sort of thing. She seemed to want to talk to me but then it was her job and she was generally friendly. She was coming back over.

'So how are you after it all?'

'Me? In what way?'

'Well your face looks pretty sore, black eye and all.'

'Yeah, suppose it is.'

'Looks like you got in a fight with the boat. Must have been really scary. I'm scared of water like that.'

'Suppose I kind of did get in a fight.'

'Guess you did. Lucky you won.'

'Did I?'

'You're here aren't you?'

'Yeah.'

'You okay?'

'Of course. Just tired maybe.'

'Okay.' She carried on polishing glasses with a big white cloth.

I wanted so much for someone to ask me how I was. And still I hadn't answered. She seemed to care. She seemed to want to know. But sitting there, I felt like if I even began to tell her all the stained things that went round and round my skull, then it would all come out in the worst way. I already felt confused and guilty and God knows what else, if she saw all that I would only feel ashamed too. More than I already did.

I sipped on my pint and kind of half kept an eye on Beth while she polished the glasses and pulled pints.

She was wearing a skirt that was a bit tight on her and a dark woollen top that was the same and that made her skin look even whiter. I wanted to touch her. She looked clean, like she might smell like lotions and stuff, though not perfume. She was nice to everyone, didn't seem angry or nervous or anything. Just kind of safe in herself I guess and liked riding her horse and stuff like that. I wondered if I could ever be like that. Sitting there it didn't seem like it.

She came back over and pushed some peanuts in front of me.

'Have some of those. I'm Beth by the way.'

'Vale'

'I know.'

'I know you're Beth.' I said.

She smiled. Then she leaned forward to fetch a glass the other side me me. She could have just asked me to pass it. Her face was right next to mine. She was so close I could feel the warm coming off her cheek. She smelled just like I thought she would. I felt like I couldn't breathe. She leaned back and went back to lining up glasses. I wish she hadn't. I wished her face was still next to mine.

'Do you want to come outside for a smoke?' I said.

'I don't smoke'

'Because your parents would mind?'

'No. I just don't need too.'

'What does that mean?'

'Just that.'

I'd never thought of it that way. Don't even know when I started, it was Tom I was with, probably five years before. Pa never said anything. Just said something about not getting caught at school.

'I guess I don't need to either.'

'Oh, no, you probably do need to.'

'Why?'

'I don't know. So you have something to do when it goes quiet.'

'Right.'

'Right.'

'Like now?'

'Exactly like now.'

I liked her so much right then. I wondered if I could kiss her. Not there obviously, but sometime.

Everything was so skew with me. Things with Tom and Pa and suddenly thinking about Ma all the time where before I managed to kind of keep out ahead of everything. I felt like I came out the water but kept on drowning anyway. But then I looked at Beth and she was all calm and beautiful in the middle of it all. I wanted to stay there just being with her.

I drank my pint really slowly. I could only afford the one. We hadn't yet been paid for the deliveries we'd done a couple weeks before and I only had the pennies from the beet haul. I didn't want to rush my drink and be out on the cold road on my own again with nowhere to go but home. So I stayed.

I didn't know what to do about Pa. Whenever we were in the same room I could feel he was trying to say stuff to me even before he opened his mouth. He'd kind of loiter around and then start by saying something stupid about how cold it was.

I knew that wasn't what he wanted to say so it just annoyed me. I felt like goading him a bit. Maybe force him to say something real. I wanted to say of course it's cold, it's winter, what the hell else would it be? But I couldn't do that either. It was bullshit.

So, instead I kept saying I needed to go see Mole Boy or something. Most times I didn't go there. I didn't want to see him either. He had come over the day before to ask Pa to make sure his numbers were good on his quote for Playford Manor. Pa said, typical of Mole, he was undercharging by over a third. I could have gone to see Mole but his father was always around and he would ask stupid questions.

So instead of going to their place, I would just sort of lie on the chestnut and smoke or take the long way home over Rabbit Hill. Up there you could see the whole farm, one boundary to the next. Ma used to make us have picnics up there when we could have just stayed at home. And Pa would grumble because he would get sand and ants in his food and then have to carry the plates and everything all the way home afterwards. Ma could only see how beautiful it was and would call out all the birds she saw. And one time a fox was there with a little kit, still more grey than red. Ma cried and when Pa asked her why, she said she didn't know.

The hill was beautiful I suppose. If anything ever went well with someone, like Beth, it would be a nice place to walk and sit. It was the only one for miles and miles. Pa said it was the highest point in that part of Suffolk, which was hardly saying much, and also I never knew if it was true.

I knew he loved the land, like it was his other child or something weird. He wanted me to have it. He always said that. Wanted me to carry it on and then he'd launch into his speech about 'we did it all for you son, so you would have your place in the world.' What a load of crap that was. I didn't ever want them to keep the farm for me. And now, because they had I guess I had to feel all guilty and sorry because I hated it. Not the farm, not the land, I didn't hate that. I was only ever quiet in myself when I was out with the dogs walking through the fields. I could get away from the rages I had by just kind of walking them off and sitting a while. But I hated the town, the people in it and all the stuff everyone always seemed to want from me. Always something.

Just thinking about the rest of my life in the same place, having the same conversations and doing the same thing every day and week and year made me feel like I couldn't breathe. The feeling would hook in and even thinking about it in the pub made my lungs feel chalky. It's the same feeling I'd get when I was at school and had to go up and do the sums on the board. I knew all the others were laughing at me. Not Tom though.

Even though I knew him forever we started school in the same class and from then on we couldn't be separated. He was a year older than me and everyone in the class on account of him starting late because for some reason his folks just forgot to take him to start school. Or that's how it seemed. Or most likely his father forgot. His Ma ran off that year, to escape all the yelling I suppose. She came back but had kind of lost her mind and from then on she drifted in and out. She'd be gone for almost a year and then turn up in the summer. Tom would take her to the doctor and buy her things and talk to her but it was like she wasn't even in her body. Someone else had taken up home in there. Tom said he didn't know who she was anymore, but she was still his mum.

'My goodly mother returned last night.'

'Really? How'd you find out? She come by?'

'Oh no. Mole called me. Said he was sitting with her outside the library in town.'

'She recognised him?'

'Not sure about that. He knew her though and went to say hello. Seems every time he started trying to you know, t-t-talk, my mother would start laughing so hard she nearly fell over. You know how she is.'

'Shit. Was Mole upset?'

'Oh no. Tell you the truth I think he did it even more on

purpose just to give her a laugh. They were having a right old time together when I got there.'

'Shit. Where's she been?'

'Couldn't say. Mentioned she passed through Norwich though.'

'You okay?'

'Sure. I enjoy her returns.'

'Will she leave again soon do you think?'

Tom chewed his cheeks. 'Surely.'

Whenever I told Pa this stuff he would look sad or upset and then when he saw Tom next he would ask all about his mother and say things like he remembered she was a wonderful dancer, light on her feet, and could sing with the voice of an angel, the sort of stuff he never mentioned about Ma. And then he would tell Tom how proud he was of him for being so good to his mother. When he did all that, I felt like I was dying.

My pint was nearly finished. Beth was filling up salt cellars.

'So, tell your friend Tom I asked after him. I know it's too soon and everything but if he gets a chair or something, he can easily come here.'

'Okay. Thanks.'

'Sorry about all that.'

'It's okay.'

I made to move. I felt like I wanted to say something, like tell her I thought she was pretty or tell her I'd made my drink last so long because of her. But I knew that was just stupid and I didn't know how to say it so I didn't sound like a dick.

'Anyway.' Was all I said when I stood up.

'Okay.' She kind of waited like I was meant to have said something else, or like she forgot what she was about to say.

'I'll see you around then.'

'Do you want to go for a walk?'

'What? Why? Now?'

Even while I was saying it I knew it was all wrong. I knew why she'd want to walk and I was just blind-sided by it but she looked surprised or maybe hurt or something and her cheeks were red and I knew I'd screwed up.

'No, not now.' I could hardly hear her. She'd hung her head a bit. I'd fucked up.

'I'm sorry.'

'Okay'

'No.'

'No?'

'No, I mean I do want to go for a walk.'

'You do?'

'Yeah.'

'Okay.'

'Not now though, is what I meant.'

'Of course not silly.'

'Well, Saturday? I've got to work before.'

'I work here Saturday remember?'

'Oh.'

'I could come a bit early, and you could come here and then we could walk?'

'Okay.'

'You won't forget?'

'Oh, no. No.'

She was smiling again and I felt like I was too. It didn't feel like me to do it. Nothing felt like me when I was talking to her. Like I had no memory of that particular feeling. I didn't really know any other girls since Tom's sister left. I never knew what to say to them.

I thought about Beth until I fell asleep. I thought about how pretty she was. She wasn't like the girls we always saw at the Hook, down near the boats, the kind of girls Tom was always lunging at and groping on the quay while I sat alone at the bar drinking, feeling like a loser because I never knew what to say or do.

Beth was different – her own kind of girl, she had stuff she was interested in and getting on with. I thought about what her skin would feel like, if she'd let me touch her. I knew it would be her letting me, her deciding and not me trying it on. I thought about what we had talked about and all the things I could have said better if I'd known how.

The next day while I was trying to fix the fencing the cows had rammed through, I was still thinking about her. Normally I would have been spitting at the cows, damn stupid animals, but I was thinking on Beth, over and over.

The cows had had gone straight through and all the posts were up-ended and the wire was all over the place. It was so damn cold I could hardly hold the wire tacks to get them in properly.

I'd had to get Mole Boy over too. I couldn't do the post bashing or get any tension in the wire with my shoulder still being bad and that pissed me off. Pa was off in town getting more crap he needed for his chickens and something about his hedgehogs too.

The fencing took all morning. Mole Boy was good to work with. He never said much which was what I liked. He asked after Tom and I said he was fine and that was that. He said there was work out towards Bury and he'd signed me up for it, I just had to phone and say I'd be there. He also told me that this guy we knew,

Gordon, from near the Sandlings was killed in Iraq and there was going to be a proper army funeral at the cathedral on the marshes with a flag on the coffin and everything, if I wanted to come.

'It's the church where your Ma's buried.'

'Yeah I know.'

'Gordon was got by s-s-snipers.'

'Sorry man.'

I didn't give a shit about Gordon but said I was sorry because Mole Boy looked all worried about it. So after that we just talked about what we were doing.

'Pass the basher', 'Is it straight?', 'We're gonna need some more tacks on the split one', and a few times, 'fucking cows'. Everyone always said Mole was a bit slow and had something wrong with him. I didn't think so. He just kept himself to himself and just because you don't say something doesn't mean you don't have your opinions and ideas about stuff. You just keep them in your head and not share them.

I always remembered that Ma had told me to look after Mole when we were little and Mole had to go to school for the first time. He was two years below us. She said he wouldn't fight his corner if it came to it and it was up to me and Tom to look out for him. I guess we still did, mostly. I know I sometimes picked on him because it was an easy laugh. I could only get away with it if Tom wasn't there. He was mad-loyal to Mole. Once Tom beat the crap out of some moron from the airbase who was teasing Mole Boy for being so small and for being called Mole Boy. The bloke went home bleeding out his ear and had his face all smashed up. So if I was going to score points off Mole, it had to be on my own.

I was thinking about telling Mole Boy about Beth, but what was I going to say really?

'Oh, so I met this pretty girl.'

And then Mole Boy would whip up straight and smile so you could see where his tooth got knocked out on the side and say something like:

'Is she p-p-pretty?'

'That's what I said mate, met a pretty girl.'

'Where'd you m-m-meet her?'

'Admiral.'

'Wow.'

'Yeah. Asked her out. Seeing her Saturday.'

And then he'd just grin and be all pleased for me, like genuinely pleased and then I'd feel like a shit for making it sound like it was my doing and that it was anything more than a walk. Still, a walk was nice enough for me.

So I never said anything. Even though I felt it was important information that needed sharing but also because I kind of wanted to have it all to myself and not have it all out there where everything was wrong and rotten and hurting.

Chapter 10

Landyn

Silence in the kitchen. The women folk not moving except for the child, just gulping back her fear and her eyes telling me that what I had done was like cursing in God's own house. And there would be vengeance. Yes, there would be vengeance. I couldn't even say where Cessie and Vale were then, so transfixed was I by the girl in front of me.

She just kept on and on, nothing to stop it, as if she were retching too, so that her whole body was near whipping from the waist up. There was such violence in it, such pain, and I had conjured it all.

Vale was out working. I decided it was a good time to see young Thomas. He sounded a little better from what the desk said when I called. Also, I was hoping to get one of those little pipettes off one of the nurses for my chicken. Small syringe would do it too. Handy too for any baby hedgehogs I came across.

When I got to hospital, I near had a heart attack to see his empty bed, knowing he'd been a little better, apart from the obvious that is. They'd moved him.

'Thought you'd gone and died on me Thomas.'

'Greetings Pa Midwinter. Ha, no.'

His face was alive to see me and that made me glad too. Still pale though and thin I thought, for such a big fellow.

'Didn't find you where I used.'

'Yeah. Seems I'm okay to come here. Not plugged in to so many old monster machines. Just these ones now. Still, a goodly fleet of them.'

'That's good then. Seems nicer here I'd say. You seem chipper. Bit of a view anyway.'

'Cars only. Cars and snow.'

'Better than that wall.'

'Yeah.'

'Got another here with you it seems.'

'Yeah. He's been taken off to do some tests and stuff. Exercises to fortify his constitution. He'll be leaving though.'

'What's his story then, do you know?'

'Iraq.'

'Ah. Always thought they went to the army's own place. Brought you some chocolate bars and smokes.'

'Yeah, no space for him in the hallowed heroes' halls. Thanks for those. Thanks kindly Pa Landyn.'

'How are you son? Much pain? They still helping you with that?'

'I guess.'

'Good.'

'It's bad at night.'

'Pain?'

'That too. Everything really.'

'Right. Getting in your head a bit is it?'

'A touch.'

'Ah. Night monsters.'

'Could say.'

'Everything gets bad at night Thomas. Aches, pains, the lot and not just the type you feel in your bones. It's all the mossy stuff, the peat, stuff you fear most. It all gets bigger, much bigger in the night with no distractions and noise and company. Is that what you've got?'

'Surely do.'

'You got to fight it.'

'Okay'

'No lad, I mean that. You got to fight it or it gets in you. It's the fear that kills a man not the other stuff.'

He looked like he knew it. Young chap like that knowing all that before he needed. Looked like he had it in him already. All dark rollers of the ocean start to rise on up through the base of you, and when the tide goes out you can feel your courage go with it. Leaves you nothing you can use. Just the eels.

'Can you fight Thomas?'

The boy was mute.

'You have to lad. You have to fight it. And you know a good fight don't you? I've seen you get in a right old collie-shangle, take down three stout lads and a sailor just on the way out the door.'

'Ha, yeah. That's just wheeling though. Hops talking too.'

'It's the same. You scrap with it and swing at it and call it every name under the sun until it runs away like a robin'd seen a cat. You can't let it in you hear me? Listen to an old man, Thomas, I know this. I've had some times too, as you well know, and there's no letting it in or it'll take the goddamned life from you.'

'Okay.'

'I've not told people this lad, but after Vale's mother passed and we were still out there, there were times when I thought I should just give up on it all. Do you know what I'm saying? The days were so long, I was reeling with the misery of it all and every morning the wound was ploughed again. But I had your young friend didn't I? Whatever I was feeling, the lad was needing me.

'You do what you have to. You have to keep fighting and if it's the middle of the dark old night, you turn the light on, read your newspaper, I forgot to bring you a newspaper, sing a song, whatever it takes to keep the darkness out your head and fill it with something else, anything. You have to fight it lad.'

'I do sing a fine ditty.'

'Well, not a fine one, but you do offer a very loud one, and that'll do.'

The boy smiled.

Then he looked downcast. All thoughtful in a way few saw him.

'I didn't go to Iraq and fight a good fight.'

'What's that?'

'Other guys like me have been to the war, all the ones on the rehab gym. I just got rightly pissed. I've got nothing to tell for it that doesn't just make me sound like a fucking loser. That guy that's in the other bed was looking for land mines and got all blown to bits and for all that he's still all full of king and country and just doing what he had to do to serve and all that stuff. And I'm just a guy that sunk a few pints of hops and nicked a sail boat.'

'Where'd you get that? Someone say something to you?'

'Not really, but they thinking it. They get all beady.'

'Son, they say that to you, you give them two choice words. And they're not happy birthday, you hear?'

The boy smiled so big.

'I never heard you curse before Pa Midwinter.'

'Not a wicked word has left my lips young lad and if it did, I learned it all from you. Son, people will talk. God knows when we came back here with our sad little suitcases and no Cessie, and I do know that was hard for you too lad, I do, and I might not have seen that then, we came back and people talked all low and strange. See the fellows down the pub and they'd all look shifty. I know they didn't know what to say, didn't know how to be with us, knowing all the mess and what had happened. But it made it worse.

'People don't know how to talk to a man who's grieving and broken. They got no words for it and the words they've got don't sound right. I was so finished, truly finished and then I'd find myself being the one who was making all the other folks feel better and comfortable, helping them be easy with me. 'In the end I didn't want to go out and about any more. Always felt looked at or ignored, so I stayed home and got myself my little Pup and chatted to her instead. Still do.'

'Sounds like a fine plan.'

'A plan for an old man. Not for a fellow young as you. You have to keep going. I would say, the old Dominos, God bless them, never a changed word from them, still as rude and rough and full of grog as they'd always been. They don't stand on ceremony for kings or earls or grieving husbands, and they saved me a few times. I'll always be grateful to them of that. Came round all the time. They'd bring cider and brandy and God knows what else, and old Roy would sit there weeping, and I mean weeping, into his jar at our kitchen table saying how he missed our Cessie and her pies. Gold fellows, gold.'

'Do you think Vale'll be coming?'

'Sure he will. Think he's out fixing a fence with Mole today. Cows took the whole thing down. Whole section. We'll have horses on the motorway if they keep that up.'

'He not want to be my brother now?'

'What? No. No. Where'd you get that from now?'

'I don't know. He hasn't come calling. Thought maybe he thinks I won't be much fun anymore or something. Perhaps he thinks our glory days are over. But I'm getting a chair. Could you tell him that? I'm getting a chair and I'll be up soon and going all over. My backs all gone as you know but with the chair I can get about a bit and I've got the sticks for places where the wheels won't go.'

'That's some good news. They're good these days the chairs aren't they? I'm sure you'll find they're good. Knew a bloke up the coast who got one, what's his name now? Ah, Wilson, Wilson's the name, got oiled up and got cut by the harvester. Terrible accident it was.'

'Yeah, that was no accident, he was being a right royal moron of the very first order. We were there, working that harvest, me and Vale and some others. Wilson was hammered and solid, solid gone and he was galloping around playing chicken with the big slicers round the back. He'd been sent home earlier but came back to cause shit, shouting about needing the pennies. The more people tried to stop him the worse he got and the guy driving, he couldn't hear dog-digitty-shit going on behind him. Damn fuckin' idiot, right? Excuse my French Pa Midwinter, but he was, well, anyway. Well. Yeah. Hope he's okay these days.'

Thomas had forgotten what he'd become. Forgotten he was the arse who drank too much and got cut up.

'Oh he's more than okay. More than okay. I saw his Pa at the Ashe auctions few weeks back. Said he's got a job cutting window frames or picture frames. Or something like that. That was a fine day at the Ashe, clear and warm, got myself a nice old brewing jar that day, forgot about that, haven't used it yet. I'll be sure I make you some good grog once the sloes are fat and ready.'

'Oh. Thanks. I'll need that. Well that's good then. Picture frames?'

'Something like that.'

'Picture frames. Righteo.'

'Vale will come to you. I know it sounds like nothing what with your legs being how they are, but he's going through it a bit you know.'

'Right.'

'He's angry with me you see, angry about his Ma not being around I think and, some other stuff to do with that. He blames me. I did know that, I did, but didn't know how much you see.'

'He never says anything 'bout her, only sometimes.'

'Never says much about anything does he, our Vale?'

'Ha, no.'

'But he blames me for her passing and I can't help him with that can I?'

'No Sir, don't suppose you can.'

'If he hasn't been here, I dare say it's because he blames himself for how you got hurt.'

'That can't be right?'

'Well, I can't speak for the boy, but he's all over the place since you both came out the water. I just don't know what to say to him. I do try, I do, only he turns away from me and next thing I hear the door and he's off walking somewhere and there I am left in an empty house, just me and my Pup. I just don't know how to talk to him Thomas. You'll need to give me some tips. I'm sitting here having a right old chin-wag with you. Couldn't do it with him though. Not a jot.'

'Yeah, but he's not a talker so you can't feel bad over that. First sign of trouble or serious talk and he gets his scopes on the exit. Huh.'

'Hmm.'

'How's your Pup-dog then Pa Midwinter?'

'Oh? Oh many thanks for asking lad, she's getting old like her master.'

'Nah.'

'I hope you're right son. I'd die without the lady, I truly would.'

'Porkers okay?'

'Ah got old Dobbler coming round next week to help get a few older growers off to slaughter. Hoping he's still got the arm for getting all the hurdles in quick enough.'

'Yeah, likes to ponder a while does Mister Dobbler. Does everything way slow.'

'Bit of a duzzy dawdler it's true. Still he just has to hold the hurdles and stake them and I'll be doing with the pigs.'

'He won't like that. He'll want to be doing the pigs. He thinks he can hear them talk. He'll be having a little Dobb-chat with them.'

'That's true, that's true. Maybe he can hear them.'

The boy was silent. I could feel him working up something in his head, keeping me close 'til he could get it out in words.

'Looks like the weather's all set in huh?'

'Oh lad, you don't know half of it. So cold it can scorch you right though. No letting up.'

'Good thing I'm warm in here then right?'

'Snug as a bug lad. I'll come back tomorrow no matter the weather. You want anything in particular?'

'Pa Landyn I'm sorry about you feeling so bad about stuff.'

'That's okay lad. The important thing is to get through it.'

'Guess.'

'I managed didn't I? You will too. You're a good lad Thomas, big heart and you've saved me a few times too.'

Tom looked up.

'Never forget you at Cecelia's funeral. You remember it?'

'Not really. Remember my own Pa was crying like there was no tomorrow and that was kind of weird. Missing the bottle I guess.'

'Well, apart from that, all you need to know is you saved me that day, you and Mister Dobbler. You two are the best friends a fellow like me could have. So, whatever you need, I'm your old pal no matter the battle.'

Tom looked all shy-like, taken aback maybe.

'Okay.'

I left Tom and could have gone home but I couldn't face Vale for a while. I knew that wasn't right. I'd spent a good hour chatting away to our Thomas and making sure he knew I was for him when he needed me. There was my own lad and I didn't even know how to share the same room with him. He raised a kind of edge in me, close to anger. Now I'd seen Tom and knowing I'd walk into my kitchen and see Vale there scowling like an hungry owl who's dropped his mouse, I know I'd be wanting to tell him off and tell him what for, for not taking the time or raise enough bottle to go and visit. But I couldn't.

I tried to remember if I'd ever felt that towards my own Pa. But I just never did. He was an easy man though, easier than I could ever be, soft in himself and even softer in the world. I knew what was expected of me though, he and my own Ma made sure of that. Sure I'd get a sulk with him when I had to help with the animals in the evening and housework when I wanted to be out playing or mucking about with Dobb along the river but it was a moment, a breath, and then it was gone.

I felt a furnace in Vale and I feared for what it would do to him. Maybe not now, but over time. There are those fellows you see, angry right down in their bones from some injustice they feel. I felt that in Chisongo from the moment I met him. He had that rage, a regret maybe, something that had grown to consume a man. Sometimes it is no more than a moment when it might have gone another way but didn't and that grows to a powerlessness for not having the gumption to turn it all around. I feared all that for Vale. I feared that his walking away from his friend and turning cold on me would mean he'd miss it, the moment you get for a second pop at it. A chance to be content, to be able to sit quiet with yourself. Call it what you will, thing is, if you're not looking for it, you might miss it. It never looks like what you expect.

For all the chat I'd given young Tom, all the way to the pub where I knew there'd be a fire and a pint for me, I carried it around me like those old harnessed ploughs, taking every last muscle and gritted tooth to get the blades through the clay. God knows that's how it felt walking up the hill to the Admiral, the wet and the ice still banked along the sides. The weight of me always felt double in the wet. God awful time of the year and it would be months yet before any shards of green took in a great gasp of life.

Heavens, I was happy to smell the hops when I swung the hinges on that door. All the Dominos and some others were planning their party in the pub, even though it was weeks off yet. They like a party those fellows and they had dragged in some of the older ones too, not including myself. I had the excuse of Vale and our troubles to let me off the hook. Not so easy in past years when I had to claim a sickly pig back home to get out of it. I wouldn't want to leave my Pup all on her own now for too long either.

Got a half pint from the nice girl that had started working there. She was a niece of one of the lads I think. Pretty thing, lovely red hair that reminded me a touch of Cessie when we first met. She always let Pup come in and rest next to the fire.

My chat with Thomas was weighing, I'd told him to fight but in truth it was sometimes just the gods above that allowed me to stay upright.

There was a night in Kabwe I won't forget, and think on it when I become complacent about life, kept it like a hag-stone to ward off the dark.

I had put Vale to bed, as I did every night, and it was the small things that made me feel so incompetent, so unqualified to be a parent. Stupid things, like the little buttons on his pyjama shirt, I just couldn't do them up for him, fat fingers and small buttons and you can mess it all up so he was never done up straight. Eventually, the housekeeper Maria pointed out that he could get the thing on and off just by pulling it over his head. I had struggled away every night. When she told me I felt such a fool.

I would catch myself watching the lad, a strange kind of vigilance I'd never known before. Was he thinner, fatter, tireder, resting enough, on and on and no one to ask when I felt I was getting it all wrong. I had to be his everything now his Ma was gone, at a time when I could just about hold my own self together most days. That's just what you do though and there's nothing left in all the damn aching of it all. Some days though I admit I was so overwhelmed by the tide of it, that I couldn't be rightly sure if it was out of love or habit. It was these small failings that did me in. Daily failures, domestic and terrible.

That night after another battle trying to get the lad to bed in a way that was organised and after a long old day with fences and surveyors and God knows, and a few hours trying to work out if we could get home to England and should we be going, again, moving. The thought of moving and packing up and again, again, again trying to make it work from the start and with another failure, the worst sort, the final failure.

The night was hot, sticky and endless, as it often was. Vale was asleep and I lay my body down on the big old bed, thick mahogany headboard. The rooms were so big in that house, and there were so many of them, echoing without Cessie's voice to fill them. The floors were always so cool though, like a balm seeping through the pads of your feet. Funny how when you feel so broken, the vaguest glimpse of kindness gets bottled to use again as ointment.

That night, years of weariness, years of failure and sorrow and the feeling that no matter how it panned out and no matter the help we got, it was too much to carry and too far. I couldn't do it. There was nothing left in me and nothing more I could do for the lad. He'd be better off without me somehow. I had a panic that I would do anything, anything to escape the grief.

I lay there trying to breathe more slowly, to get the panic to sit down.

Instead, one after the other, those jagged sweeps of pain rolled through me. No breath was coming, just gulps and retches.

I got rolled up deep in Cessie's quilt, still fresh with colour. Some of the squares showed their stitches where their neat little wounds had been sewn back together to make it such a lovely thing.

The dark had voices. It was early still. Dogs, hyenas, the whole night was alive with teeth, sharp and hungry.

I was finished, tired and terrified. Then like a funny little angel, Vale appeared around the door, his bare feet on the grass mats, pyjama buttons done up skew.

'Pa?'

I couldn't speak for choking. I knew my face was wet and eyes red, for all the things I'd told him about being brave I was done for. He looked at me in his serious little way. Always so serious. Then, the fellow walked in and climbed up on his Ma's side of the bed, walking over to me on his knees and just settled in. He pulled my tired old arm out of the covers and over him, his back to me, perhaps out of respect, so as not to expose any more of my tears.

'I'm feeling sad too, Pa.'

There we lay until sleep came, lamp on and the sound of all the moths and beetles tapping their heads against the mosquito mesh that was fixed across all the windows, all getting bruised and broken, just trying to get to the light.

When a tree full of starlings woke us to a new day, I knew that surviving was the only choice open to me.

The pub was producing a right old din. I was never one for a gang of fellows together. Vale's got that from me. I was just wanting a quiet drink next the fire.

'Colin'll be there.'

'Oh yes, Colin'll be there.'

'That he will.'

'He will.'

'He'll be there. And some others. Nigel too.'

'Oh yes, Nigel too.'

'He'll be there.'

'Be plenty of 'em.'

'Plenty. And us.'

'Oh yes, we'll be there , all of us'll be there.'

'Have us a bit of grog.'

'Oh more than a bit.'

Big old guffaws and then on and on they went. God almighty. Sometimes a man just wants bit of quiet to get his head right when he's in a muddle. I wanted to tell them to shut it all and give a man his rest.

'Fox out along the lane earlier.' Said Bill Stanton.

'Oh? You pop it?'

'No. You can't on the road can you? Law won't let you.'

'No, they won't let you.'

'Limping too.'

'Ah'

'Be gone-for soon enough.'

'That's good then.'

'It is good.'

'Vermin.'

'Filthy things.'

'Filthy.'

The hair on my forearms prick with chill.

'Which lane's that then?' I said from round the beam.

'What's that? Oh, hello Land.'

'Afternoon fellows. Lane, which one, where you say you saw the old fox?'

'Ah, down your way Land.'

'You sure?'

'Rosary Lane I think.'

'Yes, that's ours.' I nodded.

'Best mind your chooks. Got some new ones haven't you?'

'I'll mind them.'

'Though she was limping so you might be all right.'

'Ah good then.'

'Don't want to lose any of your layers.'

'No.'

Lot of old fools with their rubbish about foxes getting at chickens. Not once, not once in all my time has a fox got into my chickens. Keep the chickens behind a good proper fence and the fox on the other side. That's the secret right there. If the foxes were getting into their chickens, it was all on them. More dogs eating chickens than foxes I'd say. There was a fat old gun dog up the road, Playford Manor, where Mole was going to work. That dog had one every other day I dare say. Went by the name of Belle. She was a right bugger for it. Nice face though, noble snout.

I sat a while in the pub thinking about my vixen and her limping and wondering what could be done. I knew it had to be her. The lane was her spot. She had a nice clear view across the lower fields for hunting. I'd even seen her scratching in the hedges there for grubs. If the girl was hurt, I could help that, not sure how of course, maybe leave some food out for a while, until she healed up. She'd be okay as long as she could keep fed with all the cold about. If she was bad I'd get her in a cage-trap, tempt her in with a bit of meat and then help her heal up. I was already planning out the options.

Even as I was thinking it I could hear my Cecelia saying, 'No fool like an old fool'. But there I was, an old fool getting himself in a lather about a fox. A fox and a chicken. There's a fable in that. Still, I know what I know and I don't need others to tell me I'm wrong.

If there's a night when I'm lucky enough to get a glimpse of Cessie in my dreams, I can tell you as sure as day follows night, I'll see my fox before the next day is out. Even half a look of my vixen and I'll know it's her like I know my own heart. I know too without ever asking that it is my fox that has kept blood in my boy's veins.

Sometimes as I dream I catch just a glimpse of Cecelia reading or washing her hair, through the glass as I walk past a window. I want to go in and see her and help her with the water. But I know I'm dreaming and she's always on the other side of the glass. I'll wake and even if I don't quite remember the dreaming I know that later, I'll see my fox, step, step, stepping across the fields and the whole lovely sleep will come back to me right there, painful and hot, like a wasp sting, so as I can near hear the water running and hear her humming through the ache of it all.

Sometimes a blessing is just a breath shy of a curse.

Chapter 11

Vale

I went up to Pa's room to find the keys for the barn. He was always taking things from where they were meant to be and then forgetting where he left them.

He was off at the vet, getting Pup's pills for the month. Then he was taking stuff to Tom. Everything about it pissed me off.

Pa's room smelled like old leather and mothballs. Lately it smelled a bit like Pup too. I stood there at the door. Going up felt wrong. I knew I was the only one in the house but it still didn't feel right. I never really went in there on my own, not unless he sent me up to get something for him. Things were never where he said they were. I'd be shouting that I couldn't find it and he'd be bellowing up the stairs that it was in the dresser or next to his bed. He'd just lean up the bannister looking annoyed and arguing black for white I was wrong.

Just from the door I could see the keys and his reading glasses on the little chest at the window. He'd probably need the specs while he was out. His bed was so neat. The quilt was still the one Ma sewed. I think it used to be all kinds of blue and white but

151

now it was almost white with patches of grey. It went all the way to Kabwe and back with us. Pa always made his bed like he was in the army. Sheets and blankets pulled tight across. I tried to get mine like that, but I never could.

Over the bed hung a funny little wooden angel that someone gave Ma, as a present I think. It was a smaller version of the ones on the roof of the church at Blythburgh. It hung from a little string and just sort of floated there against the pale blue wall.

I stepped through the door. The floor board squeaked. It sounded much louder than it used to. I went over to the side table to get the keys. Next to the alarm clock was a picture frame and in it Ma and Pa being silly. Ma is laughing and Pa is kissing her cheek. He is being very dramatic so it must have been a joke for whoever is taking the photograph. His eyes are closed and he is leaning in. He is wearing a jacket and tie and Ma is wearing a nice dress. The picture was a bit faded but the dress was black with bright flowers on it. I think Ma once told me they were at a wedding. I don't think I was even born when the picture was taken. They look so happy.

I didn't really have any pictures of Ma. None of my own. But I knew there were some, a box of them. I remembered Pa kept it in his wardrobe.

The room was on a tilt so as I turned the key, the doors just flopped open. The backs of the doors were laden with hooks for belts and ties and things so they had some swing to them. The coats and jackets were all wedged in. Pa never seemed to get rid of anything and then he would come out with one of his jackets to go to town no matter how old or strange it was. When we were sitting in the caravan I could smell the mothballs coming off the one he had on. Made me feel sick. There was a shelf above the hanging rail. Hats and boxes all in rows. I knew the one I wanted. It was wood but had a leather covering. Or at least it did once. It used to be my Grandpa's. It was big enough. The first time I ever saw it I knew it was the kind of box that had important stuff in it.

I took it down. It was heavier than I expected. I had never opened it on my own before. Before that I had seen Pa's papers and stuff like that in there and after Ma died, he put her jewellery in there. She only had her rings and a gold cross her own Ma gave her when she was confirmed and a silver brooch of an oak leaf with acorns that Pa said he bought her on a holiday in Wales. She wasn't one for stuff like that though.

I set the box on the bed and sat down. I felt jumpy, like I didn't know my own skin sitting there. I didn't know what I was doing or why. Only I wanted see Ma, remember things that seemed to be getting further away from me all the time.

I lifted off the lid of the box.

I saw what I wanted right away. Under the green pouch I knew had Ma's things inside and Grandpa's watch and some other bits like cufflinks Pa never wore, was a big envelope, all frayed and a bit torn. I moved the pouch aside. The envelope felt dusty. I pulled off the rubber band and opened it. On top was a picture of Ma and below it many more of everything else.

The picture on top was taken on the beach, the day she bought her red swimming costume. She is wearing sunglasses. She looks quite serious so she looks like someone you think you know but can't remember their name. It was during the summer holidays. Tom was with us. Ma had made a picnic for the beach. She wasn't cheerful like she usually was, making us join her in singing songs as we drove, but that day it was Pa keeping us going and Ma just looked out the window a lot.

When we got to the beach she had forgotten her swimming costume and she cried which was also strange, so we went into a women's clothing shop to buy one. She kept saying she didn't need one, it didn't matter and it was probably too cold to swim but Pa insisted on getting her one saying she deserved it. I heard her say it was a waste of money they didn't have. I don't know what happened after that because Tom was being stupid about the ladies' underwear so we got sent outside. I remember being shocked by Ma's red costume. I don't know why. Maybe I thought she would get a yellow one or a blue one. Tom told her she looked like some old time actress his Ma always wanted to be. She looked pleased. I wished I knew actresses' names so that I could tell her she looked like them too.

I put the picture on the quilt. There were a few of Ma and Pa at parties, a bit like the one next to the bed. Then there were some I had never seen, and don't even remember being in them, taken in Kabwe. Ma and me and Pa in front of our house. My throat caught. The hair on my arms stood up. Ma was thinner than I remembered. Maybe she had lost weight moving. I touched the photograph with my fingers, touched her face. I know that was stupid but she seemed so real, looking straight out at me. She is smiling, just about. I don't remember being in the picture or even who took it.

I think we had only just got there because there were no roses outside the house and there were no chairs on the verandah. We only got those after a few weeks when the neighbour gave us the ones he had in his garage. Ma painted them turquoise.

The next picture and the next were all of the house, one that looked like a picture of a field until you looked carefully and then you could see there were monkeys on the fence posts. I loved all the animals there.

I kept looking deep into the pictures, trying to see something, something I missed but didn't have a name for it.

There was one of the back of the house, me and Chipo sitting with Maria on the kitchen steps. She has an arm around each one of us and we are leaning in to her. We are all laughing. And then to the side of the house, behind where I could just about see the water tanks, leaning against the big tree, is a long figure, the outline of a man, hunched over at his shoulders and smoking. And in the same moment I thought it was me, as I am now, but I also knew that it was Chisongo. And suddenly a rage that came out of nowhere started to blister through me, right through my skin, like all along there was a monster in me just sitting there, waiting and waiting for the crack in the silence of our pathetic little lives on the farm and I felt I could crush the life out of anyone but especially Chisongo for everything that he did to Ma. And it felt as if I was remembering it all for the first time. And I could hear him saying 'Where is the old man? It is him I want.' And I heard Ma saying 'He's coming back now, he's coming, you better go so he doesn't find you here.' And the other ones were saying 'Where's the cash?' and 'Where's the gun?' and Ma saying she didn't know and they started to push her and hold her hair so she cried out. I had heard Ma crying and saying 'Chisongo what have I done to you? Leave now, leave, for Sara.' And part of me remembers that maybe, maybe Chisongo had said 'Leave her. Just take the money. It is the old man we want.' But the others had fought with him. And when the first blow had come it was not Chisongo, it was the other shorter one and Chisongo had tried to stop him. And suddenly too I could smell what I hadn't identified at the time which was booze. The whole place had smelled of it and I knew for the first time how loaded Chisongo and his crew had been. 'Where's the old man? Where is he?' They said it over and over and I knew then that what Tom had said was right, I knew it right through me, that it was Pa they had wanted all along. And he could not deny it.

When we first went to Kabwe I knew things weren't good at home because Ma explained that the reason we needed to go was because there was no money in the bank. It was a time when Pa was always angry and upset and Ma would sometimes be crying in the kitchen. When I'd come round the corner to ask what was wrong she would make up some excuse about it. I knew there was stuff going on that no one was telling me. I did know it had to do with the farm and not enough money but until they told me we had to leave England I never really got it, that Pa would be in big trouble with the banks if there was another bad yield.

One night I was sitting on the step between the long corridor and the boot room. I think I wanted some milk but I didn't want to go into the kitchen where Ma and Pa were at the table with all the ledgers out and Ma had made a pot of tea which usually meant they were going to be quite a while. I spied on them through the crack that ran the length of the door back then and because they looked so serious, I decided to sit it out. They were in there talking with the door closed and I wasn't really listening, just enough to know when it would be safe to go in.

Then the smelly black labrador we had then, Badger, pushed through the kitchen door and it swung open enough for me to hear everything. Mostly they were using words that made no sense: money talk. And then they mentioned leaving and what about Tom and then Ma cried and said something about the orchard. Ma loved her fruit trees. She liked to lie under them and read her books. I would lie there too and she would read to me. And Pa then said we had to leave to keep the farm safe for me.

And now I was looking at Ma and Chisongo and remembering everything about that fucking hot, horrible place and thinking all of that was so I could have a farm I didn't even want.

We didn't have to go. Pa made up the bullshit about birth-rights and all the rubbish he always went on about. The truth is he didn't want to lose the farm for himself. His blessed woods and fields and all his animals and the place he liked to hang hag-stones from the branches that reached out over the river. It was all for what he thought was his own birthright because his Pa was the first to own land of his own instead of renting or being allowed to stay because he worked for some fancy bloody landowner.

He always said we had to, but actually, he wanted to go and convinced Ma it was a good idea. We could have sold the farm and rented a cottage off someone, even that crap-hole that the Dominos had owned for a hundred years. We wouldn't have cared and Ma could make any house nice.

I heard Pa's truck come along the gravel.

I folded all the pictures and papers back into the box and made sure to put Ma's pouch of things safe on top. I set it back in the cupboard, managed to twist my shoulder while I did it which annoyed me and even while I was doing this I could feel my chest starting to cramp up on itself. By the time I started down the stairs two at a time I was fuckin' raging and a kind of sickness was rising in my belly. I headed out into the yard leaving the kitchen door open and all the heat blazing out and started yelling for him. I felt the skin on my face wince tight as the cold hit it. It was eye-watering.

'Pa? Pa?'

'I'm here. I'm in here.' He was puffing out steam as he breathed.

I found him in the workshop. The workshop floor was covered in wood shavings. It always smelled like dust and oil at the same time. His chicken was resting up in there because it was warmer. He was leaning forward to see the bird through the wire of the cage. The bird was still alive and Pa had moved her under a lamp to keep her from going into shock. Cleaned all the blood away too.

'I know what happened.'

'What's that son?' He straightened up. I could tell his head was miles away.

'You lied.'

'I don't follow.'

'We didn't have to leave. And Ma did get killed because of you.'

'Oh God in heaven, this again?'

'Yeah, this again. We never had to go, you just wanted us to go and when we got there you fucked it up so badly, Ma was killed. It was you they wanted, but you weren't there.'

'Dear God in heaven.' He was shaking.

'No. I won't let you get away with it anymore.'

'I do not get away with it. My wife is dead. Dead, so how do you even begin to imagine I have got away with anything?'

'And what about me?'

Suddenly his eyes were red and wet but he was primed. I was watching him like you watch a sickly bull when you have to get in his stall with him. He looked no different. His face was red and his eyes were brimming, rage and God knows what else and I swear I could see his heart beating through his shirt as he breathed all short and heavy.

'You get out of here now my boy. Because if you don't there will be no censure for what you will hear, do you understand me? Get out of here now.'

'No.'

Pa flinched when I said it.

'Vale?'

'What? You going to hit me again? You going to hit me? After all those years going on about Tom's Pa and what a fuckin' monster he is and turns out you're no different, are you? First time I push you that's all you've got to answer with?'

The air was heavy. It was dark in there but it felt as though someone had thrown a flare in there with us. Pa said nothing. I could hear his lungs as he breathed.

'See? You've got nothing to say. You lied to me about Ma. I remember it all now, everything that happened that night, Chisongo, his guys, what they said to Ma. I remember it all.

'And the only reason we were even there was because you looked like a fucking idiot. You've never known how to run a farm and you still don't. We didn't have to go. We didn't. But then once we got there you had to be even more stupid. Ma died. She got killed. Because of you.' I couldn't look at him anymore.

'I lied all right. But it was the both of us who lied to you and we did it to protect you.'

'Don't try.'

'I'm not finished. You think you're all grown up, well, then you can hear the truth. You can hear what goes about between people in the real world. While I was fighting to save the land, for you. I was out all hours and late and working extra jobs here and there and so was she. And both falling to pieces. She was going to take you away from me and go back to her own blood in Ireland. Break us all apart. That's how bad we were. But we went out there to save ourselves as much as to save the farm. There is no one in the world I loved as much as your Ma and I'd have done more and have gone even further to keep us together.'

'She got killed!' I was yelling and blind.

'Jesus, boy, I am so goddamned tired of trying to keep you from everything to save you and all you do is fight me. You fight me and you blame me. I can't do it. I can't carry this for you anymore if you will keep on fighting me on it. I will not be a criminal in my own home. I will not have you judge me when I have done nothing but fought to protect you and my marriage to your mother. I fall asleep every night wishing I had done different in the way you will one day do over your friend Thomas. Not now because all you think about is yourself. But you think about that, think about it. We all make choices. Mistakes. We can't always control what happens after.'

My mouth was dry. I wanted him to stop but he just kept on. I leaned on the work table.

'So don't presume you are the victim of some evil. Whatever you think, you are a child still, whatever has passed.' He was gasping for breath. 'We did everything we did, I did everything I did, to try and protect you and to keep us all together, for love. But if nothing else I would have hoped one thing from you. Thomas' life from now on in will be nothing short of a misery. You know that. So perhaps you could just try to acknowledge that a man cannot always be kept from life. Sometimes it just comes for you. And you have to muddle through the best you can. I made mistakes. It didn't work out. But now you have made mistakes too. And you will sit with that for the rest of your life. I am sorry for that, I am. I wish for the world you had your Ma here with you, I wish you didn't know what you know and hadn't seen what you saw. I wish our Thomas was well again, that you had never ever taken the cursed bloody boat out. But you did. That's that. So enough about you now Vale. Maybe look to someone else, your friend for a start. I can't make it right for your Ma but you sure as hell can make right with our Thomas.'

Pa's face was wet, the tears were just coming out from him like the blood from the lambs when you take a knife to their throats.

'Pa?'

'No. It's enough now and until you see to your mind and your heart and make amends to Thomas, I've nothing more to say to you. I'm done here.'

He pushed passed me and I just stood there looking at my feet half buried in sawdust hearing his boots on the gravel as he headed back for the house.

Chapter 12
Landyn

I had to get away from the child and her hiccuping and Sara with her staring eyes as she held the girl to try to make her stop and Maria telling Vale to finish his meal in the kitchen.

As I turned I saw Cessie. She just stood there looking at me, the fool, the bully. I've seen her face in that moment a thousand times over, looking back at me, with the light from the oil lamps dull and gold. I turned my back on her.

I put Dog in the truck and drove up to the far side of the property. It was a fair old drive but the night was cooling a bit with the stars finding their way through the dust. I used the headlights from the truck and an old kerosene lantern, worked on the broken fences, trying to mend them, until I was sweated through despite the night air.

I was beaten, like I'd had a bloody mauling. I knew Vale was gone, had nothing more to say to me after his outburst and that was how it was. I was done in from it all too. Comes a point when a man has nothing more to give his child. Just have to let him be and hope to hell something turns for the better some time. But he'd have to get there on his own that was for sure. This old mule wasn't leaving his stable. I sat a while with Pup on my lap next to the fire. Letting her warm up properly and giving her some good attention. Always a lung rattling sigh from the little thing when she settled in. The fire looked deep. It was a good one. I could feel my bones stretch out and settle back down into my flesh as the warm got in.

Still, I had the vixen on my mind, having not seen her awhile and thinking on her left me uneasy. I decided to sit a little longer because Pup didn't seem too happy. She couldn't settle and was watching me all the time. If I so much as went to the kitchen for a cup she'd be anxious until I came back. I didn't like it. The fur around her eyes had changed too, looked pinched and drawn. I could hardly bear to look at her for fear I might see something else in her face, but I did look, right into her, so she knew I was for her no matter what came.

Some papers had arrived in the post. Papers from the insurance to say they'd not be able to cover Vale for the mess he'd made of the boat. I didn't think they would. But it was worth a pop. I couldn't face all that, not after the night I'd already had. I wrote the number I'd be owing in a soft pencil in the margin of my pig feed log and threw the letter and all in the fire. It was enough. I'd give the boy money if he needed and if I had it, but my energy was gone.

'Got nothing left Pup.'

Even though I said it I knew it was only true for the moment. Because you can have your rages against the ones you love, with warnings and final consequences. It could never be the end for me and Vale. I didn't have a choice in it. Been like that how many times since Cessie passed, all beaten and tired and nothing left.

Even before we left Kabwe I knew it and getting us both back here in one piece took it all out of me in every way.

We had nowhere to live and our lives were in boxes on two continents. The tenants were still lodged in the farm, as they had rights too, I had no work and no way of knowing what to do and how to do it.

Dobb was as solid as ever and we lodged with him for near five months though there was hardly any room for us in his cottage. I took the little extra room he had, though now I think it has reverted to a general store room for all his model boats and his thimble collection. He made Vale a little nook under the stairs, tucked a mattress under there and even fixed a small light to the wall and a shelf over his head so he could read and keep a few things to himself and a bit of curtain on a wire across the entrance and he was snug as a bug. Late into the night the curtain would glow a triangle from the lamp and I'd just hear the pages turning as he read. Vale liked it well enough I think, everything considered. Dobbler outdid himself but it was another change for the boy and me, what with our home and solace just down the way and us locked out for the foreseeable.

All of it and the rest of that uncomfortable history was playing around and around as I settled old Pup in with her blanket, had myself a second sweet cup and started to get dressed up to head out again. It took long enough to get it all on. There was a keen wind ahead of the snow, proper rafty it was. As my old Pa would say, 'That wind's got weather in it.' I took some fresh meat from the fridge and wrapped it in some paper.

It was a fair old way to the woods and heavy going in the wet. The land was beautiful. Steaming with cold on every blade. Spiders' webs all crusted in frost and every twig and bit of brush the same.

Gate posts, ploughs, fallen down trees all topped with snow and the sky promised more to come. A great wedge of geese crossed the sky calling for home. The light would be all wheezed out soon enough, though it was still bright enough for me to find my way. I got the cold rasp on my throat as my breath quickened from the effort of the walk. I could feel all of the last days' worries had been sitting in my body and they weren't ready to leave. The freeze was coming through my boots and the old toes were creeping back as far as they could to escape it. Cold could get in there like mould in a hay bale. You'd hardly notice it at first and once you did it was too late by a yard. Nothing you could do to get it out. All steel up there in all that mist and cloud, I knew it.

When we were out there in Kabwe, there was just no way of reading the sky, not the way I could back in old England. Everything out there was a puzzle; the people, the weather, the road signs that pointed in the direction of a road that no longer existed, the birdsong that may have been in a different language, the tracks of the creatures who left their paw prints in the sand outside our windows while we slept. All manner of lovely little things that seemed to accept us into their piece of earth. Birds, insects and the bigger ones too, monkeys all about, little antelope and at night, the place was bristling with life and noise so as you never knew which way it was coming from. Felt like we were sitting in a big old echo bowl and all round the creatures were rasping and singing to celebrate the cooler air.

Still, when we first arrived I knew I was walking in different shoes, and they didn't quite fit either, the leather still hard and baked with sun. To go to a new place is to not even know which questions to ask let alone the answers to them. It didn't occur to me to ask if the land had water, I'd no reason to think it wouldn't. In the end and after some negotiations and a few sleepless nights there was water, plenty of it too, just a matter of knowing the man who turned the taps on and let the great pumps do their work sucking the stuff out the belly of the earth from some great under earth lake we never ever saw but knew gave us the very life in our bodies.

The redness in the earth unsettled me. It got in everywhere. No matter what you wore or where you went, at the end of the day, the stuff was there. For miles, flat as forever with nothing but corn or tobacco and a tree here and there and bits of scrub or a little huddle of rounded huts, made too from the same curry red mud. Even thinking about it I can taste the stuff settling in my mouth and my tongue so it near dries to my teeth.

And though I got to love the creatures and recognise a fair few of their tracks across the earth, I never got a proper nose for the weather. Not helpful when you're planting the land and I knew it exposed me for the impostor I was. The other settlers from across the border, Zimbabwe way, knew the climate. They were the self same clouds that just kept moving over from their old neck of the woods.

Out there, September, or if you were unlucky, October too, was called suicide month. No rain for months and then the winds would start up blowing great curtains or red dust from left to right and all around until you choked on the stuff. Everything moving and twitching all the time and tempers fraying. They claimed it brought madness with it and they weren't far wrong. Then, maybe October and a great fat drop would plop into the dirt. Then another and another and then a great torrent would let loose and all the rain we hadn't seen for months on end would turn up in one afternoon and all the creatures would turn their faces into the rain and children too, just to enjoy the great beautiful drenching.

The trees out there always felt nervous, I felt that from the day we arrived. Later realised they were always anticipating rain, bristling for it even, and after one of those lovely downpours you could just about feel the roots ease out as they relaxed under your feet. For a week or so and then they'd be back tilted on the edge of their seat, an eye on the sky and another on the furthest horizon.

It was something to see and yet for me, what with all the seasons back to front and the skies all upside down at night, I hardly knew my own name. Perhaps that was it, all our stars were upside down and we were crossed and fated to be that way too, like some great undoing of us all.

Kraus, our neighbour, was a big fellow, not a fan of the locals on account of his time across the border but a clever fellow too, knew it was best to keep his head down and just make the best of it all. He would point up at the big old heavens and say 'Better get the young ones in. Hail coming.'

'How'd you figure that then?'

'Green. You see it? Clouds have a green underbelly? We'll be calling the assessors in the morning, Mid.'

But, he'd be right, old Kraus, within the hour there would be a storm that could terrify a standing army. Hail stones like crab apples. Corn fields stripped bare, livestock killed, a man struck by lightning and within minutes, the dry dusty flatness of it all was sheeted in white for miles and miles. Then it would melt, just like that, and we would go back to the endless heat that felt like a goddamned madness until the next storm.

From our first meeting, Kraus decided that we were the Winter family and I was Mid.

'Midwinter is not a family name,' he said, 'It is a weather condition and a season.'

Cecelia always liked him, called him 'solid', though I'm less certain the compliment was returned. His wife was a dark Christian. Mother Kraus, full of fire and brimstone. Every hail storm an apocalypse, and any gathering of more than two or three insects was a coming plague. Vale never liked her on account of her demands for prayers with hands entwined. Our house keeper Maria was happy to share in the odd prayer with Mother Kraus but after Cessie passed I had to have a word with Kraus, ask him to keep his wife from our house, so upset was the lad with all the talk of hell.

I stood puffing in the cold on the end of my fox's woods, right where the bracken meets the trees in a straight line and where a fence used to be. The fence and the fronds were russet red under all the white, my breath all short and rattling against the chill. No comfort in a cold lung my Pa would always say. He had a fence put in there to keep the deer out the fields. Fat chance he had of making that work. The deer go where they will and after he passed away, I did nothing to hold the line. Creatures should be creatures and fences do nothing but harm them. If they feel they can't move and their escape routes are closed off then they panic, don't they? Could do themselves a world of injury.

I went in.

The rest of the messy old world disappeared behind me. Even in the chill, the air was ripe with fox dung. Not often the earth is so frosted but there was still shelter in there, darker spots where the snow hadn't penetrated, under the boughs and round the burrows where all the animals are rooting and digging for grub and the like. Never known how they can be bothered to keep at it some winters. You'd have to want it, life, desperate-like, whereas we folk just slump a little further towards dying. We don't really hunt the stuff down like my fox would, chasing on the tail of a rabbit, red-alive so she'd run clean through barbs and thorns to get to it. And the rabbit, fighting too, right to its last gasp after scrabbling and crying out.

I stepped under the dark branches. Goes church-quiet all of a sudden and you can hear your own prayers again. You think more about where your feet are going and how the earth under foot has some give, some spring.

These were good woods. I knew each branch like I knew my own heart. Under them, I could see where little paws parted the way; rabbits, badgers, hedgehogs, stoats, and my fox of course.

She'd lived here for a couple of years now. She had her pups in the spring, five of them. I found where she'd made her earth then. Snuck along when I knew she was off. She'd helped herself to an old rabbit burrow, dug it wide and deep and settled in to have her brood. Of course I never saw them when they were just nigglers, they would have looked like fat old moles, all sooty and round and no sign of the red and those ears flagging up yet. Not a few weeks later they were out in the clearing below the oaks; five copper pennies. All perfect. Gladdened my heart as if they were my own.

I made my way to where I knew she lay. I had a funny old feeling as I went. All along the deer had gnawed off the bark from the branches that lay on the ground, some of the roots were exposed too and lots of digging up for tubers and morsels. The animals were hungry. The rank air made me think at least my fox had been eating. She wasn't there though, just some tracks and some scratchings. I'd wait for her. I laid out the meat I had brought her. Just as I leaned over to let it fall, I heard the snap of a twig on the forest floor. I straightened up.

'Hello?'

The air didn't breath. It was too quiet by far.

'Hello? Anyone there?'

I felt stupid for letting the dark get to me. I left the meat near enough her earth so she'd find it in the cold. I pulled my old body up the bank using the roots, nearly took a tumble too. Your lower end just has a weight to it when you're old the way I am, doesn't shift or bend like it should. The roots were all slippery from weeks of wet and cold, moss all over them. Never mind, got up there so as I could hide and get a nice look down on where I knew she'd be coming.

I settled in under one of the big old branches of the oak, my back up against the trunk. It made a happy seat, cold for sure, but as snug as I could be given the coming night. I'd wait for her, my little red.

I could feel the roots begin to creep a little closer. There, again, I heard a twig and maybe a foot or paw to follow it. My breath was too loud suddenly, sounded like those great burry rollers you get coming off the ocean in a storm, crashing their way through the shingle. I wished I were quieter. My hands were all sweated up in my gloves and my heart was racing itself to an early grave.

Then it stopped.

Nothing more, not a padding paw or twig to snap. All of it gone, just my mind playing silly buggers with me. I listened again and just heard my own heart thumping up my neck into my ears. Nothing to see.

I was exhausted. The madness of being so afraid for nothing.

Your fears get worse as you get older it seems, more superstitious. Though perhaps in my case it had more to do with our trouble.

By the time Vale and I got ourselves home and his mother too and got her buried up on the Marshes I was afraid of my own mind most of all. Couldn't sit with myself for longer than a minute or so before the owls would start flapping about in my skull. I thought they'd settle after we had her buried and they did quiet down a bit but the feathers still turned.

Somehow though, the funeral was a good thing, though I'd not have had it were it just me. It was a miserable old day, always is up there. Vale was wearing a jacket, I suppose I wore one too.

It was a large funeral, which surprised me. I had never felt so alone in my life, never felt so friendless and yet on the day it was as if there was just no end to the people who arrived. I knew Dobbler was wedged in the middle somewhere. Lots of the women came, all Cessie's ladies from about the place, they'd made a nice tea for after, the Moles were there and the Dominos, even the manager from the bank, and all sorts who you'd think wouldn't give a jot. People who'd not yet welcomed us back to the village all turned up.

I had no time for the vicar, terrible man, bad to his animals, but he was at least organised and knew the procedure which is about as much as you can expect. I did think Vale might need the whole thing to say goodbye to his Ma, on land his toes remembered, and have a place to come to remember his mother, call in perhaps should he wish to chat.

Blythburgh church is a large place, cool, light stone, hobbled old floor, fonts with dragons and painted wooden angels all along roof. A fair dose of the old Pagan in there for all the rot the vicar spouted.

The lad and I sat in the front. I had some words on a piece of paper, words that needed saying and was feeling all kinds of worry about that. Vale next to me, little knees poking out the top of his long socks, sitting as close as he could and his arm knitted through mine so we might as well have been one. The miserable organ was playing, enough to drain what hope I had left right out of me and flush it straight out those godawful pipes. I was as broken as I could be. The air was black as leprosy and all around just the desolate stone that reached from floor to ceiling. Then, off to my left the empty pew rocked and rumbled and in shuffled Dobbler, towards us. Sat himself down next to me, close. Sweet Jesus, it felt like God's own apostle had just arrived.

'Ho old friend. Can't have you up here on your own. That won't do, not today.'

Vale peaked round me and gave Dobb a good smile.

'Hullo lad, brought you a bit of sugar. You better have some too Land.' Dobb rustled about in his pockets and brought out some barley sweets. 'You'll be needing those, fellows.'

I looked over at Dobb, all eyebrows. He had a smart jacket on and there on his lapel, he had pinned a posy of white field daisies.

They took me over.

I could feel the whole place close about me and come to one screaming root in my chest where I could feel the noise start to rise. It came out first as a gulp and then as a wail and I couldn't stop it for anything. Couldn't stop any of it.

I suppose the service began. I couldn't hear it and didn't want to, just had Vale's arm in mine and knew Dobb was there and that was enough to give me a shield on either side until it was all over.

I knew nothing of it all until Dobb poked me in my side.

'They'll be wanting your words now Land.'

I couldn't speak, I looked to Dobb.

'Can you do it? You don't have to.'

'I can't.'

'You sure?'

'I can't.'

'Shall I do that, friend?'

I heard the vicar say something to me.

'I'll do that then. Give us your paper there.' Said Dobb. He leaned across me to Vale. 'Lad, will you allow me to speak on your mother, for the two of you?'

Vale nodded.

Dobbler was magnificent. He explained he'd be reading for me, read out my words with the kind of care he showed everything; too slowly and with all his own thoughts floating in the air through his pauses, so we could take them in too, like a prophet.

You never forget that sort of kindness, never. He came back to stand with us. I had nothing I could say, all in pieces. Vale wiggled in front of me and went to stand between myself and old Dobb so he could get a hold of both our hands.

One more song, some words from the vicar and we could all go out and escape that organ and the strangling misery of the place. Felt like a long old walk to get out of there. I registered a whole line of town folk behind us all along the aisle and in there a voice said,

'Pa Landyn.'

I had just about gathered my arms up to catch him when young Thomas came over the side of the pew, like a canonball into my arms. What a fantastic lad he was to do it. Hung on like a monkey too, heavy and solid, 'til I put him down so he could be with our Vale. I looked aside to see Tom's Pa there too.

Never occurred to me to look for him. He looked terrible so I knew he was off the drink that morning and he was crying and crying and crying like a man who has lost his own God. Suppose when you're away from your bottle you know you've lost your God and all else besides, and for the first time I remembered that he was a man who had lost his wife too. To lose someone, to murder or madness, makes no difference. I stopped a moment with him, to shake his hand, so he knew I saw him, saw his struggle, understood it was my own too.

After that I knew it for sure, knew that that's why you get out of bed the next day and go to work in a field that's not your own, hauling bales you didn't grow and then sit with your lad doing sums after school though your bones are so weary you can hardly stay awake; there are folk depending on it, folk who stand by you when you think you can't hold yourself straight. And Vale. He needed me to be whole.

I'd just wanted to see my vixen, she was where my hopes lay, always, I could rest knowing she was well. I felt a fool, hunting down a fox like that. I must have taken leave of my senses but in the end you just have to do what it takes to settle the madness. Tom's Pa took to drink and I took to chasing foxes. That's just how it was.

I'd had another bad old time of it, soon after we were back, been to the Admiral and feeling like no one would look at me right, couldn't look me in the eye. I had a jar more than I should have I dare say. I was so lonely that night, truly in a way that registered in my body, an ache. I got to bed, Dobb was off towards Norfolk, Vale sleeping over at the Moles' with Thomas. I just lay there in my cot with all Dobb's planes flying overhead and wishing to God Cessie was there next to me, just breathing there.

'Tell me you see me still.' I said. 'I miss you. I don't know what I'm doing and I don't feel right without you, love. Tell me you're still close enough to know it.'

The next day, my fox appeared.

So in the woods I waited. It was one of the coldest nights, and I was crabbing along through the stumps and trees, an old fool brooding over lost love and still looking for his fox. I hoped to find her well, or at least well enough that I could help her.

I must have dozed off. I don't know how long I had been there. Somehow I had slept despite my lodgings and the cold. Snow had fallen, soft and thick. The ground was glowing with it. I could just about see where I was and what I was doing as my eyes adjusted. Dusted some of the snow off me and found my watch under the folds and wool. It was getting on. The cold was marrow deep. My lungs were tight from it.

The fox-earth was just below and I could see the dark opening in all the white that now sat round it. It felt as if a silence had fallen, the woods were holding their breath and all the old trees perched on tip-toe. Then, through the snow came the lady fox. Each leg lifted high and straight as she made her way home. Left, and right she looked then up, up, up with each of the legs, the front one still dragging some as she swung it through. She looked left and then right again and then in, quick as an arrow and gone.

She was alive.

Chapter 13
Vale

I stood outside the front door blowing on my hands to keep them warm and smoking while people went in and out through the glass doors. Visitors' Entrance. Load of shit. It was hardly the County Show.

My eyes felt like they were dried up and pinched into my face. I know I looked like I'd been drinking. I'd taken a bath to try and get myself together. I was awake all night. Just lying there trying to make the crying stop and my head going round and round and round. I went outside around four to smoke. The sun was still a few hours off rising. When I went back in the house I felt as if I was the only one there even though I knew Pa was there too, asleep. He had been out somewhere the night before, only heard him come in late.

Standing outside the hospital that next morning felt like the worst option possible. I timed my visit so I could do what needed doing and then get away. I was meeting Beth at the pub for a walk afterwards. I tried to look nice for her but kind of decided I couldn't do anything about it anyway. I knew she'd be looking all neat and careful, but not in that poncy way. In a good way. My black eye was yellow now from the bruise and because I was cold I was even whiter than usual and tired so the scabs and scrapes from hitting myself on stuff in the water looked even worse. I looked a fucking mess and felt it too.

It hurt my eyes when I looked up. The sun was trying to come through which was good. It took another smoke before I could get through the swinging doors and all my energy not to run away once I got in there. Signs and noise and no way of knowing where to go. It was every bit as bad as I thought it would be.

The whole place was doors and rooms and people who seemed to know what they were doing. Apart from being in after the boat, I'd only ever been in there once before with Mole Boy when he got beaten up on a Saturday night. Fetched Tom out the front a few times. Mole hardly ever came out with us and the one time he did he got thumped. I felt bad for him. He was crying and everything. We made him come and told him he'd have a good time and in the end he landed up in the hospital having his eyebrow stitched back together. Still, he liked telling the story and we let him tell it over and over like some old duffer telling his only war story.

Standing there in daylight though, my head felt like a pumpkin stuffed in a tin can. I could feel my fingers hurting where I was scratching at my nails with my thumb. I didn't know what to do so I asked someone at the main desk.

'Hey.'

'Hey.' Tom said.

He didn't look good, so I stayed at the door. I'd stood there a while before I said anything. He went back to sleeping, or dozing, it was hard to tell. Either way his eyes were closed and he was just lying there. He looked kind of flat under the blankets. They were those hospital blankets that are all neat and white so they looked kind of funny with Tom in them. I stared at his legs while he was off dreaming. Stared hard. They seemed the same to look at. His bed had boards and rails and stuff to stop him falling out and there were hoisting handles hanging round him. It was like it was when Pa made me go with him to see my cousin. I just stood there looking that time as well. I felt like I had to breathe in deep to get enough bottle to step towards the bed. I was trying to think what to say.

'You coming in or just passing through?' Tom rolled his head towards me.

'Coming in.'

'Take a pew.'

I sat on the chair next to his bed but I couldn't look up. I felt like he was looking at me. He was dopey but I knew he was waiting for me to saying something.

'I'm sorry mate.'

He didn't say anything. He was breathing deep and low.

'I'm sorry you got hurt. I should have come before. I know that. I thought maybe you'd like to sleep and get strong you know, and I've been working so. So, I didn't come. But it's the weekend so I'm here. But I'm sorry you got hurt.'

I looked to him for some help which was stupid. I knew that. He wasn't even looking at me just through me and blinking real slow. I guess it was the drugs.

'Less hurt, more broken, brother Vale.' he said after a time.

'You're broken.'

'Yeah.'

'I'm sorry.'

'Yeah.' He looked right at me.

It fell quiet.

The way it does when you switch the engine off after a long drive. And you just sit there a minute, listening to the metal settle back on itself. I know Tom was feeling the quiet too. Then, big tears just started coming and they just came down his face and he blinked a little but mostly he just let them come. I didn't know what to do. So I sat there looking right at him and let mine come too. We stayed like that watching each other with our throats and everything else hurting like hell. It seemed like we were there forever. It was okay.

One of those noisy trolleys came past the door, rattling and squeaking.

'Man-up you pussy, there's hot nurses present.' Tom swiped his sleeve over his face in one move.

'Yeah? Yours hot?'

'Yup. Smoking. She wants me something nasty.'

'Well, if it's something nasty she's after she'll certainly want you.'

'All right boys?' said a voice. 'This your friend then?' I saw Tom's eyes widen.

'Hey there nurse.'

I turned. The nurse was as long as she was wide. She had a weird tiny head with short grey hair on top. My face was so close by her chest I thought it best to duck down a little and turn away.

'You eat your breakfast?'

'Yes Miss.'

'Good boy. I'll be back in a bit for your medication and bath.'

I turned back to Tom. 'Bath? Oh yeah, she wants you brother.'

It was a good laugh, because we both worked so hard at it.

'I brought you something.' I handed him the knife I bought at the Ashe Auctions. 'I sharpened it up for you.'

Tom took it and opened the blade. He looked much more awake. 'It's a good one,' he said. 'Thanks, man. I better hide it though. They don't like us to have stuff like that in here.'

'No?'

'No. Think we're going to top ourselves or something. I'm more like to top the bastard that makes me do exercise every day. Comes in all perky in his little white hospital uniform. Swear he's queer. Makes me wheel over to the gymnasium, I got a chair did you see? He makes me do some terrible stuff. Hurts like a bitch and I try brother, I try hard, but Jesus he's a serious bastard. Says we need to get my legs moving again, maybe. But I sense they object to the idea. Not much movement, just hurts like a bitch.'

'Your dad come?'

'Yup.'

'That's good.'

'You know how he is.'

'Sure.'

'Sometimes best he doesn't.'

'Okay.' I could tell Tom didn't want to talk about his dad.

'What else been going on with you while I been in here? What news from the western front Commander? Any high jinx?'

'Well, nothing really. Been trying to get some pennies together, beet haul with Mole, Randall gave me shit.'

'Arsehole.'

'Proper.'

'He does take a tone.' He took a big breath in and shuffled his top half a little before exhaling.

'Yeah, well things have been a bit off, you know?'

'Same here.'

I knew that was a warning shot. Don't bring your sorrows here, you've got it easy brother, type of thing. I didn't know what else to say though.

'So Mole has a good contract at Playford. All excited too but feeling like he needs a new car and all. His keeps conking out. He's had it forever hasn't he? Going to try for a bank loan.'

'I'll loan it to him. No need for the bank. Mole's a good sort. Keeps his word and all that.'

That felt like another snipe, telling me off because Mole had visited and I hadn't.

'You don't have anything.'

'Well, brother, that's where you are wrong.'

'Don't be stupid.'

'Not stupid at all. Quite crafty.'

'You drink your last copper the minute you get it.'

'True. But only after I've taken out 20 per cent. To get that you take a zero off what you've got and times that number by two.'

'What?'

'Indeed brother Vale. Zero off, times by two.'

'You have savings?'

'Not so much savings. More a maternal tithe.'

'I wish you'd talk English.'

'I save it up for my goodly mother. She's a woman who will one day be in need of a monthly stipend. Well, if she's still alive, and let's be honest brother, she probably won't be. You seen her around at all while I've been in here?'

'No. Not since the summer.'

'Me neither. Gave her some cash and a couple new books I

nicked out the library, Thack-er-ay, but then she was off again. Cargo ship or something. A new development in her career.'

'How did I not know this?'

'You did. You were with me when she turned up at the Anchor. I whacked that dodgy Polski for touching her, remember? Loathsome fucker. Got him smartly too.'

'Yeah I know about your Mother. I didn't know about the savings. Anyway. Doesn't matter.'

'Anyway, tell Mole I'll help out if he needs. He can drive about all over once he's set and that way you'll all have to come visit me all the time. Regularly.'

'I'd visit you anyway. That's stupid.'

'Well, you might. Or you might not. But this way, you'll feel bad when you don't.' He paused as his jaw tensed suddenly. I could tell he was in pain. 'You know I'm joking right? Not about the money though, that's genuine.'

'Yeah. In the way you know I'll visit you.'

'Well. We'll see.'

The room went quite. I tried to look at him without him seeing. I couldn't work out how angry he was with me and whether it was about the accident or from not visiting. Or both. Mostly he looked uncomfortable, like he had started to rearrange himself but just stopped halfway through. His face looked all bent out of shape too. There was nothing wrong with it but he looked hard round his jaw and his eyes were kind of puffed up and grey. I felt like I needed to say something.

'So, is it a good chair?'

'What?'

'How's the chair?'

'How the fuck would I know? I only know this one.'

'Right.' I'd screwed up.

'Mostly the chair is fuckin' horse shit, as you can imagine, oh, hang on, no, you can't imagine can you?'

'You're right. I can't imagine, I'm sorry.'

'And really I'd rather have my fucking good legs than a fucking good chair, wouldn't I?' He was really riled.

'Of course, yeah of course, I'm sorry. Tom come on, it's okay.' I tried to go to him but he shook me off, he was still so strong on top.

'Just fuck off will you, don't come here again.'

I just kept agreeing and saying I was sorry, but I was talking to his back. He was lying there shaking, twisted away from me, with his legs still facing forward. I didn't know what to do.

'I never want to see you again.'

'Don't say that man, you're just angry.'

'Fuck you. Don't come back here, ever.'

I felt like I'd been hit all over again. Really gut-smacked, or fallen overboard into the water and I knew I should never have come. It was always going to be like this in the end.

I found my way out of the hospital again, although I don't know how, and just walked off down the road towards town. I didn't feel like waiting for a bus. I was angry and hurting like hell in a way I knew I deserved. But I still felt confused by it. Even though I was expecting it, it still felt like I'd been hoofed out of the fucking blue.

I was walking so fast and so angrily that I got to the Admiral early. Beth wasn't there yet. I sat on the wall outside the pub. I felt kind of obvious there, people walking past would see me there and know I was waiting for someone. I hoped no one like a Domino came along. They'd want to talk and ask why I wasn't going in and how was Tom and the truth was I was hating him a bit as I sat there. And then maybe Beth would turn up and I'd be telling the Dominos how crap everything was and it would all be ruined, all of it.

Even the sky was noisy, two crows were battling and jousting over me, the one trying to see the other off. The noise was terrible and it was hard to tell which one was being the thug or which was winning.

Another day I might have been excited about meeting a girl, any girl, but especially someone like Beth, and I was excited, kind of, but I couldn't stop thinking about Tom. I shouldn't have mentioned the stupid chair. Walked right into that one like a sap. But what the fuck was he expecting me to say anyway? Like it was only my fault, always my fault that he got hurt, like none of the decisions were his. I always felt bad, guilty. And for what? I wasn't sure about him saying he had all that money either. It was true he did love his Mum but that had to be bullshit.

Beth came down the road. She had a brown coat on over a dress and she had lipstick on. I'd never seen her wear it before. I was looking at her and her mouth and I was thinking, she's made an effort to look nice. She likes me, she's not just here because she feels sorry for me because my friend is hurt. She looked down quickly when she noticed I was gawping at her like a fucking idiot. She was so pretty. It felt like a relief to see her.

'Hi.' She was smiling.

'Hey.'

'You ready to walk?'

I just looked at her face. I remembered that I'd wanted to try and kiss her. She was clean and nice like I never was. She wasn't

185

really a girl who would go for someone like me. She looked like she had nice manners and knew how this should work, what I should do next. I felt like such a loser next to her. Just seeing her made my jacket too old and too small.

She was looking like she was expecting me to say something important. Or, maybe to be someone, a guy who is nice to walk with, who has nice things to say. She was like the perfect girl. I would need to do things in a certain way and use the right words. But I couldn't. I had nothing nice to say. I was a shit to Mole Boy, my friend couldn't walk and I'd turned up at his bedside and fucked it up even more and he wasn't talking to me.

'Walk?' She repeated. She was smiling. She was inviting me to go with her.

I just stood there. Like I was too tired to move or something. Some days it's all I could do to keep myself upright and breathing. I felt as if I should walk into that stupid hospital and ask them to keep me there until I felt safe again.

I wanted to say to Beth, I don't feel safe. I don't know you, your type of girl. I wanted to say, standing here with you feels important, but I can never be enough. You are too pretty and kind for someone like me.

I knew I would just fuck it up and just thinking about trying to make it work out, know what to say, know what to do, was already too much.

She was looking nervous. She reached out her hand to my arm and I don't know why but I backed away, just a bit, like an inch, but she saw it and I saw she felt it too.

'Vale?'

'No.'

'No? What do you mean?'

'I'm not ready to walk.'

I turned around, I turned my back on her and walked away. I walked away.

'Vale? Where are you going?'

I just walked faster until I was up around the bend and I knew she couldn't see me anymore. I knew I'd hurt her. She looked hurt. Fuck. I wanted to be able to tell her I'd like go for a walk with her and maybe another one after that. But I felt like everyone was needing something from me and whatever I tried to give wasn't enough, or it wasn't right.

I went straight home and took the dogs out without even going in. I left Pup in her bed next to the fire. There had been big snow in the night. The roads were clear but walking across the fields was hard going. The smaller dogs had to leap in arches just to make their way through it but I think they liked it anyway. We were out for a long while and I don't think I had a single thought the whole time. Not Beth or Tom or Pa, none of them, just a blank. Clean as the snow fields. It felt so good. The wind was getting up again, razors in it, but it felt so clean. I could breathe.

When we got back I threw some hay at the cows and pigs before taking the pack inside. I could hear Pa crashing around in the sheds so I ignored him. I ate, then put some fruit and newspapers and cigarettes in a bag. Found some playing cards too and some chocolate though I wasn't sure how old it was. I took a couple of Ma's books off the shelf and headed back to the hospital. By the time I got to the end of the lane, I was done in, so I waited for the bus, and when it eventually came I could hardly breathe for the cold. I didn't care.

I stood outside Tom's door like I had that morning. The door was shut though.

'Hello. Can I help?' It was a different nurse from earlier.

'Hey, nurse. Can I visit? Tom Walker.'

'Well, he's in a bit of a sorry old way, for his sins, so we're letting him rest up a bit.'

'Sorry way how?'

Turns out Tom hurt himself after some struggle with the physical trainer. Tom had got angry because he couldn't do what was wanted and he'd hit out at the gym guy. Got him too, but also hurt himself while he was doing it. He fell over on himself. He was real hurt and tired and had to have injections for the pain and to calm him. I watched him through the little window in the door. He was out. Just lying there all heavy so he had sunk low into the mattress.

I went in and sat there anyway, in case he could see through a dream whether I was there or not. I told him I'd finished the fencing he'd helped me with and the younger pigs were being moved up to the barns already. Told him about the beet I hauled with Mole Boy and the kinds of cars Mole might need for his business. I know he didn't care about all the people I delivered haylage to but I told him about all of them anyway. I told him that Mole Boy was doing so well and Pa kept going on about it. Still, I might get him to help us for the next couple of months while all the moles were snoozing. I nearly told him about Beth, told him I didn't know what to do or what to say. But I stopped myself. I felt as if stuff to do with her shouldn't be shared about. Even though I had walked away. All along, Tom just lay there, breathing deep and slow.

'Do you remember what happened on the boat? I don't really. I feel like I've just made it up sometimes.' Tom carried on sleeping. 'Only I was under the water. I came up and I could see the boat, right there. I grabbed hold and I got myself in. I was shouting for you. Did you hear it? I couldn't see you. I was shitting myself thinking you were drowned. Then I heard you. Scrabbling against the side of the boat and shouting out to me. You tried to get in the wrong end where it was too steep. I called for you to hang on to the ropes and get round the side. I did hang on to you and then, Jesus, I don't know how it all happened I got alongside you and the wind was coming off the sea like a fuckin' monster and the tide was rushing out in that gully. I guess we were further out towards the sea than we thought because suddenly you were shouting that there were rocks and you were hanging on the side and I couldn't get you in even though you had rocks behind you and then the boat just fucking swung, it just swung and I could tell you could feel it. You let go and pushed away so you had your legs up against the side trying to get the boat away from you with your legs, I could see you were straining hard, but it kept coming and I was screaming and I didn't know what to do to make it stop coming at you.'

'It smashed you Tom, it fucking smashed you. Jesus, you were screaming like a beast, a fucking beast. But it was worse when you stopped. You'd let go and the only reason you were still there was the boat had you pinned into the rocks. Jesus. I got you in though, I got you in. You were bleeding everywhere from the rocks on your back and you couldn't feel your legs or use them to help get yourself in. But I got us back, got us back with the motor. I thought it would never start and I thought you were gone. Yeah. Thought you were gone.'

I left Tom sleeping to go and smoke outside. I didn't feel like I could breathe in his room suddenly. I smoked slowly and tried to burn away the boat and the water and those white blankets with Tom lying under them. I lit another one.

Chapter 14

Landyn

I stayed out until it was nearly morning again, the one time of the day there was any cool in the summer months, just before daylight. The crickets eventually went quiet and gave way to that time of the night that is too dark for hope but then, the birds. One then two, then all together. Beautiful birds, big and bold with great sweeping songs. As the sky changed, their voices started crying out and rolling forward out of the hills, like a big old storm was on its way.

I don't know when they came.

Chisongo and his crew, drunk and rabbling in the way groups of young men can be. I had humiliated him, and then terrified his wife and child. And he came for me, to frighten me, but it was Cecelia he found.

Slaughter day. Vale was up but he didn't want to speak. I hadn't seen him all weekend. Just heard the door open and close a few times. It was miserable for me and he looked done in, like the darkness had got him. Not just mardy, something more wicked.

But, I held that if he had something to say to me he'd have said it already. Saw to my Pup, who somehow looked the worse for it every day, then got myself together. It's always a long old morning when we have to get the piggers off to chop.

There seemed no end to the goddamned cold. Usually it would come for a day or two and then leave us with all the clay bleeding its insides out so that even the tractors struggled through it. But this was set in. Vale was climbing into his overalls in the boot room, then hopping on one leg and another to get his boots on but left the room without a word and went to load the truck with stakes for the hurdles and got the sacking out and what not. I could see him walking back and forth across the black of the open barn doors, fetching this and bending for that. His shoulder seemed to be holding out. To be fair, I hadn't expected him to be there to help us, but there he was anyway.

Dobbler arrived. He always came down the lane like a rocket in that old truck of his. Huge black thing that just seemed to go on forever. He was out and ready before I'd even got down the stairs properly.

I was moving slowly, even though I'd had the first good night's sleep in a while. I was late in after another visit to the goodly woods and had rest without my Pup that night. She was agitating and kicking, couldn't settle, so I took her downstairs to sleep with all her little pals. She hadn't done that for a long time, not since I'd had her in with me those past months. I'd carried her down and set her in a warm bit of bed between Buckshot and Jessie. Jessie was a good one, I knew she'd look after my pup.

'Ho there Landyn.'

'Mister Dobbler. How's Queen Victoria running?'

He patted the bonnet of his old truck. 'God save the queen.'

'God save the queen.'

'Good day for pigs.'

'Good as any.'

'Good 'n clear for once. They'll be pleased with that.'

'They will. Bit rafty though.'

'Certainly is. Where's your lad?'

'At the truck. Tiffling about with the bits and bobs.'

'Eager then?'

'Something.'

Dobbler knew his pigs. In the proper way, understood what they were about, not just the price on their rumps.

We went out to the arcs, the three of us wedged in the cab of the truck. Dobbler always liked to sing a little as we went and then whistle too, though his whiskers got in the way of that. Vale wasn't saying anything to me so I was grateful for Dobb being in there between us.

'So lad, how you been?' He asked.

'Okay. Thanks for asking.'

'S'alright, been worried for you all.'

'Yeah.'

'How's Thomas doing?'

'Okay.'

'You know, one of his nurses at the hospital, that's Margery Curtis, she's my cousin, distant, but, you know, family. Known her for donkeys. She says he's a strong lad and though it doesn't look good for the legs, she's seen weaker boys come back from it. So that's something then isn't it? Have you seen Margery there then? If you haven't gone calling yet, keep an eye out for her. You can't miss Margery, if you get my meaning. Ho, you'll know her.'

'I know who she is.'

'Do you?' I had to interject.

'Yeah.'

'How's that then?' I knew I was pushing him.

He took longer than he should to reply.

'Because, Pa, I met her and we talked some about Tom and how he was having a bad day.' He was hissing.

I wanted to slap him for his insolence but I was so flummoxed to hear he'd been at the hospital I held my tongue, near bit it too as we rattled over the frozen rabbit holes and ditches to the pigs.

'Oh, sorry to hear he had a bad day of it,' said Dobb.

'Yeah.'

'There'll be some more of those I dare say. But he's a strong lad.'

'He's strong.'

'Ho, fights like a bull. But you're both solid lads, you'll all do fine.'

Dobbler resumed his half-whistling through his whiskers. I wanted to get a look at Vale's face for some sort of reaction but I couldn't.

I aimed us at the far corner of the birch fields. There were thirty or forty pigs of a size in there and we needed the ten largest. Vale started getting out the stakes and stacking up the hurdles, ignored myself and Dobbler who I hoped didn't notice the chill between us and I don't think he did, being fixated on the pigs as he was, walking up and down looking at them and getting his plan organised in his rum old head. He had a kind word for each of them too.

After some sorting out and deciding which ten we wanted I got the trailer reversed in, we staked in the hurdles, deep as we could with the earth all frozen up. The pigs had rooted under what was left of the snow which helped but it was hard driving.

I was happy to have Vale to do the bashing and only when we'd done with all that did I notice there was no straw in the back of the trailer. Just the cold metal base and bars, nice and clean as I like them, but no straw.

'Vale son, we've forgotten the straw for our piggers.' Of course I wanted to say what the hell's wrong with you, you had half an hour faffing around and you still couldn't remember the straw.

'Oh dear, we must have straw for the blighters,' said old Dobbler.

'We'll keep them busy, if you go back and get some then. You've got the turnips?'

Vale was chewing on his cheek looking like a storm warning.

'They're over there'. He gestured with his chin over his shoulder.

'Ah good, straw too?'

'No.' God I could feel the tightness in my throat coming on.

'You can get that then and we'll finish getting ready here.'

He muttered something.

'What's that son.'

'Nothing.'

'All right then.'

'They don't need it.'

'Oh that they do', said Dobbler, 'It's cold and they'll move a bit as we go and scrape the flesh without straw.'

'They do need it son, they always have the straw.'

'They're going to be killed, we're taking them to the slaughter house, right? What difference does it make?'

'Well, it makes a difference to the pigs how they get there.'

'Do you know how stupid that sounds?'

'Nothing stupid about it. These are my pigs and I like them to be treated right. I don't want them cold and fearful and cut up. They've lived well and they should die well too.'

'Good man,' said Dobbler nodding.

'Jesus.' Off Vale went, kicking up the frost like he had no intention of coming back.

Dobbler got his tobacco and rolling papers out and leaned against the fencing post as we waited. I took one for myself. It was fine out. Chilly but compared to the spirit sapping freeze of the past few days it almost felt like summer had come. We were in a slice of sunshine, clear and crisp and biting. It was one of the most fetching views of the farm from that corner of the field. The house set up against the slope, thin column of smoke coming out the chimney and then the trees cutting a clean line through the snow where a stately old avenue used to grow. Their roots would have cut deep through the soil, and good soil it was, occult black. You knew the trees were drinking that oil right in. Crows were pecking through the snow for anything to eat and from time to time a funny old pheasant would let out a clanging call. Dobb always called it the dinner bell. Liked his food. Pigs looked good too. Snow always makes them cleaner and pinker than usual. I went over to see them.

'You've been good fellows. Thanks for that.' I said to them. 'We'll get you some straw for the ride though.'

After some time, no doubt part of the protest, Vale brought the straw and made a right fuss of spreading the bail round the trailer, muttering for all the free world while he did it. The bale made a good deep nest though. As it should be. Nice bed of straw in there and some broken-up turnips along the ramp to tempt the little fatties in. That's what you need.

'All right then Dobb, let's get going.'

'All right Land.'

'Son, you stand by the trailer and Dobb and myself, we'll send them forward through the hurdles, but nice and easy, one at a time so as not to worry them or they'll be off.'

He said nothing, but went to the trailer. The pigs were good and calm, chatting a little but sniffing on the breeze for the crushed turnips and rolling on forward where we needed them. Dobb and I were using the boards, but hardly needing them, and had the ten we needed nicely separated out and heading in the right direction at a waddle. Vale had the slats in place, so straight ahead, along through the hurdles and into the trailer they could go. Same as ever. Dobb and myself walked along behind them to keep them moving forward. Dobb was nattering away to them in his own sleepy world so I had to be the one to keep an eye out in case one of them ducked out the side or suddenly took a start and turned. Then they'd all go screaming off.

First one went in easy enough, snuffled through the turnips, next one took his time though, stopped for a think along the way.

'Hurry up.' Vale was getting impatient with the fellow.

'He's coming, just thinking things through, having a little look around,' said Dobb.

'We'll be here all morning at this rate, damn idiot.'

'Don't be making any fuss now. Pigs don't like fuss. If he goes to duck out you just move the hurdle in,' said Dobb.

The pig wasn't going anywhere.

'Come on!'

'Easy lad, don't rile them.'

'Pa, just shunt them.'

'No hurry, we'll get them in.' The boy was being more trouble than the pigs.

'Damn pigs.'

'Er, lad, you turn away then,' said Dobbler.

'What?'

'We got a clever one, he don't like being stared at.'

'What?'

'You look away and drop your shoulder a little, all hunched-like, submissive, and the pig'll come to you.'

Dobb was right as ever. Vale was leaning over the entrance to the trailer staring at the pigs and shouting, no pig in his right mind would get in that trailer. He was upsetting them. They didn't like it and nor did I.

'He's right son, you stand to the side and I dare say they'll just go ahead. They'll go in for the grub.'

'You're both mad you know that?' As he turned away he kicked the hurdle, just to let us know what he thought. The metal clattered out a warning and the wary pig out front started, screamed and turned, and made to bolt back towards the open field.

'Move the hurdle, pull it to, pull it to,' I say.

But it was too late, the wily pig and all his chums were gone.

'Oh, oh that's a shame,' said Dobbler. I could tell he was disappointed. 'Pigs don't like fuss lad, you have to . . .'

'I know what I'm fucking doing you old git.'

Silence.

Vale's face went red as if it were stained with a beet straight out the pan. Dobbler seemed to be in some distress, confusion mostly, blinking, his mouth moved a touch but no sound came. I near exploded.

'Apologise to Dobbler, Vale.'

'I won't. I'm not ...'

'Apologise.'

Dobbler found his voice,

'It's all right, I suppose. Just a touch startled is all.' He looked more than startled. Speared right through I'd have thought.

'Apologise Vale. Apologise at once.' I could feel the rage returning.

'I won't.' He was livid, veins coming through his neck, eyes red. 'I've had enough, I hate this whole place. It's bullshit.' He was storming away as he shouted, 'I hate this place!'

'Dear God Dobb, I'm so sorry, he should apologise, he will, I'll be sure. That was meant for me. He meant to say it to me. I can't tell you how sorry I am old chum.'

'No, no, I fair know it was aimed at me.'

'He aimed it at you, but he meant it for me.'

'I am slow, Land, I do know it. Only, you know, I do worry for the piggers a little.' Dobb was all at sixes and sevens, twitching and fretting with his hands.

'It's me he meant to curse at. He does it all the time too, I know, but not to my face, that he can't, he chose you, I'm sorry to say. We aren't speaking. God Dobb, I'm sorry, fellow. We had a quarrel you see. About his Ma. I think I've lost him but in the meantime, he means to hurt me. He does.'

'He's got some language in him.'

'That he does and some fire to back it up.'

'Hmm, head of steam there.'

'Oh yes'

'Ah, knew a boar like him once.'

Dobbler had a pig for any situation. He had his tobacco out again and was rolling a smoke, a little shaky though.

'Oh? What you do with him then?'

'Parsnips.'

'You saying I need to give my boy parsnips?'

'Ho, might do the trick, might do. No, no, I just found out what he liked, something to get him on side. Oh he ignored me, turned his back on me, trod on me, ran at me, tusks out. I was quicker then, mind. But like I always say, pigs don't like fuss, you just got to leave them to it and let them find their own way and time, whole heap of it. But you can't leave their field though Land, no. They need to know you're there 'til the job is done, set your boundary, but show you got time to do it right and do it easy.'

'What did you do with the parsnips then?'

'Nothing. Remembered he liked them, threw one over his way every day and ignored the old bugger, few days later, he was coming over all lovely-like.'

'I do think it'll take more than a couple of winter roots with my boy though, Dobb.'

'Never know.'

'I'm still sorry for what he said, truly so. You've saved us so often these years.'

'Have a smoke.'

'Thanks for that.' I took the offering.

'He'll come round.'

'He blames me for his Ma's death Dobb, over and over. That's what the last round was about. Said it right to my face.'

'Oh, Land, that's not right, not right at all old pal. How has he come to that then?'

'Well, I took us out there didn't I? Lost all our cash then convinced Cecelia we'd be better off at the other end of the world.'

'Well for what it's worth friend, and I'd never say it, I'm not sure you had too many options. Money all gone and I dare say it was fair tricky to be in a room with the two of you some days.'

We were silent a moment.

'Things were bad weren't they? With how terrible it all was after, I suppose I forgot it was bad even before. In its way.'

'Land, I'll remind you of the Blyth Show. As dark a day as ever and that was just the one.'

'I didn't behave too well did I?'

'No. I dare say you didn't. But sometimes we can all be a bit awkward when we can't see the way ahead.'

'You're a wise old bugger aren't you Dobb?'

'Not sure about that. Do know a good pigger though.' He chortled through his whiskers. 'So, let's get those frosty ones in the trailer then. Don't expect your lad'll be back to offer a hand.'

The Blyth Show had been a low point. Dobbler was with me as usual. It had become such a big event with all the breeders and such, they were holding it over two days instead of one for the first time. The boys were off with a ration for sweets and rides and Cessie was with the Institute ladies serving their cakes on the tea stalls. She'd been baking all through the night. All kinds of lovely sweet treats.

Dobb and I were readying our prize boar for the ring. We'd been up late the night before giving him a bath so his thick curly bristles were all shining and he was all lovely and pink beneath it. Really enjoyed us scrubbing behind his ears that one. Rosary Rufus was his show name, a real charmer. Never forget him. We were tired but in good spirits and I was keeping the pig in the harness while Dobb went round with his paintbrush putting cooking oil under the eyes and on all the black markings to get them all shiny, bit around the snout too and a few dabs on the trotters. The boar looked magnificent.

We'd be on within the half hour and Cecelia was mean to be back already to get a good view of the ring and help a little in case anything went awry. We had quarrelled again the night before and we hadn't yet made it right between us. We never did, we eventually just forgot why we were angry or another fresher spite was ignited. I dare say I wouldn't recognise the man I had become; quick to anger and defensive, feeling I was wearing every last failing as a husband and a man on my back like a target. The money was falling away like paint off an old wall, most days Cessie and I were hardly talking let alone loving and everything I tried to right went wrong before I had got it off the ground. I was so ashamed. I can name it now. At the time I only felt the whole world was accusing me, now I know it was I who had the harshest words.

The Blyth Show was a welcome respite and Dobb and I had really worked to give ourselves a good chance. I wanted Cessie to see us do our round. We knew Rufus was a good boar and, I suppose, I hoped she might be proud of us, of me. Dobb kept an eye on Rufus while I rushed off across the paddocks and down the lovely old avenue of yews they had there at the ground, towards the tea stalls. Place was heaving with visitors. The hot weather had brought them out.

I took a short cut round the back of all the tents, having to hop all the ropes. There was our Cessie chatting to a man I knew. Had some fields near Orford way, big orchards too. Since that day I had tried to remind myself what I saw. And the truth is, nothing. There was nothing to see. Only that she laughed and her hand reached out to lightly touch the man's arm as she did. That was all she did but the sin, as I saw it, was that she did it with such great joy, no censure nor thought. None of the wariness that had found its way onto our conversation, none of the silences, the closed doors, the turned back in our bed. To be Mrs Midwinter gave Cessie no reasons to laugh and yet this man, hardly known to us, had made her laugh.

In the space of an in-breath I knew my reaction was wrong, there was nothing amiss, but still felt I had to shout or run and all I felt was a terrible, terrible fury and panic. I turned and took off back to the pens and the pigs like a man outrunning his own death.

'You alright Land?'

'Yes. Yes.'

'You don't look it. Have a swig of rum. I've got a half-jack in my coat pocket for the nerves.'

'Thanks. I'll take a measure.'

'Didn't find your missus-wife then? Never mind, we're on next but this one, so we better get a shift on.'

I suppose I got my white showing coat and hat and numbers on myself and the boar. Can't remember a thing about it. I assume we did our turn, parading Rufus around to some effect as we took home second prize that day. As we got the pig out of the ring and back into his pen and were getting his water and pellets to him, Cessie came rushing in across the straw floor.

'Oh Landyn, you and Dobbler did the most wonderful job with a prize for Rufus. I didn't miss a thing. I saw you, I saw all of it.'

I could have left it. Should have left it. But I couldn't could I? All injured pride and speared right through by a laugh.

'So did I, Mrs Midwinter. I saw you too and God knows I saw all of it.'

I knew Dobb was still there and I didn't care.

I watched Cecelia's face. It went from confusion to understanding and then outright panic in the space of a second.

'Landyn?'

'Going about laughing and carrying on with other fellows.'

'What? You mean just before? Will? Land he's my friend, your friend. There's no carrying on and you know it.'

'No.' I was losing ground already and I felt an even bigger fool than I had before. Dobb was shuffling out. I could hear him talking to Rufus to distract himself.

'Yes. A friend.'

'Cecelia do not insult me.'

'It is you Landyn who insults me. You take your mind out of the place it has gone and you wash it clean before you ever come near me again.' All tears she was, shaken and cut raw. 'How dare you? How can you even think such a thing when I have done nothing but stick by you through all of this mess? You are a shameful, horrible man and I am asked to call you husband.'

'Maybe ...'

She raised her hand to stop me. 'No. I'll hear not a word more from you. Shame on you.' And with it she ran out of the tent and that began a long old, bad old time of falling apart and trying to get ourselves together and falling apart again and more trying.

I couldn't bear to look at her, hear her speak for weeks. I'd escape the house before the sun was up and stay out past dark. Not hard to do when you work the land but I took no Sundays. Eventually I could bear to cast an eye across her but she looked so changed. I caught myself looking for signs that she might have softened, knowing that the misery was all my own fault, my own wounding but not knowing how to be the first to break the silence.

I felt such pain. Almost as if my body had lost a part of itself. When I felt distressed it was her I would turn to for solace or comfort and now even that was denied me. My closest friend could not comfort me. She shuffled around and sang and cooked and chirruped in the garden. I suppose for Vale, to keep him feeling safe but even that irked me, that she could even summon up the song in her voice when I felt so silent and broken.

But what was to be done? Nothing.

The pigs still needed to be slaughtered and there was no sign of Vale returning. He was seething. Dobb and I had finished our smoking and the slaughter house wouldn't wait. If the pigs weren't there by noon they'd have to stay over there for the next day and I didn't want that. They'd be worried being away from their friends.

'Let's do these piggers then Dobb.'

'Right you are.'

We got them in, Dobbler and I, no more than twenty minutes, one after the other, nice and neat and no fussing, because the pigs don't like it. The ten looked pleased in their straw bed for the journey even though it was a squeeze and by the look of them, we'd get some good cash. Dobbler would take them, do the doings, take his cut and bring me the rest in the morning. He would always take less than I thought he should and then I'd have to protest but he'd never relent and so I'd send him home with some hooch and some eggs and so forth.

With the trailer gone, I stacked all the hurdles nice and neat under the oak tree that stands proud on the edge of the field. Couple of years back we thought it was a goner. Branches dying back and some disease oozing out the trunk. We cut it right back and lo and behold the tree came back. I patted the trunk. I felt encouraged by that old tree that day. It had history to it and healing. There was one like it on our farm in Kabwe, local tree, I never knew its name but I knew its heart. You get those sorts, let you into their shade on a hot day. Let you sit deep and close.

* * *

In the days after Cessie passed I couldn't be in that Kabwe house. Quite apart from the mess and the police keeping us out until they had done their job, I just couldn't be still there. Police inspectors, officials, neighbours and the weight of death always in the air.

All the workers had to be interviewed of course. There were near three hundred of them and it took five days but on the very first day we knew Chisongo was gone, and his good-for-nothing brother too. His girlfriend Sara, who worked in the house, was interviewed again and again. She sat with her child in her lap and answered the questions over and over, quietly and calmly and only once when she turned away from another hour with the inspectors, did I see a tear roll down her cheek. She brushed it away as soon as she felt it and held her child all the closer to her chest.

They found them in the end, heading north. Four fellows in all. Made a mistake and tried to steal some gasoline from a small holder up there and it was that which exposed them. The small holder shot at them and tied them up until the police arrived.

Eventually I was summoned to court, a plain pale blue building with stairs outside that led to the entrance. It smelled of stale cigarettes and bleach. The four admitted what I knew, that they had come to scare me, give me enough pause to send me packing after I had humiliated not just Chisongo but his family too, Sara and the child. He had brought his friends with him to make sure he gave me a proper fright. Instead, he had been surprised. Cessie was alone and had run to press the panic alert on the two-way radios that connected all the farms. Chisongo and his gang had rushed at her, she had recognised him, shouted out his name, even begged him to be kind. That was, said Chisongo, the problem. The others had told him that they had no choice but to kill her after that. They were drunk he said, he was sorry, hoped that God would forgive him.

Chisongo looked terrified, tearful too. It surprised me. I realised how young he was for the first time, twenty, twenty-two at the most, the same as Tom and Vale when they took they boat.

Sara, smart and neat with a green and yellow wrap on her head and another for the child, sat with her head bowed behind him. He apologised to the judge. His voice was softer than I had ever heard it. He asked the family, me, to forgive him, he had made a mistake, he had only meant to frighten the Englishman.

Something in his face, his frowning and the way he was rubbing the back of his neck, looking down at his hands, made me think, this lad has a father and somewhere a mother who had loved him, may still love him. But I pushed that from my mind, dowsed that small flame, because I had to worry about my Vale and the mother he no longer had.

The judge asked if I had anything to say, but there was nothing. I sat there, weeping like a small lad. I had no words for the judge, for Chisongo, for any of it. Eventually, two of the four were convicted, including Chisongo. Sara and the child tried to cling to him as he was led away.

I lied to Vale. I told him they were all locked away forever.

I hadn't thought about Chisongo for some time. He'd probably still be in the clink. Hard to say. I couldn't forgive him. Not for that, not ever, but there was, now, a feeling of distance. If you could call it that. Was he so different to my lad, to Thomas? Too, angry, too injured and one too many jars at the pub, one bad decision that ends somewhere you could never have imagined when you set out the door with your gang of friends. Young hotheads all. I understood what had happened, I understood how it could happen. What if Thomas had died on that boat, or they'd taken a truck instead of a boat and set it through a cottage wall?

Because I was older and closer to the end of life perhaps I was more willing to see his ways were down to other things, not of his making. He would not answer my questions about where he was from because to speak of his place of origin would, perhaps, demand that he raise his own ghosts which he had come all the way to Kabwe to escape. And who was I to ask this information of him? A fuddle-headed foreigner, coming and going. And Sara and his child, what of them? They had left the farm, obviously. The last we heard Sara had a job cleaning at a hotel, badly paid, terrible hours but close to the prison so she could visit Chisongo each Sunday. At the time I couldn't understand why she did it. Let him go, let him rot for what he did. Who would want their child to know their father who has done such a terrible thing? But then you realise, slowly and after years have passed, that he is still the father to her child, he has only shown her kindness, she knows he did not mean to do it, he told her so, he told the judge the same. She knows he has some darkness of his own, for where were his parents? Where was his home, his solace? Only in Sara and his child and her only solace was in him.

This was Chisongo as I came to see him after all those years had passed, I saw him for what he had lost too, for what Sara had lost. But no, I could never forgive him. There is always, always that breathe of a moment before the knife falls when you could do different. There is always another way. And he chose the wrong one. The worst one. So, I could understand the fellow, but in the end I lost everything to him, and if the past weeks had shown me anything, I could still lose more. There could be no forgiveness, even when my tired old bones went to their grave.

The bitter night was frosting, I started the walk back to the house, needing a hot cup.

Then I saw her.

Straight copper back, limping, out across the horse field and along the hedgerows where she was wont to stalk of an evening. All along she went, hunting, hunting. First when I saw her I hoped her gait was off with all the mud the snow had left behind, struggling to get through it maybe but she was hurt all right.

Beautiful lass she was. She hadn't seen me. She was too busy listening as she went her head cocked to the one side and taking soft careful steps so as not to let whatever she was listening to hear her footfall. But she couldn't, her leg was dragging a little so she had to add a little hop into it. She'd never catch anything like that. She stopped, knowing her quarry was gone. She leaned herself towards the woods. She was headed back to her earth, that was clear, her keen snout was pointed right at it. She had caught nothing.

Chapter 15

Vale

I took the gun. Just took it out the cupboard, loaded two in the chamber, dropped a few in my pocket, and laid it on the front seat of the truck. I covered it over with Pup's blanket that was always there, and I left. I'd already put the booze under the front seat just before. Two bottles of the Dominos' homebrew rum. They always gave Pa some when he helped them with stuff but he could never drink it. He said he was sure it was just battery acid.

As I drove, I got one out by feeling for it and pulled the cork with my teeth. Even as I did that I could feel my nose tingle from the smell. I took a swig. Burned like hell. I couldn't really taste anything only the hard fire hitting my stomach and then a flush of heat rising in my chest. I took another larger taste. It roared right up my throat and nose so that I just shouted out like a fucking mad man.

Pa and Dobbler were done with the goddamned pigs. Pa had gone to put hay out for the cows. I knew he'd look to his beaten up hen and then take a nap and then go into the woods again. He'd be busy in there for hours looking for some fucking fox or a badger or something. If it wasn't a bird it was Pup, or his hedgehogs or that crow we had when I had the measles. He left me to go and feed the bird and nurse it. I know he was gone not even an hour but it felt like he was never coming back and I lay there all sweating and aching and wishing the bird would fucking die so that Pa would come back.

When I left I never said where I was going. Only that I wouldn't be home. I wanted to test Pa. He said nothing. Just kept his head down. He was so busy with his goddamned hen I doubt he would have noticed me anyway. I turned away from the sheds and walked towards the truck. My eyes burned.

If he'd stopped me it would have been a relief. But he said nothing. So I had to go, get in the truck and start driving. There were no other options anymore. Since he whacked me he was too scared to even talk to me, except when we quarrelled. It was bullshit. So, there was nothing more to do.

Since Tom and me took the boat nothing was the same. It wasn't as if I had it bad. Tom's legs didn't work. He was doing all the exercises and therapy but his nerves weren't yet showing signs of life. Didn't look like they ever would either.

All I was doing was moaning about Pa and missing Ma so much as if I was still a baby. Anything I felt or wanted could never be important because it was Tom that had lost everything. And I knew it was my fault.

I wanted to tell someone that when we were on the boat I didn't care if I drowned. There was a moment when I nearly told Pa that there was that second when we were just rocking back and forth in the dark and I thought if we went under or froze out there, it would be okay. I was just tired of fighting every day. I could have just stopped trying to get the boat home. But Tom was there and just when I was about to give up it had all gone so quiet on the water, and I felt so held. I can't say by what, only that it would be okay. I got us home.

The music was even louder on the radio, dark metal drums. I turned it up and took another swig. The brew was terrible.

I went straight back up the way we went to the Ashe Auctions. Fog was coming in. Looked like the road was floating. I had to concentrate on the line down the middle. I couldn't see too far ahead like I was just cannonballing through the dark. I was drinking that shit-awful rum and had the radio on, drums going, and it was loud and crazy with the engine screaming and me burning and suddenly I felt so safe. Knowing it would soon be done suddenly made it possible to be alive. That there was a way out, finally another option, made everything okay.

Almost too late, I saw the sign and had to hammer on the brakes and pull off for the Blyth. I felt sick. I had the bottle between my knees. I'd hammered a good measure already. I stopped on the side. My body was fuckin' thundering. I saw the church sitting on top of the mist, all the turrets and gargoyles coming and going as the wet rolled over. My breath was short. I took another finger-full for it.

I sat in the car a while. I don't know how long I was there but the fog seemed to have gone. As the booze did its work, I felt the panic sit down again. I sat some more and took another drink. It felt okay. For the first time in forever I knew what to do. I knew it was right. Everything was just falling into place.

I knew where Ma's grave was. It was up at the end, looking out across the marshes and then out to sea. Most days you couldn't see the sea, just smell it. I knew it was hard getting Ma home, expensive too, but Pa wanted her back here so we would have somewhere to come. To speak to her I guess. I never did. Usually I just stood there with Pa looking at the stone and then he would put some flowers down, always white daisies. She loved those.

I got out of the truck and looked at the sky. Only about an hour of daylight left. The air was bitter and as wet as it can be without raining. I was raging. I didn't even feel the cold in my body. I went round the other side for the gun and the other bottle. I locked the doors and left the key on top of the tyre where someone would know where to find it.

There were a few steps up to the church. From where I was, it was just a mound with the church on top of it. But on the other side there was a steep drop down into the reeds and salt and mud.

There was no one there. I knew that already. There never was in the week, only the vicar but he never left his house unless he had to, like if someone died or it was Sunday. Pa saw him kick his dog once and Pa went over and told him he was going straight to hell. The vicar went all red and sweaty and went off on one.

'Don't give a monkey's what he says. Not going there to see him am I? Am I?'

'No Pa, you're not.'

'If there's a God he knows that man's heart through his dog's bruising. That's how we're all judged in the end and that man is guilty.'

He could go on for ever on stuff like that.

I was struggling to carry the bottle and the gun with my hands being so cold and wet. I thought about Pa getting back from the woods or in the car with his hen and then taking Pup upstairs for a nap. He'd curl around her like she was an egg. Both of them snored. I could see him there.

I could see him so clearly in my head but when I was with him, I couldn't even look at him.

Not just him. I felt so shifty, kind of guilty just for being alive. It felt like people were talking about me even before I walked through a door. Then I left Beth in the road like that. I fucked that up too. But she was just someone else to disappoint. One huge fucking mess after the other and no one to tell me how to fix it. Ma would have known. I knew that. She'd have answers or at least better questions. And if she had none of these she'd have comfort.

It felt like it was so, so long ago that I last saw her. I couldn't even really remember her voice let alone anything she might have said. Sometimes Tom or Pa or someone would tell me something she'd said or done and I'd need to hear all of it, so I could hold it close.

Tom was always coming up with shit he remembered. He loved my Ma. I knew he did. He was always so angry though, fighting, and I didn't always know what to do with that. Sometimes I wished we could go somewhere and not have to defend our corner all the time. When guys started goading me I just turned away and let Tom take them on if he felt like it. Then the one time I nearly beat the crap out of some air-force guy in the Hook. I really beat him and after I was thinking why did I do that? Tom was always getting in fights and stuff, but with me, there was no excuse really. Mostly guys just ignored me because I had nothing to say ever. But that night, someone said something to Tom about his sister being a whore and I fuckin' lost it. Tom got me out in one piece.

Later, we were sitting on the quay, skimming bottle tops off the water in the dark and drinking, like we always were. The night was good and hot.

'Jesus, Vale, what the fuck you do that for, mate?'

'He had it fucking coming.'

'Yeah. Well, still, give me some warning next time, brother. Jesus. Anyway, why you so righteous? She's my sister, and you know what? She is a bit easy with her virtue. She really is. Your nose is bleeding again.'

I dabbed at it with my sleeve.

'I don't know. I just got angry.'

'Yeah I know what you did brother, I just don't know why. If you start going off on one with no warning like I do, we'll be done for. You're meant to be the one that quiets down the crazy. You're the volume control remember? I'm afraid it won't do to have you provoking the fine gentlemen of the airborne divisions.'

'Yeah I know. I don't know why. I just got in a haze. And that guy was a dick right? All that bullshit about him being a real man, been to war, and anyway, how does he even know your sister? Does he even know her?'

'Brother Vale, the combined defence forces of the free world and probably some of the others, all know my sister. But still, he did take a tone and as for your mad an' crazy haze, I invented that didn't I?'

'Yeah, guess you did.'

'Don't worry about it. You're just angry 'cause you're keeping all that fuckin' huge sorrow at bay.' He was swigging on his bottle with his small finger extended like old ladies with fancy tea cups.

'What? What did you say? What you talking about?'

'You get angry so you don't have to feel the fuckin' huge sorrow that's in you.'

'Where'd you get that from?'

'Your goodly mother told me.'

'That's bullshit.'

'No bull about it brother. That's what she told me.'

'Why'd she tell you something stupid like that?'

'I don't know. I was in your kitchen one time and she was patching up my face with a wedge of ice after my Pa had come at me like a fuckin' windmill. Taken a bit of a pummelling, brother, and I was blubbing and wailing and carrying on and I asked her why he did that to me and why he got so angry. So, she said most people got that way because they have great sorrow in them and being angry is the only way they know how to say it without saying it. That's what she said.'

'She said that?'

'I just told you she did.'

'Right. So you must have a shit load of sorrow in you then?'

'Epic, epic sorrow. I express it well, don't I?' He pretended to punch. 'But, she also told me that if she ever saw my father again she'd break his neck with her bare hands.'

'She would too.'

'I know it, brother.'

Tom dug out another beer and I thought about all the other things Ma should have told me before. Stuff you might need to know, about sorrow and being angry, how to be in your own life when is feels like you're just drifting and sinking.

I found a space to sit in the churchyard in that cold, in the bitching wind. Swigging away on that bathtub rum, I still knew nothing. Three tombstones in a row had angels on them, two had their heads bowed, the third was looking up, wings out across the top of the stone. I kept thinking she was looking at me. So I turned away.

I was babbling in my head trying to just focus on what I needed to do next. I tried to think better thoughts, good thoughts, but there weren't any left. I was beaten and I knew only the two bottles and the gun would make it stop. I felt as if I was just following instructions, all neat and clean. First this then that. Just follow the order of things, get the gun, the bottles, take the truck, drive to the Blyth. On and on, just to find a way through the noise to the end. The churchyard's not right. Get to the place where the earth meets the marshes. That's the place. Two in the chamber. That's what I would do.

I went round the back end of the church. There were steps down the far side of the graveyard that went under a short arch of trees and down and then out along the marshes through the reeds and the bullrushes. Looked like the tide was out for the most part. The mud was oily and grey. There were birds all wading in and picking away at stuff. It seemed too cold for there to be anything alive in there worth finding. Sun was four fingers from dropping away. I figured I'd wait until it was gone.

I got myself along the banks without losing the second bottle or the gun. I could hear the water but just kept watching for hard ground. I knew I didn't want to land in the mud. It was covered in ice on top but I knew underneath it was a rancid bloody bog. The wind was snide and full of sea. I had to lean into it and it made my skin all tight and dry. I kept on, trying to close my fingers tighter around the barrel of the gun, like I was feeling for a handbrake in the car but couldn't find it. And in my head too, stabbing around trying to pull up the brake. I couldn't, so I just kept on along the banks. I could hear birds gathering, crows maybe. I couldn't tell if they were in the sky or if the noise was coming from the marsh in front, maybe from one of the sandbanks.

I came to the big bend in the reeds. The water was still high there. Cold as a gravedigger's spade. I couldn't see into it and the reeds had their winter on. On the bend I knew there would be an old tree stump.

I sat. I was spinning. I put a foot further out to the side to steady myself. It helped. The sky had some huge clouds whipping across. Other birds, smaller than crows, all on the move. They knew something was coming.

After another drink, I laid the bottle to my left, cork out. I pulled the foot that was acting as an anchor back towards me. I put the butt of the rifle between my feet, barrels straight up. I looked at it. All clean after I'd used it a few weeks back for the rough shoot. I could hardly remember it. I suppose it was like any other. Tom was there for a while but he mouthed off to one of the fancy city guns and that was the end of that. They sent him home with no pay for his time. Could hear him effin' and blinding all the way across the fields. When I told Pa that night he said any pheasants they would have shot would have been hiding for the rest of the day for the shame of all the language they heard.

'Regal birds they are, don't like foul language. Get it? Get it son? Fowl language?'

Then he chuckled to himself about it all night. It wasn't even funny the first time. I don't know why I remembered that, then and there. The stupidest joke ever. Fowl language.

I just sat there a while thinking about that stupid joke and about Pa. For the first time I knew how cold my face was because my tears felt warm at first and then colder. I couldn't stop the crying, not for anything. The wind gusted so hard against me it felt like the salt just froze to my cheeks.

I didn't feel crazy anymore, just dull and tired. It was okay because it was so calm suddenly and everything made sense.

Take the gun, get some booze, into the truck and on until the end even if I couldn't always see the way.

I took a great swig from the bottle, and another, then threw the bottle to the side. I leaned my chin forward onto the barrel, I knew there were two in the chamber. It wedged in quite deep in the soft cup behind my chin bone. I just kind of rested there.

I felt so safe. Relieved even. The noise had stopped. No more questions or ways to make everything better. There was no longer any reason to try to make life possible. Nothing left. Just me and the reeds and the rushes and those big oily marshes and the crows and seagulls.

I said, 'I'm sorry, Pa.'

Crack. Eyes open. The sky broke. Black. Crows. Mobs screaming out across the rushes. Cracking and flapping, blazing and black. And an egret. Pure and white and beautiful in the rush of dark wings.

Was this it? My breath tore through me. It burned. No. I was breathing. My chin dropped back onto the barrel.

'Jesus.'

I pushed the gun away.

'Jesus.'

Something else had frightened the birds. Someone else.

I was retching and all of what was inside of me was coming up all over the place. Great pools of it heaving out of the belly of me and into the mud and reeds. It didn't stop. Bile and booze and foam. Coming out my mouth and nose and burning me all through while it did. I was like an animal with its guts spilt all over the slaughter room floor. An animal that should be dead but isn't and is still breathing while it dies and you can still see its heart pumping away even though it's hacked right open.

I was on my hands and knees thinking I should stand up. I felt the bottle on the grass next to me but it felt spongy, like it was part of the mud and moss.

I lost time, but I could hear water bubbling and sucking like it was coming through the bottom of a boat and the briny stench of the stale sea. I felt like I was rocking back and forth like the bottles on the deck that night with Tom. Out to sea. I thought, I have to get back to the harbour. I have to get home. The sky was so dark. I had to get back.

I woke up from retching. It was darker than I thought and my head was all over the place. The wind was whipping up through the rushes making that noise Ma said sounded like witches hair.

I was buzzing. The tide was doing something too, probably coming back in but I couldn't see. It made the mud bubble and spit. I wanted to get away from it.

Once I thought I was pointing back towards the church but fell down the banks towards the water. I just needed a light to know which way to point myself. Even the mud was icy and the reeds cut me bad. I thought, I just need to find the harbour. Pa will come and find me.

I got back up the drop. The jolt focused me long enough that I could see which way I wanted. Pa's gun kept sliding off my shoulder which didn't help.

The air went roaring through my head and ears every time I took a breath. The noise was unreal, like being stuck under a huge wave. I couldn't make it stop so I held my breath a few times just to get some quiet to think where I wanted to go. I felt so lost.

Exhausted. I stopped trying to find my way. I shut my eyes, just for a minute. I leaned on the barrel of the gun and felt it sink into the earth a little. It was so quiet, even the wind eased. Angels passing.

Then ahead I saw a small light, it couldn't have been bigger than a single bulb on the church porch. I was close. I found the steps that went back up to the church. I wanted to sit there but it was too cold so I dragged myself along the railing until I was up them and the church was in front of me. There was the light out front. I just about managed it to the door. I guess I left the gun on the bench outside. That's where I found it after. The door opened, not without a fight. It was better just for being out of the wind.

The floor was uneven under my feet. There was a small light on over the altar at the far end. Down the middle of the rows of pews there were shiny slabs, they looked slick and dark. The rest was all cobbled and patchy where different stones and bricks had been laid into the floor. No one had ever bothered to level it. I tripped up on the floor a few times.

It was the first time I'd been back in there since we had the service for Ma.

I woke up later when I near fell off one of the pews. The wood was hard and cold. The air smelled like damp paper and vomit. My head was humming and hot even though I knew I was half frozen with cold. My skull felt bruised and my hip was wedged into the seating. I had a fat tongue. I knew how sick I'd been.

When I could, and it took some time, I turned onto my back and knew I was in the Blyth. I knew how I got there too.

I was still breathing.

I felt the weight drop back over me. For a moment when I

222

woke and had only the cold and the hard floor to think about, I forgot it all.

From where I lay, the roof was just about as far away as it could get before it disappeared. There was light starting to come in through the windows that ran along the top. All along the ceiling there were wooden beams, tight packed. I couldn't see how they were held together. They used to be painted all different colours. You could kind of still see that. Every couple of yards there was a huge carved roof angel. The wings were spread out right across to touch the tips of another one which faced the other way. The wings used to be gold and green.

There was one right above me. She looked right at me. She looked sad. Like she was trapped up there or something with her wings pinned into the beams like that. She looked smaller than the other ones. She was as long as the others, but her cheeks were thinner, or her eyes were bigger. Something. She was tired. My eyes burned, and my throat.

'I don't know what to do.' I said

She just kept looking at me and I felt something I couldn't name. Not then anyway. So, I just lay there, looking up at the angel on the roof, feeling broken.

The sun was getting up. I decided I had to get up and out before anyone turned up. I couldn't have anyone see me there like that. Everything hurt. Birds and squirrels and things were moving, even in the cold. I sat in the truck a while before I managed to start it up. I didn't want to go home, but I had nowhere else to go.

When I got back to the farm it was gone seven o'clock. I couldn't remember what day it was. There was a burn of red. The sun had got trapped under the clouds. I sat for a bit, my whole body thumping to my heartbeat, like I was just one pulse. I was alive.

I knew Pa would be in the kitchen drinking coffee with the dogs. I didn't want to go in. I had to breathe deep and hard to get enough spine to open the door.

Pa looked up.

'Been out all night then?'

'Yeah.'

'You don't look so good son. You okay?'

'No.' I could feel tears coming quick.

'You all right?'

'I wanted to see Ma.'

He nodded. 'I know.'

He didn't know.

'I'm tired.' I said. I didn't bother to hide my crying from him.

'Of course you are. Come, sit. You've got mud all over you too.'

The room felt big. I stayed at the door.

'Pa, I ...'

'I know son.' Pa was crying too.

'I don't know what to do.'

'You will. Just keep a weather eye out.'

'For what?'

'You'll know it. You'll know it in your heart.'

'I thought maybe she helped me find the shore the other night.'

'I don't doubt it. Not for a second. She always keeps a watch for us, useless as we are.'

We sat there awhile. Pa brought me tea, too sweet, and toast with honey. I managed it and felt more solid for having eaten. He read me bits out the newspapers. Things about football teams and farm insurance and God knows what else. I didn't care about any of it but we just sat with the fire kicking in the stove and the dogs stretching and groaning in the warm.

Chapter 16

Landyn

I still don't quite have a way of being with what I found when I got back. You forget it, it fades, thankfully, and then it claws back in when you least expect it. The sky was light, steel grey and wide. And I knew something was off axis. It was too early in the morning for the front door to be open and when Dog went in ahead of me he came back out across the polished concrete leaving his prints in blood. I scrambled from the truck calling for Cessie and calling for Vale over and over and neither one replied. The sight as I came in the door was glass, upturned lamps and curtains down. Our worlds rent this way and that. Calling their names. Through to the corridor that lead to the bedrooms and there she lay, outside Vale's bedroom, a great soak of blood behind her and her finger tips lightly touching his closed door.

The boy came in from God knows where, all covered in mud and sick and looking like he'd seen a ghost. Maybe he had. 'I wanted to see Ma,' he said.

I didn't know what that meant but he broke my tired old heart saying it.

We were all full of hauntings those past days. Feeling the chill of something else about. Not that I was fearful, only trying to be vigilant in case there was any change on the wind. Hauntings aren't about being afraid, they're about longing. If you don't crave the thing that stalks you it's just a thing, or a person or a fox, maybe, because it has no meaning. What a haunting is, though, is all your longing for someone in a shape you can wrap your brain around. So we allow the thing that haunts us to take up home with us and then, the magic happens. That moment, just as I had with my vixen, when instead of her haunting me, or hunting me, I began to hunt her. I started seeking her out, imagining I'd seen her tail and pursuing it, following her tracks through the mud near the water mint and watching her with her pups that red evening. We start looking for the thing that had us so terrified. Not just the fox though. I know the boy's mother haunted him. He looked for her everywhere, leaned in to any word spoken of her.

Vale went for a bath and then I heard him go up to bed. I took him another cup but he was asleep.

I went to call on young Thomas. He was asleep too, as if the two had planned to meet up in a dream, so I left him a pork pie and a newspaper with a note. When Thomas lived with us, the little lads would have to share a bed, and often, while off in their slumbers, they would turn over or stretch or wiggle a little just at the same time. I thought maybe they were doing that as I watched Thomas rest. I had a word with a nurse too.

I didn't know what to make of what the boy had said about his Ma that morning. He struggled so much with all that. But what does an old man know? I only knew what he saw that night she died in Kabwe but I couldn't speculate on how he was for seeing it.

Popped in at the Admiral on the way home. A neat half for noonins was in order. I was still rattled by my seeing Vale, how he was that morning, coming in half drenched in misery. The lad had been out jousting with beasts the night before, I could tell that much, and smelling like he'd bathed in the River Styx.

The pretty lass was there.

'Hello there.'

'Hiya.' She looked a little quieter than usual.

'Usual, half though.'

'Cold out, right?'

'Oh yes. By a long mile.'

'Where's your dog today? She okay?'

'Oh, she's not good today. Definitely under the weather. Thought I'd let her stay next the fire.'

'Here you go.' She pushed the jar across. 'Want something to eat?'

'Oh, what you got? I'll have some scratchings if you have?'

'Sure.' She stood a moment, a strange pause I thought, then turned to get a bag. 'Here you go.'

I took a deep drink. Medicine, from the earth's own apothecary.

'Oh that's good. You've saved an old man's life today. It's been a mardy one already and I've almost forgotten it all.'

'Sorry to hear. Is it to do with Tom, Walker?'

'Oh? You know him?'

'Not really. He comes in here, well he used to with you know, Vale.'

'Ah then you've had the pleasure of my lad's acquaintance too.' I may not have minded my expression and offered a frown as I said it.

'Yeah. Well, in a way.' She wiped the counter in front of me. 'Can I ask you, is he, I don't know.'

'Is he?' I looked at the girl properly. Blue eyes, clear and open.

'Is he okay?' She said it softly. Near a whisper.

'Oh. Oh, well.' I took a breath for it. 'I'm not sure what you're asking really, but I'd have to say he probably isn't.'

'Okay. That's fine then. Not that he isn't okay, that's not fine.'

I was not on solid ground, not being prone to having girls getting upset with me over my lad. But then she struck me as a girl who just came out with whatever was on her mind. The open heart came with the open eyes I dare say.

'He's a bit tricky at the moment. Bit antsy. I would say though, if he's been unkind, you tell him off for it. Don't let him get away with it.'

She enjoyed that. A small flush in the cheek told me.

'Maybe I will.'

'Oh you tell him off. And then, maybe, if you can, give him another chance. Only if you think he's worth it. He is a good lad. He's honest and true. You may eventually find you like him again. But I admit I've not helped him much with the niceties.'

'I do like him. I don't think he likes me though.'

'Ah well, I can't speak for that. But, I would say it's him he doesn't like more than anything and he doesn't like me either. Going through it a bit.'

'Okay.'

'And he'd be a fool not to like you. We Midwinters always like a girl who takes no nonsense from us and has a lovely head of red hair.'

She smiled.

'There you go. If he's been unkind, tell him off and then decide how things feel after that. I dare say he'll be as sorry as a pup that's eaten a shoe and try make it right.'

When I got home there was a note on the door from Mole Boy to say he'd called and with it a blue and white business card saying that he was the Mole Man and his number and so forth. Very smart. I was pleased he was doing so well for himself. He was the softest of the group of lads and to be honest, didn't have a whole lot going for him, and yet while the rest were all over the place, he was quietly working away to make a life for himself and being a good sort while doing it.

The house was still quiet, heavy even, and I felt a walk would be a good balm for a bristling brain. Thought I might head down the North side of the woods and look for some tracks to see if my vixen had been out. The fresh snow meant I'd be able to tell if she was still dragging a paw.

I looked for Pup. She was next the fire and showing no signs of moving.

'All right little one?'

She twitched her ears to show she'd heard me and looked up with a tired old eye. Not herself. Thought it best to leave her to it.

'I'll see you soon old friend. I'll bring you a pine cone to gnaw on and make sure it's good and damp so as you can sniff the woods on it. How's that?'

I straightened up and went outside, whistling for the rest of the pack to follow.

It was perfect. Clear and cold and just a bit of cloud clooming across the sky. The snow would be back later but for the moment, there was respite.

The dogs were happy to be out. Two in the hedges, one rolling in something, one digging, one watching the digging, old Jessie sitting as usual a few yards from me, all lazy whiskers going nowhere. She was a descendant of my own Pa's collie dog. That one was named Mollie. Mollie the Collie. He thought it was funny even after the old thing died. Off we went and after two flat fields I felt my settle return.

I stopped at the old oak avenue and turned to look up the side of Rabbit Hill. The woods made a line along to the left of it. I passed a moment breathing in the loveliness of it all and, I don't mind admitting, letting my breath come back to me in a more regular way.

As a boy I would scamper up those fields every day, hunting creatures, finding this, hiding that. In one afternoon I'd be a pirate, a thief and a king, and I'd get home and my Pa would say,

'What you been up to, son?'

'Nothing,' I'd say.

'Busy up there?'

'Not so much,' I'd say.

He'd wink at me and I'd be cagey, say nothing. Then later, when I was eating my Ma's stew, all hot and runny and sinking great big bread ships into the deeps, she would say, 'Fine day out, dear?'

I'd say nothing and shrug and Pa would wink again and I would have to think hard so as not to smile.

I dare say I had a bit of the young Vale in me at the time, probably nine years old and I could have gone the same way. But then I had my Pa and Ma a bit longer than he and when they passed, I was twenty-two, no time for worrying about this and that. Had a farm to run and business to learn and I wanted to make them proud so that folk would say they raised me well.

Not our Vale, when he was nine or so, he'd sit there bristling like a badger who'd been cut off from his sett. Cessie would laugh at him and that could help, she could do that for him. Once she was gone, it got all the more difficult and he took to disappearing. Half of the Finn Valley would be off looking for him and then just as the night changed from slate to black he would come in the kitchen door as if nothing had happened. When I asked where he'd been he'd just said, 'Walking.'

'Walking where?'

And he'd shrug, not for being cheeky, but because he didn't know. He'd just walked until whatever he was feeling was gone and then he'd came back – ten or eleven years old.

'You can't be doing that son, it isn't safe out there in the dark.'

'It is.'

'Safe out?'

'Yes.'

'How'd you figure that?'

'Only fields and animals. Better than indoors.'

'What's wrong with indoors?'

'Stuff.'

'What kind of stuff?'

'Stuff, Pa.'

'What you saying?'

He shrugged again but didn't manage to hide a rising tear.

'What did you see indoors lad? Do you, do you mean your Ma?'

'Maybe.'

'Maybe? Can you tell me what?'

He shook his head but couldn't hide the tears rising in his eyes.

And then I knew with a sickness in my belly that he couldn't tell me not because he hadn't seen anything but because he had seen everything. And there could be no speaking of it. None at all.

So, the boy went walking. I never stopped him again. And as every new year came and went, he looked more and more like a boy with a skull of angry rats all gnawing away at him, his head always dropped over like a late apple.

There were a few dead rabbits left on the fields. I was always surprised they survived so far into the winter. Still, they made a meal and from the sound of it, the crows were getting hungry. My own dear Pa always said,

'Funny birds, crows, cleaning up the dead like that. They'd have to have some sense of humour, crows.'

But I said, 'It's only their job, Pa. It's not about a sense of humour. It's about work. They take the meat to keep things clean and to eat.'

'Funny birds.' Was all he said.

In the end, when dear Pa was bristly about his face, and his bones were poking out his chest and he had more beard than breath, he passed, quiet and thoughtful, as he would. He was a young man too, but he just seemed to run out of lung. I had to get the undertakers then, but I did wonder if he'd have preferred the crows. When his old dog died, on account of a broken heart those few days later, I took him for the crows, up Rabbit Hill. It's a good place for it. They got stuck into that old dog and cleaned him up in one swing of the sun.

I sat a moment on a stump. My heart was thundering in my chest, tight and sharp. I mused at a rabbit skull sitting near the opening of a warren on the bank behind me. For a few months after we got back to the farm and the tenants had moved out, and we shuffled back into the house, I seemed to find the little skulls on every walk I took. And I walked a good deal. It was too difficult to be in that house some days. Never had it felt so desolate. The day we first pushed the door back to find our home as we had left it and yet without the one thing that made it all sing, was a dark one indeed.

Around the time I began a collection of the rabbit skulls. Can't say why. Just picked up one and then another and soon had a whole little line of them along the windowsill in the workshop. Various stages of disrepair too, jagged little teeth and big gaping eye sockets but all white and bleached. I looked down at the one behind me. Force of habit or amusement meant I leaned back to retrieve it and put it in my pocket with my knife and smokes. I lit one up.

Cecelia. There was no one I had ever loved more. What hadn't I done to her? The misery I became; jealous, defensive and then moving us all. And the end. All for nothing more than my own fear and failure. I'd failed at the farm but then, worse than that, I had failed to love her too. To show that love.

Nothing more than foolish pride to wager the happiness, the very life of the one you love, just to keep your hands on some green acres and a few barns.

'I wanted to see Ma.'

Lord above. A shiver, right across, hair on end. He'd had the gun, came back in with it. 'I wanted to see Ma.'

The crows began rabbling and cawing, black wings flapping about. Something was about, something with teeth. My face was wet, tears, hot and monstrous. 'Oh Jesus. Oh lad. What have I done to you?' I stood, all at sixes and sevens and calling to the

233

dogs but feeling they were all gone up the hill. I needed them near. I wanted to get home to my lad, wake him and tell him we'd make it through.

'Come on, come on muttlies.' My voice stuck. I tried to whistle but didn't get it out either, my throat was clogged. I turned to look for them. And even through the tears and the panic I saw her.

The copper of her pelt near winded me. She was like a bonfire, a comet even, flaming across the white snow. She stopped, at the boundary of the dark woods and the clean snow fields, perfect and pure. And she looked right into my fresh broken heart.

Chapter 17

Vale

There was shit everywhere. Pools of it. Pup had been walking through it so it was dragged and slopped all over the place.

'Jesus, Pup? What a fuckin' mess.'

I didn't know where to start. She had no control anymore. She just went when she had too and it came out like water, but it was never this bad before. I managed to tiptoe through the pools to the kitchen door to get some fresh air in.

I had felt a little stronger. After I got back to Pa I went to bed and had slept all day and into the next. I think I had heard him go out with the other dogs about an hour earlier.

Pup was under the kitchen table. Her ears were down flat and she was all shivering and shaking. I felt like maybe I shouldn't have shouted at her like that. It wasn't like she could help it or anything, but Jesus, it was disgusting. I knew I'd be the one to clean it all. It stank. Sat in my throat so I could near taste it. I knew once Pa got home he would just rush to the dog and forget there was cleaning to do.

She didn't look good, all small and her whiskers were all

quivery. She looked whiter than usual under the the dark of the table.

'Pup? You all fine there?'

She stayed shivering and she looked all dopey. She didn't come when I tried to call her either. She normally came over with her nails making that annoying scratching noise on the floor boards.

'You okay? Want some porridge? Want some meat?'

I could see she was sitting in a dark pool too. Jesus, it was horrible. I thought it best to start cleaning her up. Then I could get her into a different room and start on the kitchen. I was pissed off though.

Even when I picked her up I could feel she was shaking and she felt cooler than I expected through the coat, which was always terrier-wiry. She stank. Her arse was covered in shit which was dripping off her, all thick and oily. I'm not a pussy about that stuff. I've done all the calving and lambing and the like, and when Mole Boy's older cousin got whacked with the combine we were all there. Had his foot cut off. Left the thing on while we went round to see what was stalling it.

This was different. Don't know why. I got her outside to the cold room where there's warm water in the sink and a hose. Also, all the old dog blankets and stuff I guessed she'd be needing.

I put her in the sink all quaking and clinging on with her toes like a freakin' monkey.

'For fuck's sake Pup, you've been in here a hundred times.'

I turned the tap on and as the water hit her hind it turned red. Jesus, I got a fright. I kept on a little. She was bleeding out her rear. Big pools of blood coming out. It didn't matter even once I'd cleaned all the crap away there was still red coming.

'Jesus Christ.'

I wrapped her up in the old towels and a blanket and rushed her towards the house, nearly fell over too, with all the snow being so deep. It was near over my knees in places, the heavy sort that squeaks when you lift your foot. I could hear Pa coming across the gravel and the other dogs barking.

'Pa? Pa? Come quick!'

'What is it? Are you all right son?'

'Hurry up. It's Pup. She bleeding. It's not good. Are you coming?'

Pa looked strange. We reached the kitchen door at the same time.

'Oh Jesus.' He looked down at the floor.

I handed the dog to him, she was all wrapped up.

'Don't let the others in.'

'What happened in here? Oh, poor Pup.'

He was hugging her close and trying to rub her snout through the blankets but she was burrowed in deep. I couldn't watch him. It was pathetic.

'There was crap everywhere when I came down and I was cleaning her in the cold room and then I saw it was all blood, too. She's bleeding badly.'

'Oh sweet Jesus, we need the vet. Go telephone the man.'

He picked his way inside, carrying the bundle of dog and went to the fire.

I went off to call and I was dialling it but I was thinking, I wish the dog would just die now and then we wouldn't have to do all this. It only ends one way.

I got the vet's wife on the phone. She said he wasn't in and she thought he was up towards the Sandlings with a horse. He wouldn't be able to get to us to help soon enough what with the roads still all iced over.

'Pa, Mrs Alvis thinks we need to help Pup ourselves. Charles can't get here.'

'Why not? We need him.'

'He's past Sandlings and it's snowed heavier there last night. So she says we need to decide, you know?'

Pa just sat there kind of rocking Pup in the blanket and she was just lying there shaking away. The dog looked bad. But I didn't want to be the one to tell Pa. I wished he would just get on with it and it all be done but he was chewing on his lip and was all welling up suddenly. I didn't need to see that. Didn't help anything.

'Pa go back in the living room. I'll clean up and then make coffee.'

'I can't do it, Son, I can't do it, but she can't go on being sickly. But maybe with the bleeding and all she'll pass out? Because that would help wouldn't it? If she passed out. She'd feel rather better then. But she might still be hurting. I don't think we can trust that, she might be hurting. I can't do it though. I won't. I can't this time.'

And then he looked at me, all a mess and said, 'I'm sorry lad.'

He was shaking worse than the dog and spit was coming out his mouth and his nose was running. He was twitching and blinking. I wanted to slap him, just to knock some fuckin' sense into him and make him stop babbling. I couldn't think with all the noise.

'Lad, think we should go to the Sandlings? Take our Pup there? Where the vet is? It's just about an hour or more? We'll be there in a jiffy I'd say. Think that's the plan? I need him to do it. I just can't do it. son. Not this time.'

Pa was looking right at me like he'd just seen his own death. His pupils were black and wet so I said, 'I'll do it.'

I sent Pa upstairs, he didn't want to give me the dog. He was a right mess. It pissed me off. He was jabbering and sniffing and carrying on. I just didn't want to see that. I was feeling sore myself. Pup was whimpering. I wanted to tell her to shut up, too, but I knew he would lose it if I did. Jesus, what a fuckin' mess. We should have taken her to the vet weeks before but he just kept saying, 'Our Pup's doing fine.'

And I kept wanting to say, 'She's not our Pup she's your Pup. She has nothing to do with me, and she's not fine.'

I was tired of his doting on her all the time. He never wanted to be out too long, always had her as an excuse to rush home from wherever we were. Guys at the pub, like the Dominos and some others, teased him and I know it was just a joke, but I bet they thought he was just a stupid old git. I did too, about the dog anyway.

I cleaned the kitchen while he was upstairs with her. He came down a couple of times to change her blankets. They got all messed up with crap and the blood. She was done for the world. I knew it and Pa did too, but he just couldn't do anything about it. He cleaned her up and then he'd put his face near her and she'd do the thing she always did where she'd lick his nose and all on his glasses too so he'd have to take them off.

'Still got love in you my Pup.' He was wiping his specs.

Jesus I wanted to run right out of that house. I could feel myself fucking dying in there alongside Pup. I just couldn't watch it. I couldn't watch him.

'I need to walk Pa.'

'Right. We'll be here.'

'I'll take the others out again.'

'Right.'

I couldn't get out quick enough.

I got the other dogs and headed straight for the river. The snow was deep so it was hard going, day after day of new fall. But the cold fresh air felt so free and there was sunshine. I had a smoke to warm me. My cheeks ached as I drew in. The smoke felt good. It made me think of Tom and everything I wasn't doing and should have been. I thought I would try see him later that day. I didn't feel as brave as I should. I felt unlucky suddenly. Difficult times make you superstitious.

I got another smoke out. I heard the Moles' tractor clunking up the valley behind. You could hear that thing from town it was so fuckin' old.

I didn't know what to do about Pa or about Pup. I'd wanted to tell him that I was lost in the world these days but every time I tried to ask him what to do about it, he just brushed me aside and said 'you do what needs doing son'. He acted like somehow I knew what to do, like I already had in my head what it would take to fix it.

I just needed him to be straight with me. Do this, do that and in this order. Ma would do that. First you say sorry, then you fix what you broke, then you plan how not to do it again. I let my face find the sun which was starting to streak behind the clouds. I needed Ma so badly.

Above me a huge skein of geese, holding their course, flying straight and true for home.

I finished my smoke and took the long way back to the house, around the side of the woods, across the stables and back. By the time I was at the house, the clouds had come over again, from nowhere it seemed. I stood at the door awhile. When I eventually opened it, Pa wasn't in the kitchen.

I found him in his bedroom. He was lying on his side on the bed. He had Pup still in her blankets and he was kind of curled round her. Like a baby or something. I think they'd been there for some hours. I couldn't even see the dog in all the bath towels and stuff.

'Pa?'

He didn't say anything.

'I'm going to take her now. It's time for her.'

'A little longer.' He was just mumbling really.

'No. It has to be now. It's getting dark out, weather coming again'.

I took a step forward. I felt kind of scared I guess, mostly of what Pa would do if I tried to take the dog from him. In the end I just lifted her off the bed and he didn't move. When I was back on the landing I heard him starting to weep. I couldn't deal with that, I had to get the dog outside while there was still enough light to see what I was doing. I'd got the gun ready. There were still two in it from before. I looked at them in the chamber.

By the time I went to get Pup from the kitchen to get it done, I'd taken the rifle and left it in one of the stables and I'd put straw down, for the mess. It's always a mess, no matter how it goes. She wasn't moving in the blankets so I figured she was near gone anyway.

I put the bundle on the straw and pulled the bottom half of the door closed. It was snowing again, lightly. Soon the valley would be deep in it. I leaned on the door and lit a smoke. I felt heavy in my legs after the walk, from just getting one foot in front of another, just trying to get home. Everything was catching up with me and my bones as I stood there. My one eye felt tight, the one Pa had hit. I don't know why.

I turned to look in the stable. Pup was there. She'd come out of her blankets. Her back end was stained with blood, even though I'd cleaned her earlier. She was sitting there quaking away and looking at me. Jesus. I chucked the smoke and lifted the gun off the floor. It was just as well it was all ready and waiting.

I raised it and she just sat there, looking at me, but she was moving about, swaying and looking around and I was thinking, where's the bullet going to go with all these flint walls? I couldn't just take her outside, the snow was higher than she was. If I didn't shoot clean, if I just hurt her, I knew she'd scream like a fucking banshee. I hadn't thought it through. I'd done it for a cow once and once me and Tom had shot a deer that we found on the road. Been hit by a car. It was pulped but it was still alive and struggling. They were big animals though. The shotgun was just too long for this job. I couldn't do it. I put the gun down, crouched down to Pup.

'Come here girl.'

She came to me. Slowly but kind of wagging some, I guess. I lifted her and put her across my knees. She lay there like she always did, kind of bony and comfortable at the same time. Her breathing was slow and steady. Her eyes were closed. Her body was warm. I played with her ears. They felt cold. I looked out the top of the stable door with the snow coming down. Ma would say it was raining down prayers from heaven. Pup was asleep.

I flipped her. I grabbed her throat to crush it.

I held her down with the other hand.

She screamed, she screamed and fought me. I wasn't ready for that. It frightened the hell out of me. I didn't think she would. I thought she'd know she was beaten. Jesus she thrashed and growled and screamed like she had a fuckin' beast in her. She had foam coming out round her nostrils from trying to get air in. I was getting cut from her nails, thrashing and scrabbling to get lose. I was telling her,

'Just shut the fuck up.'

And her eyes were wild and bursting out of her head and she looked right at me, right at me.

There was blood coming out her mouth because I was ramming her face closed and her teeth had gone through her tongue. I just held on and pressed into her fur even harder and then I felt her windpipe under my thumb, all ribby, so I just fucking rammed it. I rammed it in and she screamed and then it felt like something that was nearly a noise, something like a popping. She stopped thrashing. She just stopped. I let go.

She seemed to hold her breath in her still, even though I'd let go, and then her body or whatever she was now, breathed out. As she let it out, I guess all of her gave out and I felt a warm rush over me, all down my front and legs. I was soaked in her blood. Everything that was pooled up inside of her, all that shit and bleeding just spilled out. I could feel it on my skin, suckering through.

I just sat down in the straw. I was breathing short and my eyes burned from the tears.

I hung on to her a bit while I got my breath back and all along I was thinking why did she fight back, why did she fight? I laid her on the straw but she looked so bad, all mangled and messed up. So I picked her up again and held her close again, mostly so I didn't have to look at her anymore. I just sat there with her and let the tears come. It was so quiet.

In the straw with the shit and the blood with the snow coming down again and settling all round the stables and the light going out all over the sky and knowing what I'd just done and all the other stuff that I could never do, something was changed.

It was a feeling I remembered or a way of being that I used to know. I couldn't name it but something terrible had sat down in me and another part of me had returned, something stronger. Or maybe something had leaned out of the way, just an inch or two, so that I could finally see past it. I don't know what that thing was, a shadow maybe. Or a memory. And in the end I had killed Pa's Pup. She still had life to fight me like that and I had killed her anyway. I could never tell Pa that.

Later, I picked Pup up. I had to close her eyes. I took her out into the snow to clean her. I took my time. Her white fur looked yellow against the snow that settled. I ran my hand along her back. 'I'm sorry.' Then I did the same again with snow in my palm and over until she looked cleaner. When I was done and the snow was stained behind us, I dried her with some straw and wrapped her back in her blanket. I did it nicely. Pa would like that. He'd take her to the woods or maybe to Ma's orchard or even up the hill.

I got to the house but I didn't think it would be right to take her in. I took her into the cold room and laid her in there and locked the door. I had to take a bath. I was covered in blood and shit. I was laying in the water for a while. I didn't want to get out because I still didn't know what to say to Pa. I knew he was still upstairs.

I wanted to go back to before everything, before the boat and Tom, before Ma, before we left. I wanted the long summer holidays and sweets from town. I wanted Tom to stay at ours for weeks and weeks and Ma to be there making us dinner. I wanted to spend hot nights sleeping in the barn and wake up itching right underneath my skin. I wanted to not care if I got caught in a rain storm and not wonder if I was enough before I even walked through a door. I wanted Pa to teach me how to fish again, stand right close behind me with his arms out along mine even though they were twice as long and show me how to make the line whip and arc out along the river and then crack it back as the hook stuck in through a fish's lip. I wanted to try over with Beth, take a walk with her. I even wanted Pup back, for Pa and also for me. I wanted all these things to still be out in front of me.

All of this washed around me so that it felt as if it clung to my skin even once I got out of the water. While I was dressing I felt something that was painful but outside of myself. Something was reaching outside of me towards something. Like a yearning for something you can't name.

I sat on my bed and then stood up, and walked around and sat again. Pa was across the hall lying on his bed without Pup.

I opened my door and went to his. I pushed it aside. I felt both pain and relief reach into my throat and my face. It came out of me all at once. I tried to say something. Instead I made a noise that might have been crying. I fell to Pa and curled around him on Ma's quilt. He held my head close like he hadn't done since I don't know when. And we lay there together, broken and wrecked and not speaking.

We stayed there until it was black as black outside. The room was so quiet apart from the clock ticking and the pheasant clacking outside. Pa moved the big flat of his hand across my head and then again and then left it soft on my face. Then he sighed, right deep from out his belly somewhere.

And it sounded like a long, flat wave finally rolling into shore.

Chapter 18

Landyn

I found him in the wardrobe, curled up like a kit, small and tight with his arm over his ear and asleep to all the world. He had seen what he should not have. I woke him as softly as I could, I was still trying to stop myself retching and shaking.

'Vale son, it's your Pa, I'm here lad.' He opened his eyes so slowly, so thoughtfully and just looked at me. Not a moment of recognition on his face. I pulled him to me, as close as I ever could so that we could become one. 'It's your old dad here. I'm here.'

He lifted an arm around me but held something in the other hand. I opened his fingers to find the panic switch from the main bedroom. The light was still green. He hadn't pushed it.

By late March the nights were still frozen. Snow fell most days and settled a fair few too. Probably just from the habit of it, daffodils and tulips looked to come through in the garden but they were soon enough covered over in a few inches after another fall. Not just a scattering though, it was drifting too, up along the banks and the near side of the hills, scant as they are. Lambs though, come the same weeks every year, early in the month, and so through those bitter nights we were bent over and crouched in the barns getting the ewes to right themselves and hoping the little ones would be as they should. Mostly they were that year, but when the last great wave of cold came over the ocean with all the bile and spleen it could muster, it killed near half of them. There was no room to have them all sheltered. All night as the winds cracked and whipped through the bare old branches and you couldn't sleep for the horrible bleating and crying of the ewes as their little ones died, one by one. In the morning, the fields out the back were strewn with their small bodies, rolled in on themselves to stave off the ice that now covered them. Their eyes were frosted shut and already stiff from the cold and the dying. The mothers kept on calling for some mercy, but the lambs were dead and as we all walked along the fields in a line picking them up and laying them on the back of the trailer, you could feel the mothers' eyes follow you and mark you for what you were.

The lad was still muddling through in his way. But he had changed, his rage, the almighty furnace in him, seemed to have softened a little, edged closer to sadness. And that was perhaps all one could ask for.

'Pa?'

'Son?'

'I need to talk to you.'

'Yes.'

'About Tom.'

'All right.'

'He's leaving the clinic soon, they just need to do more stuff with him. Teach him about moving around in a house and stuff. Then he can leave.'

'That's good news.'

'No it isn't.'

'No?'

'He'll have to go home.'

'Right.'

'Only his Pa at his place.'

'And he's no good.'

'No.'

'No. I see what you're saying.'

'So.'

'So.'

'That's it then?' Said Vale.

'It is.'

We decided it might be best if we went together to ask Tom if he'd like to come back to live on the farm. I wasn't sure how to ask him, not wanting to insult the boy, make it feel like charity.

I was a right old mess when I got to the hospital and Vale was saying nothing as usual. Chewing away at his lip. He'd not seen Thomas too much. Just dropped stuff off for the lad from time to time. But there was still a bit of messiness there. Silences came across them, the same ones that came out the sea behind them that night and none of us seemed to know what to do about it all.

I drove along slightly too slowly, mostly to give myself time to rehearse my speech I'd be giving. Vale couldn't ask him, well, he could but if it came from me, Thomas would be more likely to get off the high horse he was on those days. All full of that 'I don't need anyone's help' type of rubbish. The lad was fighting on all fronts.

'Ready son?'

'No.'

'Me neither. So here we go.'

'He doesn't want to see me.'

'He just thinks he doesn't. It'll all be fine.'

'What if he says no.'

'Parsnips.'

'Huh?'

'He'll come round. Ask Dobb to tell you about a pigger he had trouble with. Got him round with parsnips.'

I was worried though. Tom wasn't in a good way. He liked Mole Boy visiting. Though he did complain that once or twice Mole got a little teary-eyed and he hadn't been prepared for that. Given the Mole just got on with things in his funny old way, it was easy to forget he had his own sorrows to carry about. I visited Tom as much as possible and once a younger Domino even wandered through illegally late on a Saturday night after a run in with a pavement. Seems he got tired of waiting to be seen and went to find Thomas to pass the time.

When we got to Tom's door, it was open and he was awake, which was good, but it also meant he saw us coming and turned away as soon as he did. I thought it harsh, I did. Vale had been going along over the weeks and leaving bits and bobs for him every few days through the winter. Books, newspapers, sweet treats. He was doing what he could, in his way. They never seemed to speak much though. Didn't seem to know how.

When I'd visit Tom though, he'd find a way to ask after Vale, though never directly. He'd ask a sly old question about any work we were doing or ask 'any news Pa Landyn?' and I'd take that as my cue to tell him all about Vale. I told him about the night Vale went off with the truck to the church. As much as I knew anyway. After I finished the sorry tale, we just sat without a word. The sun was coming through the window. We rested there awhile with our cups of tea steaming between us.

'Well that was a fuckin' bullshit idea wasn't it?' Said Tom.

'On this one occasion Thomas, I approve your language. I truly do.'

There was no sun the day my boy and I dragged our way along those corridors to ask Tom home. When he saw us and turned away Vale saw him do it.

'Oh Jesus.'

'Keep walking lad.'

I dare say I was a bit relieved to find nurse Margery who I'd come to see quite often, faffing about in there with all his pill bottles and the like.

'Oh, hello there Midwinters. Both of you today. Must be Christmas all over again.'

I'd spent some of Christmas with Thomas. Vale was off up the coast running rough shoots with the Dominos. The money was good as no one else wanted to do it. Couldn't make it back on time for the day on account of the weather, or so he said. I didn't push him on it. It was a pity he wasn't around and it did pain me some but young Tom and I made the best of it. I'd brought a few fingers of grog in a little flask for him and hid it in my coat like a crafty old drunk. You'd have thought I'd brought out the baby Jesus himself to see Tom's face. Brought him a fruit pie from the shops too, though I'm not sure he noticed the pie until much later.

Margery was counting out pills on a tray.

'Be going home soon, Tom. Pleased about that?' She said.

'Yeah, be pleased to see the back of you and your righteous sponges.' He was ignoring Vale and as a result he was having to ignore me too, though I saw him try to catch a glance, perhaps to let me know it wasn't me he was blinding. The air was a little chill.

'Now don't be fresh young man or I'll really use that sponge.'

Tom didn't say anything. The boy looked heavy and grey. Guess he wasn't in the mood for jokes with Nurse Margery. She knew it too.

'You'll be just fine. You have to come twice a week to me and three times to the gymnasium to keep you going, and see the doctor of course, and you've got your father and your friends here, the Midwinters, so you'll be fine then.'

'He's a real quality arsehole,' said Tom.

'Thomas Walker, that's very, very rude.' She was clucking and handing Tom the biggest mitt of pills you ever saw. 'These have been good friends to you.'

'Not him, not Pa Midwinter, my own.' Tom took the pills all at once with a whole cup of water. 'My own father is a right royal A-hole. Told me last week I was a waste of space getting messed up like this. He's not far wrong either, can't work the land now, can't drive or haul. It's bullshit.'

'I'm sure he didn't mean it.'

'Oh, he did.'

Nurse Margery looked to me for help.

'He did.' I said.

'Well that's not right.'

I knew I had to say something but Tom was chewing on his nails and ignoring Vale and ignoring me and it seemed we'd chosen a day when he was all weighty with temper even before we turned up. There was still bad weather there. I dare say he had no idea what to do with the two of us, and Vale standing at the bottom of his bed saying nothing wasn't doing it all any good.

'Tom's old man is a well known A-hole,' I offered.

'Legendary,' said Tom, still chewing.

There was one of those awkward pauses you think only young folk are supposed to have. Vale looked up. He cleared his throat a little.

'That's why me and Pa are hoping to have Tom come live with us when he gets out.'

Nurse Margery had turned from her pill bottles. Vale went back to frowning. Tom said nothing. He stopped biting his fingers. He spat out a nail.

'Could do,' he said.

Thomas moved in the same day the first daffodils fought their way through the ice and cold for the final time. Dobb was there of course and Vale and I got him in the truck between us and got him out the other side. Thomas was worn out by it all, I could tell. He was thinner and quieter but I was happier for knowing he was home with us.

Vale had had Mole come over and between them they had taken time to make up a room downstairs in Cessie's old sewing room. They put in a bed with all the pulls and boards the lad would need and put in a table which they worked out Tom could wheel under to sit at. They added little lifts to each leg to make it a touch higher. I liked hearing them working. The Mole was a kind sort and I do think Vale had warmed to him a bit over the winter, seen him for the solid pal he was. They never said anything of consequence but I liked the noise as they hammered and chatted.

'We using g-glue?'

'Yeah, but nails too and then a bit of rubber under each leg so it doesn't move.'

'You're g-good at this.'

'New job for me?'

'Yeah.'

Later when the room was fixed up, Vale put things in the drawers of the table for whittling and carving and God knows. On top of the table was a photograph of the two of them with a carp they caught one afternoon when they bunked out of school. The biggest fish you ever saw. They were so proud they didn't even bother to explain how it was they came to be on the riverbanks when all their friends were in school studying geography and history. They ran all the way home with the fish and demanded a picture. Two boys with all the madness of joy they could muster. Vale had placed the picture right next to the clock. He thought Tom would like it. I watched Vale going back and forth with pieces of wood and hammering away, digging out quilts and pillows like an old mother hen.

'Son, it looks fine. You've done your friend proud. And me.'

He looked up from where he was flattening some nail heads that were sticking out of the bed. He looked so serious, busy with his purpose, not speaking it but showing all the love he had for our Thomas with his hammers and ropes and things.

The air held as it does when something's understood. I could tell he was pleased I'd said it. He gathered up his tools and went outside.

The worst March in decades said the weatherman as it shuddered to its miserable old end. As the snow had thawed and I was able to walk out along the far fields again, Tom was settled in and we had all found a way to be together. Not always easy, but that's family for you. I missed my Pup still and caught myself turning to look behind, where I would expect to see the old girl limping along.

That day I walked out further than I had for a while. The dogs were feeling the relief of the warmer days and the sun on their fur even though the air still had early morn bite. We crossed over on the steel bridge and started along the old paddock fields towards Cessie's orchards. The air was lime green and bursting as we found the footpath that crossed the fields to the river.

There I found my fox, dead.

The valley held its breath. All comfort fell away. She lay where later, lush waves of barley would suddenly give way to a barren bank where nothing would grow. The dogs sniffed her out, but finding no life in her they let her be. On a different day, a day full of blood and chase, they would have run her down 'til her legs gave out.

'Oh, heart, little one.'

Carefully, I prodded her with my boot. She was still flaccid, and it being morning, and early enough that I could still taste coffee on my breath, I decided she had died in the night. I looked her over a little bit more, half expecting to find bullet holes or the mottling of buck shot. Nothing there. No snare either, nor the bite of one that let her go free but kept just enough that she would bleed out in the clay.

Oh, she was beautiful, and apart from some swelling in her tongue and mud and all sorts around her rear she was truly perfect, as I had always known her to be. Her whiskers made perfect rows and she lay so soft on the ground. I extended a hand to her shoulder to touch her. I stopped. I felt as if she might suddenly make a start from her dreams and rush off with the dogs after her. But she was gone. My hand had rested light on her fur. It felt like a moment I had always known. Yes, I thought, you are real.

I lifted her then, her ear brushing my face as I embraced her to my chest. She lay with such sweetness. I paid no heed to the muck coming off her. I whistled for the dogs. We walked the long way home. I held my fox close, though she grew heavy.

When we got home, I went passed the chickens and into the cold room. I left my fox there before quickly pushing the dogs through the kitchen door. Back to the cold room and the light hummed to life. There she rested.

I knew what I wanted to do, what was needed.

I fetched a bucket. I filled it half with cold and hot and got some sponges. New ones. I cut the corner off one and saved it to the side. I touched my fingers to her forehead. Oh, what a lovely girl she was.

I started with the feet, dousing and bathing. Her nails and pads showed she was hardworking and strong. I fancied her quite brave. The muck ran in great tides down the side of the table. Even under the light that cast my own shadow over her, her strong cinnamon shape emerged. Her pelt was soaking from my sponges and made her seem smaller as she flattened with the weight of the water, but her form was still impressive.

I flushed out the bucket and wiped down the table so she lay on a great silver slab. Then I took the blue sponge corner I had saved, and filled and squeezed and filled it again under the tap. I leaned into my fox's face; our noses were nearly touching and her whiskers seemed to awaken in the space between us as my breath passed through them. I raised the triangle and passed it over her sleeping eyes. First the left, then the right, between her brows then back across one and then the other eye, making sure to clear any mud from the instep of each. I was holding my breath though I hardly knew it. When I was done I breathed out, heavy and straight, so my fox let loose a drop from her sponged eye. I stayed there, bent over, nose to nose with her for just a little while.

'Pa?'

It was Vale. Probably wondering why the dogs were in and I wasn't.

'Here I am.' I rustled out the door and switched off the light. I didn't want him to see her. I can't say why.

'Everything okay?'

'Oh, fine. Well, not.'

'What?'

'Found my old lady fox in the fields.'

'She hurt?'

I wanted to say she died but I began to feel all teary and tired. So I dropped my head and felt a terrible shame, knowing Vale would see me for the old fool I was.

'Do you need help?' I was surprised for the offer.

'I need to take her body back. To her woods. Or up the hill.'

'She's dead?'

I nodded. I felt him stiffen a little. I assumed he was riled by me being my duzzy old self again. 'She is.'

Vale paused. He was searching my face for a cue, before I gave any, he said, 'I need to tell Tom I'm going out again and change my shoes.'

He turned and I heard him calling as he went through the kitchen door.

'Tom? I have to go out with Pa. He found a fox.'

'What? It's not coming back to my bed brother. No way.'

'I think it's dead.'

'Oh, then definitely not.'

257

I couldn't hear what Tom said, only that Vale said, 'Wait, I'm coming. I'll help you before I go out.'

I went back to see my vixen.

The bulb hummed up to light. She had mostly dried, and the copper of her near winded me. She was crazy red, like a bonfire, blazing alive on the cool metal with the light hanging over her like that.

So, I laid out a square of cotton from the cupboard, nice and straight on the table beside her, then lifted her on top, making sure to keep her neat. She lay smartly on the linen, paws crossed at the ankles, though she was starting to stiffen a little. I made sure her ears looked good; you'd want your ears to keep their look about them if you were a smart vixen. Same for the tail. These are the things that define you as a fox. I wrapped her and tied the corners together to hold her safely in.

I heard Vale coming across the gravel.

'Pa?'

'I'm coming.' I met him as I came out of the cold room. His eyes fell to my linen bundle.

'You wrapped her.'

'Seemed the thing to do.'

He frowned. 'Okay.'

'Our Thomas all right? You don't have to come.'

'Do I need a shovel?'

I paused. 'No. The hill I think.'

We had a long way to go. I could have slung her over my back; might have been easier, but it didn't seem right. So I held her to me, across my chest as before, and started to walk.

Out past the horses we went, around the fields of early beet, and all along the hedgerows, where I knew we'd not be spotted. Through the gates and across towards the woods and Rabbit Hill.

Vale walked along next to me, having a smoke as he went.

He wasn't talking so I spoke to my fox. Not loony talk, but I said, 'Don't you worry, we'll be there soon enough,' and 'Oh, mind your head now,' and sometimes, 'Sorry about that,' when I nearly dropped her on account of her weight and the uneven ground and the fences.

'Do you want me to carry, Pa?'

'Oh no, I'll manage. Just don't want to drop her, you know?'

'Okay.'

It wasn't easy going. 'Tom okay?'

'I guess. I'll take him to the pub later. See Mole there.'

'Oh, Admiral?'

'Probably not.'

'Pity. Nice girl there. Always asks after you.' That got his attention. 'Saw her there Saturday. Said she hoped to see you about.'

'Okay.' And I dare say he looked as pleased as he ever had. Not a smile, heaven forbid, but at least something in his face with a little life in it.

I offered. 'Tom likes the Admiral. Easy to get him in there on his wheels.'

'Could do.'

'Be a nice evening for it. Let's rest a moment.'

At the base of Rabbit Hill, I sat a moment. Vale next to me looking ahead with his arms wrapped around his knees. I had laid my fox down on the grass, already snake green and deep. My arms ached though I'd never admit it. Still, there can be no half measures with this sort of thing. You need to do a good job of it.

'I did think the woods, but they feel too dark today.'

***

Up on the hill time passes differently. So after a spell, and I couldn't say how long it was, I started to untie my fox from her bundle. I thought she looked a little shrunken but still magnificent. I lifted her off the square and placed her on the rock I had in mind, a nice wide slab. As I laid her down I had half a thought to cover her up with the linen, like a clean blanket over a sleeping kit. I folded it away to stop any such thought.

It was cooler. Up there you got a snide wind that came right off the sea. The air could taste of salt if it was blowing right.

'Ready, lad?'

'Sorry about your fox, Pa.'

'She's been for both of us, son.'

Vale looked up from where he had been looking at her lying there. He looked at me like he hadn't for years; into me even, as if he was looking for something. I could feel my tears stacking, sharp and then letting loose.

He replied with his own. 'Pa. It'll be okay.'

'S'all right son. I know it will.'

I laid a hand on his shoulder. He let me use it to steady myself as I stepped off the slabs and turned from the wind and so, too, our fox.

I knew the crows would come. The longer we waited the longer they would too, shuffling around on their starfish feet, restless for the feast.

We went down and along the edge of the hill, all the quiet in the world holding the space between us, like a lovely ribbon between trees. Behind us, the dark old woods rested, empty now.

Acknowledgements

There can never be enough gratitude for my agent, the unsinkable Jo Unwin. Her trust in me and this Suffolk tale has been a constant comfort and one for which I am eternally grateful. Thank you for all that you are. To my editor at Corsair, Sarah Castleton, for her immense care and her sensitive, intuitive reading of my manuscript. I feel so lucky Midwinter found its home with you.

Gillian Stern has been a true and generous mentor. The first person in UK publishing to say "yes" to me; the most valuable gift. She has given both time and precious energy to me and this novel and I shall always be grateful to her for her support.

To all at Corsair and Little, Brown UK and their affiliates: Caroline Knight, Olivia Hutchings, Rachel Wilkie and Helen Upton. For her apt and quite magical cover design Raquel Leis Allion.

To my family, particularly in Suffolk. To my sister-in-law and in heart, Fiona Swaffield for her determined support of me on every level and for being my first and most enthusiastic fan as she read earlier drafts. My brother Adrian for making sure I always had a working computer and a desk in lean times and for forcing me onto social media where wonderful and fruitful literary friendships were formed. Thank you.

My precious nieces Imogen and Clara, are acknowledged simply for being who they are.

My mother who has shown her quiet support despite harbouring an entirely rational wish that I should go back to "a proper job". Thank you.

My literary confidante Karin Salvalaggio for our daily missives over the ether have kept me motivated and grounded. Writing is a lonely old business and we have travelled a long road together with our scribblings.

To Julia Bell at Birckbeck, University of London, for her teaching, advice and encouragement and others on the course, students and teachers, too many to mention, for their kindness and thoughtful feedback.

Eternal thanks to Suffolk friends – most dear Jane Hamerton, Judith Wiesner, Felicity Devereaux, Hillary Legard, Anne Curtis and her Pup, and so many more.

Thanks are due to my friends in South Africa. Christoph Hoffmann for the author pictures and Emma Jesse, Michelle Kriek and Taryn Millar - who never doubted I was anything other than a novelist and assumed the best for me - and Beate Schulte-Brader, her magical intuition and friendship.

Final gratitude must go to Suffolk. To all the old Suffolk lads I met in fields walking labradors, shooting rabbits and catching pigs. To the younger boys, the lost ones, who never seem to find their way home. To all of those who inadvertently let me steal their language, insight, history, knowledge, even their names, thank you.